Another famous 'Gypsy Series' book; written by Aad Aandacht

a Boy loves a Man -1- Gypsy Heir to the Throne

Aad Aandacht is a Dutch psychotherapist who loves writing 'books with a message'

This heartwarming story is written for all the people on earth who have children of their own, deal with children on a regular base, or simply love kids.

Copyright © 2012 by Aad Aandacht

All rights reserved.

No part of this book may be used or reproduced by any means, graphic, electronic, or mechanical, including photocopying, recording, taping, or by any information storage retrieval system, without the written permission of the publisher, except in the case of brief quotations embodied in critical articles and reviews.

AandachtPreSS books may be ordered through regular booksellers, or by visiting the appropriate homepages or contacting:

www.aandachtpress.com
www.gypsyseries.com

First print, April 2012

ISBN 978-90-79092-07-9

NUR 341

Aad Aandacht is a Dutch psychotherapist who loves writing 'books with a message'

www.gypsyseries.com
gypsy@gypsyseries.com

a Boy loves a Man
-1- *Gypsy Heir to the Throne*

Another famous 'Gypsy Series' book
- Written by Aad Aandacht -
Dutch psychotherapist and writer
www.gypsyseries.com

*

Inspirational Fantasy
Age: 12 and older
Words: 83900

*

"*Books with a message*"

Our famous ongoing 'Gypsy Series' consists of:

a Man loves a Boy -1- my little Gypsy Soul Mate
a Man loves a Boy -2- a little upcoming Shaman
a Man loves a Boy -3- our quickly growing flock
a Man loves a Boy -4- my boy gets a new face
a Man loves a Boy -5- claiming our Gypsy roots

a Boy loves a Man -1- Gypsy Heir to the Throne
a Boy loves a Man -2- training my Shaman skills
a Boy loves a Man -3- becoming a Real Trapper
a Boy loves a Man -4- our caravan burns down
a Boy loves a Man -5- recognizing my new Dad

Throw-away-kid -1- born as a halfblood Shaman

Please visit www.gypsyseries.com to stay informed.

Table of contents:

1. That first day of my life as a Gypsy Prince. 7
2. Being named after my Great-Grandfather. 15
3. Discovering ; developing ; experimenting. 23
4. Talking to my Dad; and what is Real Love. 31
5. Sitting upright; seeing my possible future. 41
6. Daddy, Mommy, Harry luvyou deawly too. 51
7. Restricted; I am teaching myself crawling. 59
8. Walking; and a wandering question mark. 69
9. My first birthday; exploring Mother Nature. 79
10. A metamorphosing little caterpillar friend. 89
11. Second birthday; and Michail's marriage. 99
12. 'Black magic'; and Felicia gets twin sons. 109
13. Four years old; discovering tasty 'spices'. 121
14. From now on, I am our little 'Chief Cook'. 131
15. I am dry and allowed to enter our woods. 141
16. Entering our woods for the very first time. 149
17. Emptying traps; girls don't have peckers. 159
18. Setting up my own trap; and showering. 169
19. Drowning; and us boys differ from girls. 179
20. As stiff as a dead tree; I catch a real pig. 189
21. Washing and our ancient bonding ritual. 199
99. You've reached the end of my first book. 209

I want to thank our Spirit Friends and Beloved Ancestors for their invaluable help. You've helped me tremendously, by staying with me and patiently offering me your much appreciated Inspirations and Stimulations.
May our Highest Supreme Being Love you and Bless you!
Aad Aandacht; Dutch psychotherapist and writer.

www.aandachtpress.com
aad@aandachtpress.com
www.gypsyseries.com
gypsy@gypsyseries.com

"Books with a Message"

1. That first day of my life as a Gypsy Prince.

"Here comes our little Crown Prince! Could you please ask our Wise Woman to assist his birth?"

"Yes, I can see a small piece of his crown; and I think he will have blond hair, just like his Mom."

"Then, I hope he has her blue eyes as well. That would be very special, for our future Leader!"

"Look; the imp already wrestles with all of his might, as if trying to enter our world all on his own..."

Smiling inwardly, I listened to the people who crowded around my new Mom while waiting for me to show up. Although their voices sounded muted and were accompanied by my new Mom's heartbeat, my inherited Shaman abilities sensed the energy of their spoken words and thus understood who they were and what they were saying. I could feel my new Dad around me who acted a bit nervous; next to my new Grandmother who seemed to be even more nervous; and Michail, my loyal friend from several former incarnations, who would help me grow up during my first six Earthly years and defend me with his own life if necessary.

Of course, they were right, and I WAS wrestling with all of my might, to leave my too tight shelter as soon as possible. Since this morning, my steadily growing baby body had started to feel too cramped in my new Mom's womb; and I wanted to show up and greet my waiting subjects. Fortunately, labor had already set in, and I would be born soon.

For nine long months, I had waited to be born again, while dreaming away as a growing little fetus in my new Mom's uterus. During the first few months, I had just floated around in her cozy womb, feeling like the famous tadpole that wanted to turn into a Prince. Now, after nine long months of waiting, my baby body had finally metamorphosed from a tiny lump of cells into a real human being. From now on, I felt more like a too big frog that was crammed into a too small aquarium. It was time to leave my new Mom's womb, be kissed by our Gypsy Queen (that is my new Mom too), and greet our Gypsy

King (that is my new Dad) and a few others around me who eagerly awaited my arrival.

Several Earthly years ago, in our Timeless Eternal Realm, many devoted Cosmic Friends and I had started to prepare ourselves to descend towards our so terribly confused Planet Earth. Guided by the Gods themselves and working closely together, we would try to turn our degenerated playground into a much better place to live on; by using our Divine Cosmic Powers, and by teaching our fellow Earthlings how to use much more Humanity, Love, Understanding, Gratitude, and Happiness. Not surprisingly, everybody immediately chose ME to become the next Gypsy Leader. Because, during many past lives, I had trained myself thoroughly to be a very powerful Shaman and Cosmic Mage; my Soul now possessed all the necessary abilities to perform such an important task on Earth.

Before I left our Timeless Eternal Realm, a few devoted Friends and Helpers had already preceded me, to prepare my Earthly arrival in advance. During my first six Earthly years, they would help me grow up in this secluded Gypsy camp. Then, the Royal Gypsy Family and I would have to flee to a foreign country, where we first had to redeem some old and very nasty Karma. Both my new Mom and my new Dad would perish in a blazing fire, and only I would survive.

Two Earthly years later, I would meet my Very Best Friend and Eternal Soul Mate who once had been our 'Beloved Gypsy Monarch Harold the Great'; while I had been our Vice Leader in this same secluded Gypsy camp. During my last life on Earth, he also had been my 'trapper Dad'. Now, during my present life, my reincarnated 'trapper Dad' would adopt me as his own son and therefore be my Dad again. We would again love each other dearly, while he would help me and teach me everything that I had to know, until I would be old enough to become our next Gypsy Leader. From then on, all our Eternal Friends and Earthly Helpers would start working together as a powerful Cosmic Team, to transform our so terribly confused Planet Earth into a much better place to live on.

Eagerly, I waited to be reborn as our little Gypsy Crown Prince and only Heir to the Throne. Nine earthly months ago, I had left our Timeless Eternal Realm, to descend towards this secluded Gypsy camp and reincarnate here as a brand new human baby. Patiently, I had waited until my new Dad and Mom made love, and one of his sperms swam to her ripen ovum and kissed it.

---

8   Aad Aandacht is a Dutch psychotherapist who loves writing 'books with a message'

Chapter 1. That first day of my life as a Gypsy Prince.

Feeling full of anticipation, I had attached myself to the tiny lump of cells, to embody it and bring it to life. From then on, I had waited until I would be reborn, while my Cosmic Friends and Eternal Helpers assisted me by keeping my Soul awake, so that I could bring all my Shaman and Cosmic Mage abilities into my steadily developing Human Awareness.

Unfortunately, most remembrances from our Timeless Eternal Realm were already fading away, making me feel a bit unsure. My awakening human brain was already taking over and forcing me to start thinking; while, at the same time, it closed down the memories of my soul. Soon, I would be able to remember my Eternal Origin only through my 'intuition' or 'inner awareness'. Fortunately, my inherited Shaman and Mage skills would still provide me with several 'supernatural gifts' and 'psychic abilities'. And, all my Beloved Ancestors, Cosmic Helpers and Spirit Friends would always be there for me, whenever and wherever I needed them. I could always reckon on them, and they could always reckon on me.

By extending my enveloping aura and feeling around, my clairvoyant Shaman abilities told me that my new Dad tried to assist my new Mom, while he waited for our Wise Woman to show up. I also sensed my new Grandmother around me; and my loyal friend Michail who again would be my Big Friend and powerful Cosmic Assistant, next to being our Gypsy Vice Leader and my new Dad's best friend. They all crowded around my new Mom, while talking about their unborn little Prince with very much love and reverence. Although their voices sounded muted and were accompanied by the ever-present 'bump-bump, bump-bump' from my new Mom's heartbeat, my Shaman abilities helped me sense the energy of their spoken words, so that I could understand most of what they were saying. Now, I was very happy to have inherited all those useful 'sixth senses' that let me feel the surrounding energies and translate their muted words into a meaningful conversation.

During the past nine months in my new Mom's womb, time hadn't existed, life was good, and I had nothing to worry about. All the time, my steadily developing baby brain had been dreaming away; until slowly, nearly imperceptibly, my new Mom's womb started to feel too tight. From then on, my growing baby body became too big to float around, so that every involuntary movement pained my new Mom. Fortunately, she never complained but always told me she loved me dearly and would endure her inconveniences in joy.

To read all our famous 'Gypsy Series' books, please visit www.gypsyseries.com

I sensed the meaning of my new Mom's words, felt her motherly love engulfing me, and knew I would be more than welcome. Being loved like this, in advance, was a wonderful feeling; although my new parents still didn't know who I was, and our Wise Woman only found out I would be a boy. Therefore, I already started to love my new parents very much in advance; and I even tried to help my new Mom, by restricting my movements as much as I could.

Now and then, my new Dad had put his warm hands onto my new Mom's belly, as if trying to contact me and wanting to feel my moving and kicking. At first, my tiny baby body had been too small to be able to do much, because its undeveloped muscles had to grow some more first. Now that my body was bigger, it was easier to feel where my Dad's hands were; and I pushed my feet towards them to greet him. I wanted to let him know I knew he tried to contact me, and that I was very happy to have him as my new Dad.

My new Dad reacted elated when he felt our first real contact, and he exclaimed:

"Maria, I think my son recognizes me, because he kicks my hands on purpose. What a wonderful boy!"

"Yes, Janov; I am sure your son recognizes you as his new Dad, and he already loves you in advance."

"Thank you, Maria, for giving me such a wonderful child; and I love both you and him with all my heart!"

As a growing fetus in my new Mom's womb, it felt wonderful to be loved like this by the people who soon would be my new parents. Now, it was time to show up and greet them. Labor had already set in; and my clairvoyant abilities sensed how my new Dad helped my new Mom squat down onto the floor of our caravan, while he waited for our Wise Woman to show up. In advance, I had already worked my baby body upside down, instinctively knowing this would be the correct way to enter the world. Now, my new Mom's contractions started to push my head into a narrow gap, to where my instinct was sure my way out would be. Slowly, the steadily widening gap opened up more and more; until the crown of my head suddenly showed through, obviously having blond hair... Earth, here I come!

Impatiently, I tried to help my new Mom, by kicking around and pushing my baby body down with all of my might, until my entire head popped through the expanding opening; and I opened my eyes and tried to look around. However, much to my disappointment, my

10   Aad Aandacht is a Dutch psychotherapist who loves writing 'books with a message'

shoulders seemed to be stuck inside my Mom's womb, because they didn't follow my head. The rest of my body stayed inside, although I still tried to kick around and push myself down with all of my might, to free myself. I surely hoped I wouldn't be stuck in here for the rest of my life. Could anybody please help me?

Fortunately, our Wise Woman showed up in our caravan, just in time to assist my birth. Hastily, she squatted down, next to my heavily panting and wheezing new Mom. Immediately, she tried to free my stuck shoulders, by grabbing my head and pulling at it while trying to turn my unwilling body around. Her too cold hands were wringing at my neck, while she tried to pull my stuck shoulders through the too narrow gap... Ouch, that HURT! Couldn't our Wise Woman be more careful with my new baby body? Ultimately, it had to serve me for the remainder of my life! Feeling helpless and a little bit angry, I sent my thoughts to the Wise Woman and asked her:

"Could you please try to be more careful with my new baby body; because you are hurting my neck!"

Although I was sure that the Wise Woman had picked up all my thoughts, she only answered me to be quiet, while she just went on wringing and pulling at my head. Now, I became really angry with her, while I started to fight her too cold hands. Why didn't she listen to me? Ultimately, this was MY body, and she had no right to do anything I didn't want her to do! Stubbornly, I continued to send her my anger; until my shoulders suddenly popped through the widening gap, and the rest of my baby body followed automatically.

Without any more help, I just flopped out of my new Mom's belly, straight into the cold hands of our Wise Woman. Within a few seconds, the air around me felt too chilly and the too bright light dazzled my sensitive eyes, so that my newborn body started to cramp and shiver from the sudden cold and the unexpected shock.

Still feeling angry with the Wise Woman, I admonished her:

"It's too cold here and my neck hurts. Therefore, I order you to push me back into where I came from, immediately."

Of course, the Wise Woman didn't push me back into my Mom's warm womb; but she only sent me her own thoughts:

"Greetings to you too, my beloved Crown Prince! You are very welcome in our Gypsy community, and I hope you will soon feel more at home here. In the meantime, I will place you where I am sure you will like it even better."

Then, the Wise Woman laid me down onto my new Mom's belly, in between her already opening arms! At seeing her baby boy for the first time, my new Mom started to cry from happiness, while she folded her warm arms around my shivering body and started to cradle me. That felt wonderful! My anger quickly faded away, while I enjoyed the warmth and safety of her embrace and our close togetherness very much. Suddenly feeling ashamed, I again concentrated on our Wise Woman, this time to send her my humble excuses:

'Sorry for being too cheeky; and I didn't really mean it...'

Fortunately, the Wise Woman wasn't too angry with me. She only responded it was okay and that she understood, while she took a pair of scissors out of her purse and adeptly cut the umbilical cord that still connected me to my new Mom. Within a few seconds, I got a strange feeling in my new organs that, what I later on discovered, were called 'lungs'. My new chest started to feel too tight and upset, while my squirming baby body started to heave and gasp for air. Then, I inhaled my first breath of earthly air and pulled it deeply into my quickly unfolding lungs. Yes, that was what I had been waiting for all the time! Finally, I was back on earth and born again, this time as a little Gypsy Crown Prince and only Heir to the Throne.

Instinctively, my new baby body started to cry, probably because it wanted to unfold its crumpled lungs even more, while a strangely deep and sonorous sound escaped my throat... Feeling confused at hearing such an unexpectedly deep sound coming from my new baby throat, I stopped crying while trying to think this over. Was really my new body making such a surprisingly low noise? Why was that? Tentatively, I filled my lungs with fresh air and exhaled again; and, again, my throat produced the same sonorous sound, this time even louder! What the heck could be happening to me?

By using my clairvoyant Shaman abilities, I sensed that all the people around me initially reacted rather surprised, at hearing such a deep and sonorous sound coming from such a tiny baby. Then, one by one, they started to laugh and nudge each other, because they also felt very pleased to hear such a healthy crying coming from their newborn Gypsy Crown Prince. The Wise Woman even started to chuckle, while she exclaimed:

Chapter 1. That first day of my life as a Gypsy Prince.

"Wow, our little Crown Prince has a real baritone voice! I think that, once he is a grownup, he will have a low bass. He has a LOUD voice as well. That could be very handy for our future Gypsy King; as such a loud and sonorous sounding voice certainly will make him be heard by everybody!"

While my onlookers complimented my Mom with such a healthy child; my Shaman abilities sensed that my Grandmother approached me, and her warm hands lifted me from my Mom's belly while supporting my wobbly head. Silently, she took me to our couch in our living room, where she laid me down onto a nicely warmed and fluffy towel. Adeptly, she washed my squirming little body, dried it, powdered my sensitive parts, put a warmed diaper on me, and finally laid me back into my Mom's already waiting arms. Immediately, my Mom refolded her warm and cozy arms around my now spotlessly clean baby body, kissed the top of my blond head, and tenderly cradled me.

Feeling thankful for my Grandmother's much appreciated help, I concentrated on her to send her my love:

'Thank you very much, Grandma, for caring for me like this; although I sense you cannot pick up my thoughts.'

Now that my new body was clean and warm, I started to feel wonderful; while I basked in the pleasant sensation of being loved and cared for by all the happy sounding people around me. Unexpectedly, a nice and soft thing touched my lips; and, instinctively, I opened my mouth and started to suck on it. Within a few seconds, the most delicious nourishment I could ever imagine entered my mouth. Yummy, this liquid food tasted wonderful! Enthusiastically, I started to suck on my Mom's soft thing with all of my might, while I closed my eyes and forgot everything else around me.

In the background, a door opened, and an enthusiastic voice shouted to the waiting people outside our caravan:

"IT'S A BOY! WE HAVE A NEW HEIR TO THE THRONE!"

Instantly, loudly cheering sounds filled my sensitive baby ears, making me flinch from the unexpected noise. At the same time, the happy sounds also filled me with lots of self-consciousness and pride. While my inherited Shaman abilities scanned the energy of the joyful words, my 'sixth senses' told me what they meant. Outside our caravan, my quickly gathering subjects were cheering and congratulating each other because of ME!

Two violins started to play beautiful Gypsy melodies full of joy and happiness. Soon, the sound tore at my heartstrings, so that I got goose bumps all over my body and stopped drinking from listening intently. Were my subjects playing these heart-warming tunes because they felt happy with their newborn Crown Prince? Then, they already loved me very much! By extending my aura, my inherited Shaman abilities sensed more and more enthusiastic people gathering outside our caravan, celebrating my birth while talking to each other with happy voices. Of course, my 'sixth senses' tried to understand what they were talking about; but all these different energies were blurring my sensitivity too much. Yet, I still felt their combined love and happiness, making me feel even more accepted and welcome.

After a long time of celebrating and crowding around our caravan, at last, my happy subjects left us and went home. Our violin players stopped playing, and all the sounds slowly diminished and finally went away. Only now and then, a few people knocked on our caravan door and asked to be allowed to take a look at their newborn Gypsy Crown Prince and only Heir to the Throne. One by one, my visitors stepped inside, looked at me, and at first reacted a bit surprised at seeing my curious bright blue eyes and unruly blond hair. Then, they smiled at me, congratulated my proud parents and grandmother with such a healthy child, and went outside to make place for even more visitors. Every time, our caravan door closed immediately to keep the winter cold out, as it was March the third and still freezing.

When finally the last visitors had left our caravan, everything went quiet again. Slowly, I started to doze off, while lazily sucking on that yummy soft thing that still was in my mouth. Sleepily, I sensed that my new Mom got up, removed my soiled diaper, cleaned my smelly bottom, dried me, and put another warmed diaper on me. She brought me to a neatly furnished small sleeping den, put me in between a pile of colorful pillows, covered me with a cozy blanket, and tenderly kissed my little forehead, before she returned to her own bedroom to take her own much needed rest.

Her motherly love made me feel safe and cared for; and I enjoyed those feelings very much, while I almost immediately disappeared into a deep sleep. It felt wonderful to be a newborn little baby!

2. Being named after my Great-Grandfather.

A couple hours later, I woke up in total darkness, and for a moment didn't understand where I could be now. I suddenly missed my Mom's cozy womb I had been living in for nine months; and I also missed her reassuring heartbeat sound of 'bump-bump, bump-bump' that always accompanied me. Feeling uncertain, my new baby brain tried to find out what could have happened. Where had I landed; and where was my safe shelter? Could this unexpected darkness be my first earthly 'night'? Feeling more and more helpless and lonely, I didn't know what to do, and my confused baby body reacted to the unusual sensations and started to cry while again producing its deep and sonorous baritone sound.

Within a few seconds, I heard some unknown noises, and a night light switched on so that I could look around. A broadly smiling face showed up and hovered over me; and I stopped crying while staring at it in wonder. In vain, I tried to focus my still very unwilling baby eyes on that vague and misty thing that moved nearby and produced reassuring sounds. Two warm hands gently lifted me from between my pillows, while at the same time supporting my still very wobbly head. Now sensing her already well-known female energy, I recognized my Mom and immediately felt safe again.

My Mom took me into her arms and happily cradled me; until she suddenly sniffed the air and told me:

"Son, I think you have pooped your diaper! Just a moment please, because I have to clean you first."

She took me to our living room, where she laid me down onto my fluffy towel. Adeptly, she removed my again soiled diaper, washed and powdered my smelly bottom and other sensitive parts, and put another warm and clean diaper on me. Next, she carried me to her bedroom, took me onto her lap, and YES! There was that yummy soft thing again! Immediately, I started to suck on it with all my might, until my stomach was filled to the brim with that delicious nourishment. Unexpectedly, I had to burp and spilled half of it; but who cares. My Mom just cleaned me up and let me drink some more.

Feeling cared for and happy again, I fell asleep in her warm and cozy arms, and didn't even notice her putting me to bed in what was now my own small sleeping den with my own cozy bed and my own huge pile of brightly colored pillows.

Some time later, I woke up again, because the bright morning light tickled my sensitive baby eyes and made me sneeze. Immediately, my clairvoyant Shaman abilities sensed the presence of another person who approached me from our living room. Obviously, somebody had heard my sneezing and now wanted to know what I was doing. This time, I sensed a totally different energy, full of power and strength, engulfing me with lots of love and safety. Instinctively, I knew this had to be 'male' energy; and the person hovering over me was my new Dad! I tried to focus my unwilling eyes on him; and, much to my delight, I really succeeded in getting the vague picture a bit sharper. This much darker face that was adorned with an enormous moustache, was producing louder and more sonorous reassuring sounds. My Mom's eyes had been bright blue; but the warm eyes full of love and happiness that looked at me now, were deep brown, nearly black.

When my new Dad saw me concentrating and trying to focus my still unwilling eyes on him, he started to smile broadly, while his enormous hands lifted me out of my pillows and gently supported my still very wobbly head. Happily, my Dad took me to our couch in our living room, where he sat down, took me onto his enormous lap, and folded his strong arms around my tiny baby body. Immediately, I tried to melt away into his warm and cozy aura, already feeling totally safe and welcome on his huge lap and in his strong arms. His powerful love and tender care engulfed my entire body, and I basked in my happy feelings of being loved and cared for like this, while I tried to melt away in his enveloping aura even more.

Within a few seconds, my Dad sniffed the air and chuckled:

"Son, I think you've pooped your diaper again! What shall I do; wake your Mom to help you, or shall I try to clean you?"

Without waiting for my answer, my Dad laid me down onto my fluffy towel, removed my again soiled diaper, and cleaned my smelly bottom. After drying me, he tried to powder my sensitive parts; but accidentally spilled some powder into the air, which made both of us sneeze at the same time. Looking ashamed about his clumsiness, my Dad continued to put a clean diaper on me, while I wiggled around in his enormous hands and showed him my joyful face.

Although my new Dad did this for the first time, I already LOVED it when he tried to pamper me! To be honest, I still do...

Still trying to focus my unwilling eyes on my Dad's lovable face, I stared into his dark brown eyes, where I contacted his soul and immediately started to smile broadly when I recognized him. I was now sure that my Dad and I were kindred souls, and I felt very happy to have this wonderful and lovable person as my new Dad!

At seeing my first smile, my Dad suddenly got tears in his dark brown eyes, while he told me with a choking voice:

"Boy, your bright blue eyes are looking straight into my soul. What an enormous amount of power do you possess! To me, you already are a real Prince. And, although you are not even one day old, you were already smiling at me... My dear son, you really are a special child, and I am very proud to be your humble Dad."

Looking proud, my Dad scooped me into his arms, turned around, and slumped backwards on our couch. Then, he placed my tiny baby body on top of his enormous chest... That felt marvelous! Immediately, I tried to spread out onto my Dad's broad chest as far as I could, while I let myself melt away in his powerful and lovable male aura. Accidentally, my nose disappeared into his left armpit. At that same moment, when I smelled my Dad's strong manly odor for the first time, I was sure that I would be hooked on this manly scent for the remainder of my life! To be honest, I still am...

For quite some time, my Dad and I enjoyed our togetherness very much, until I tried to put my small arms around his broad chest, to let him know how much I loved him in return. Unfortunately, that turned out to be very frustrating, because my still undeveloped arms and legs absolutely refused to do what I wanted them to do. Much to my disappointment, my baby limbs just flapped around, because I couldn't find the proper muscles to control them. Obviously, my small body was still way too immature; and I had to learn how to use its uncooperative muscles first. After some more trying, I started to feel a bit disappointed, stopped my idle efforts, and looked at my Dad.

For a few seconds, my Dad stared back at my disappointed face, obviously not comprehending why I suddenly looked distracted. Then, our mutual love and togetherness made us smile at each other again, while I basked in his powerful manly aura full of love and happiness.

Feeling totally safe on his broad chest and in his enveloping arms, I slumped down, put my little nose in his left armpit, closed my eyes, and almost immediately dozed off into dreamland. Within two minutes, both my Dad and I were sound asleep, joyously snoring together.

Since that first day, I was addicted to sleeping on my Dad's stomach or lying curled up in his safe arms. Soon, my Dad started to call me 'my little octopus', because I always tried to drape my limbs all over his chest and belly. Well, I just couldn't help loving him, and I also wanted to have as much bodily contact with my Dad as I could muster. To be honest, I still do... Besides, thinking about it, doesn't a real octopus have eight limbs instead of only four?

An hour later, I suddenly woke up again, because my inherited Shaman abilities sensed another very powerful male energy that approached our caravan and clearly planned to pay us a visit. Obviously, another 'special gift' had kicked into action; and it turned out to be absolutely right. Within ten seconds, Michail, who was our Vice King and my Dad's best friend, opened our front door and stepped inside our caravan, on his way ducking his head to be able to pass the doorpost. Michail was a HUGE man, always clad in his inseparable fur coat, today also wearing a pair of leather boots and warm gloves because of the cold winter weather. He started to chuckle when he saw my Dad, still peacefully sleeping on our couch, while having his proudly beaming little son spread out all over his chest and belly...

My Dad woke up when he heard Michail's chuckling; but he first looked at ME, to see if everything was all right with me. When he saw I was awake and smiled back at him, he seemed to feel relieved. Carefully, he sat upright and took me onto his lap and into his safe arms. Now, my Dad welcomed our still chuckling visitor:

"Sorry, Michail, for oversleeping; but I have to baby-sit my son because Maria is still in bed and recuperating."

"Yes, I see; and your son and you absolutely are one of a kind! Just look at those over-curious bright blue eyes. What an enormous amount of power and intelligence does our newborn Prince radiate! Although he is not even one day old, he already stares at me as if he recognizes me and understands everything that I am saying, while he looks straight into my soul with his piercing blue orbs..."

Indeed, I WAS staring at Michail's lovable aura, while my Inside basked in the happy feeling of recognizing my most loyal friend from our Timeless Eternal Realm and from many shared past lives.

He still had his beautiful and vibrant aura that stretched out into all directions and engulfed both my Dad and me with very much Love and Respect. My Inside was sure that Michail and I still loved each other dearly. In our present lives, he would again be my faithful and totally devoted loyal Friend and Cosmic Helper; until I would be six years old and my parents and I had to flee to a foreign country to redeem some old and very nasty Karma. Two years later, I would meet my Eternal Soul Mate and Very Best Friend who once had been my 'trapper Dad'. He would become my new Dad, after I had reached eight Earthly years and was living in some foreign country...

Unfortunately, my meddlesome baby brain restarted to think, so that my clairvoyant memories faded away into oblivion until I just couldn't remember them any more. Feeling frustrated, I tried to shake my wobbly head, to get rid of those suddenly appearing cobwebs. Had I really had a 'trapper Dad', during my last life on earth? And would I really meet my 'trapper Dad' again, after I became eight years old and lived in some 'foreign country', whatever that might be?

In the meantime, my present Dad answered Michail:

"My newborn son certainly is an extremely special child; and I am already very proud of him! This morning, he suddenly smiled at me, just before we fell asleep; and he smiled again when I woke up and sat upright to look him over. Now, my precious Gypsy Crown Prince and newborn Heir to the Throne, let's go outside and meet our already waiting subjects; to let them have their first official look at you..."

My Dad lifted me off his lap, rose from our couch while supporting my still very wobbly head, and first laid me down in between a couple of colored pillows, before he started to look for some warm clothing to wrap me in. Soon, he found a nicely colored plaid blanket; and covered my entire body in it, letting only my face show through so that I could see where we went. Together, my Dad and I followed Michail outside and stepped into our cold winter world full of blinding snow. Helpfully, my Dad turned me around, so that I could look around and see where we were going...

Feeling totally overwhelmed, I started to look around with bulging eyes, and just didn't know what I wanted to see first. Desperately trying to focus my still way too unwilling eyes, I stared at a blurry circle of snowy caravans around a brightly glowing campfire. Lots of happy looking people seemed to be waiting for us, while their children were frolicking around and throwing snowballs at each other.

Everybody started to cheer when my Dad and I showed up from our Royal caravan, and all the people bowed towards their Beloved Gypsy Leader and their newborn little Gypsy Crown Prince, obviously to greet us and make us feel even more welcome.

Two violin players started to play beautiful Gypsy melodies full of hope and glory, while my Dad and I stepped into a circle of wooden benches around the brightly glowing campfire. Immediately, all the grownups went to their own benches and sat down; while all the playing children left their snowballs and climbed onto one of the inviting laps, to be cuddled and feel loved. Now that everybody waited for us with expectant eyes, my Dad started to walk me around the circle, still carrying me in his arms while supporting my wobbly head. Happily, he let all our beloved subjects have a closer look at their newborn little Crown Prince and only Heir to the Throne.

Again, the people who saw me for the first time, reacted surprised; and many of them told my Dad how amazed they felt at seeing my over-curious and intense looking bright blue eyes. They were sure they had never seen such alertness and Inner Power in such a young child. For our future Gypsy King, having blond hair and bright blue eyes had to be an absolute first in our long row of preceding Gypsy Leaders. If this were a sign from our Supreme Being, our newborn Crown Prince would certainly become something VERY special!

By using my inherited Shaman abilities, I sensed the energy of their praising words, understood what they meant, and involuntarily started to blush. Were really my beloved subjects thinking I could be THAT special? Wow...

After all my beloved subjects had seen and admired their newborn Crown Prince, my proud looking Dad announced:

"Today, we present our newborn Heir to the Throne to our entire Gypsy Community, to our Beloved Ancestors, and to our Highest Supreme Being. The official names of our newborn Gypsy Crown Prince will be 'Harold Janovski Romani'; because his Mother and I have decided to name our first son after his long ago deceased but never forgotten Great-Grandfather who once was and always will be our beloved 'Gypsy Monarch Harold the Great'. So be it!"

Immediately after my Dad announced my official names; all the men with little children on their laps rose from their wooden benches, while lifting their kids high into the air. After they kissed their kids, they threw them upwards into the sky, as high as they could, to thank our Beloved Ancestors and our Highest Supreme Being. When their kids landed, the men caught them adeptly into their strong arms and retook them onto their laps. The kids enjoyed the fun immensely, and many of them shrieked with delight while begging for more.

Unexpectedly, I too had a sensation of flying up, even higher into the air and far above the other kids! Immediately, I felt ecstatic and free as a bird, while I nearly cried from my suddenly overwhelming emotions and just wanted to fly even higher. This intense sense of total freedom strongly reminded me of our Timeless Eternal Realm, where my Inside still remembered that my Soul belonged in reality. During a way too short moment, I felt like flying Back Home...

Too soon, my earthly body started to go down; although I tried to fly even higher by flapping my unwilling arms and legs around. Then, my flight was over. The moment I landed, my Dad adeptly caught me in his strong arms and quickly took care of my still very wobbly head. For a few seconds, he looked me over from head to foot, to see if everything was all right with me. Still feeling ecstatic and full of energy, I showed my Dad my broadest smile!

Feeling reassured, my Dad smiled back at me and kissed my nose. Then, he lifted me onto his broad shoulders; while holding my body with one hand and supporting my wobbly head with the other. Again, he started to walk me around the circle; this time to let ME greet my own Beloved People! One by one, my Dad stopped in front of my Subjects and told me their names. One by one, my Subjects bowed towards me and touched my feet, thus vowing their eternal loyalty to their newborn Crown Prince and future Gypsy King.

Of course, I tried to greet my Beloved Subjects back, to thank them for their trust and loyalty. Only, much to my disappointment, my idle attempts turned out to be in vain and extremely frustrating. My way too unwilling baby body just didn't know how to bow back; and the only things that left my mouth were air bubbles and a lot of saliva. After several more idle tries to bow back to my people and speak to them, I started to feel annoyed. I became angry with myself because my tiny baby-body was too small to be able to make myself understood; and I felt frustrated because my still underdeveloped muscles absolutely refused to do what I wanted them to do.

My happy looking Dad saw me drooling; but he clearly didn't understand what I was trying to do, and he only laughed at seeing my frustrated face and still mumbling mouth.

After my last Beloved Subject had bowed and touched my feet, my Dad just handed me to Michail, and asked my huge friend to take me back to our own Royal caravan, where my Mom would clean me up and put me to bed to have my next nap.

Of course, I tried to protest fiercely, because I wanted to join the fun outside for a much longer time! However, neither my Dad nor Michail seemed to understand what I tried to tell them. Without saying another word, Michail just took me into his enormous arms and carried me back to our own snow-covered Royal caravan.

Inside our nicely warmed caravan, my Mom was awake and happily greeted us. She smiled when she saw me drooling, and first cleaned my wet face and bubbly mouth with a few tissues. Then, she removed my colored plaid, took me into her arms, and let me drink from her soft things she called 'breasts'; until I was stuffed to the brim, had to burp, and unintentionally spilled some.

After my Mom cleaned me up and applied a fresh diaper on me, she kissed my little nose and put me in between my pile of brightly colored pillows, to have my afternoon nap. Within a minute, I fell asleep, dreaming of a beautiful future and being able to speak...

3. Discovering ; developing ; experimenting.

During the next months, my extremely fast bodily development turned out to be the most exciting time of my life as a newborn baby! The next day, much to my disappointment, my baby body only wanted to sleep, drink from my Mom's breasts, and sleep some more. Then, my developing new brain woke up from its annoying sleepiness, so that I became more alert and started to look around. Much to my delight, my new baby brain was suddenly able to learn so many interesting new things, in such a relatively short amount of time! Immediately, my insatiably curious mind wanted to learn about every interesting thing or fact that it saw, heard, or came upon. Although my tiny brain almost felt overloaded with all those possibilities, I just went on. For a while, I even disliked sleep, because it prevented me from discovering even more fascinating abilities.

First of all, I started to teach myself how to focus my unwilling eyes, so that I could see everything around me more clearly. For a couple of hours, I tried to exercise them by alternately looking at nearby and far-away objects. Unfortunately, my quickly tiring eyes started to see double and more blurry; but they returned to normal after I had some more sleep and woke up again. Then, much to my delight, I found out how I could use my eye muscles without straining my eyeballs too much. From now on, I was able to focus my eyes properly on anything interesting I wanted to look at!

Immediately, my over-curious eyes started to focus on every person who showed up in our caravan or who just happened to look at me. I also started to scrutinize every other interesting object that moved, was colorful, or made appealing sounds. Within a day, I also tried to turn my wobbly head, to have an even better look at all those new and fascinating things that caught my always-curious attention.

Many surprised visitors who entered our caravan and saw me looking at them, told my proudly beaming parents they felt truly astonished about seeing such an extremely fast developing little baby. According to them, I had to be the fastest developing child ever in the entire universe!

By using my inherited Shaman skills, I sensed the energy of their praising words, understood what they meant, and involuntarily started to blush. At the same time, I felt very proud of my early achievements and all those newly found abilities! Ultimately, my newborn baby body was only a few days old; and therefore, I really had to be 'extremely precocious', according to what several surprised looking visitors told my proud parents.

The next day, now that I was able to see properly, I also wanted to be able to turn and lift my too wobbly baby head as soon as possible! Therefore, after some heavy thinking, I decided to start concentrating on training my still way too unwilling muscles. To begin with, I wanted to find out which individual muscles were controlling my neck and my limbs. I already knew how I always moved all the parts of my body at the same time, by floundering and jiggling when I became excited. Only, how could I perform all these different movements at will and independent from each other?

For quite some time, I forced myself to feel excited, so that my tiny baby body started to flounder and jiggle around, while I tried to make sense of all those erratic movements that seemed to occur only randomly. After I started to feel too tired and had to take some much-needed rest, I suddenly decided to stop trying and start thinking first. Clearly, I had to stop getting excited and start doing something totally different, but what? After some more heavy thinking, my developing little baby brain thought I could best concentrate on flexing only one single muscle at a time; while, at the same time, observing which part of my body suddenly moved. Much to my delight, this turned out to be an extremely interesting experiment!

Unexpectedly, my Mom showed up in my sleeping den, lifted me from between my pillows, and took me onto her lap, to change my smelly diaper and let me drink from her breasts. Normally, I always enjoyed my Mom's close togetherness very much; but, this time, I felt almost angry, because I wanted to go on with my experiments that had caught all my attention! Unfortunately, my Mom had no idea why I suddenly looked distracted, and she reacted rather worried. At first, she thought I could be ill, looked at my tongue, and felt my forehead to check for a fever. Then, she wanted to dress me in my warm plaid blanked and take me to our Wise Woman, to ask for her advice...

Immediately when my Shaman abilities picked up my Mom's thoughts and I found out what she wanted to do, I started to smile at her, to reassure her and let her know I wasn't ill but only felt excited.

Of course, it had never been my intent to make my Mom feel worried about my health! If only I could talk to her and explain what I had been doing... Looking apologetically, I tried to talk to my Mom; while, at the same time, I sent her my thoughts:

'Sorry, Mom, for worrying you; and I promise I will make it up to you once I am able to talk properly.'

Unfortunately, my Mom only smiled at seeing my mumbling mouth, while she took a few tissues and removed my excessive saliva and air bubbles. Obviously, she couldn't pick up my thoughts, as our Wise Woman had done so easily. After cleaning my smelly bottom and putting a fresh diaper on me, she seemed to feel relieved that I still had a healthy appetite. Happily, she let me drink from her breasts, burp, and drink some more, until I was filled to the brim. Then, she put me to bed in between my brightly colored pillows and covered me with my cozy blanket, to have my afternoon nap. Although I had planned to go on with my interesting experiments as soon as possible, I fell asleep almost immediately.

The next morning, after my Mom had bathed me and let me drink from her breasts, she laid me down in between my pile of brightly colored pillows on our couch in our living room. Immediately, I went on with my interesting experiments of flexing only one muscle at a time, until I suddenly found out how my little baby brain could concentrate on only one single limb, without flexing all the other ones at the same time. Yesss, that was what I had been trying to do all the time! Finally, I was able to move my baby limbs at will and one by one, without involuntarily jiggling my entire body!

Happily, I started to play with my baby arms, by moving them into every possible direction while following them with my eyes. That was a lot of fun, now that I was able to steer them around more or less properly. Unfortunately, and way too soon, my untrained arm muscles started to cramp and feel too tired; so that I decided to stop playing and waited until my Mom had changed my again soiled diaper and I could go to bed and take my next nap.

After I woke up again, my too strained arm muscles still felt a bit sore. Therefore, I decided to let my arms have some more rest until their soreness had disappeared. Instead, I tried to crane my still very unwilling neck, because I wanted to take a closer look at my small legs at the other end of my baby body.

Unfortunately, I could see my tiny legs only now and then when I kicked them up and down, because I still couldn't lift my too heavy head to properly look at them. Obviously, my tiny baby body first had to gain a lot more strength in its undeveloped neck muscles.

Fortunately, now that I knew how I could steer my baby muscles independent from each other, I was also able to turn my head around from left to right and back to left. Only, every time I wanted to look aside, all those colored pillows were in my way and obstructed my vision. Would I be able to get them out of my way, so that I could look around without craning my still too unwilling neck? Tentatively, I used one of my tiny arms to push against the nearest pillow... And, yesss, very much to my delight, the nearest pillow-in-my-way suddenly moved away from me!

Although my strained arm muscles still felt a bit tired, I started to spend quite some time pushing my pillows away from me while trying to rearrange them around me. Now and then, an unruly pillow fell off my bed and disappeared to the floor, making me wonder where it suddenly went. When the pillow didn't return, I forgot about it and just started to shove the next one around; until that pillow too disappeared from my vision. Unfortunately, my still too tired arm muscles started to cramp again from the unaccustomed workout. Therefore, I just laid them down next to me, while I tried to shove my pillows around by kicking at them with my hitherto unused legs.

Immediately, I found out that my legs were less flexible than my arms, but they were able to kick my pillows around with a quite lot more force! Feeling enthusiastic again, I started to kick at pillow after pillow, while trying to follow them with my eyes by turning my head from side to side and craning my neck. Suddenly, one of my pillows jumped up into the air! How in the world had I done that? Feeling even more enthusiastic, I again kicked at pillow after pillow, until I found out how I could kick them high into the air deliberately, by using both legs at the same time.

In no time, my sleeping den was a total mess, because I had kicked all my colored pillows around everywhere! As a very welcome result, I also felt much freer, because I now could look around without tilting my head or craning my neck. Enthusiastically, I started to kick at my remaining pillows; until all of them were out of my sight or disappeared onto the floor. Although both my arm muscles and my leg muscles were painful and started to cramp, and my worn-out little body felt dead tired; I was truly satisfied with my progress!

26   Aad Aandacht is a Dutch psychotherapist who loves writing 'books with a message'

Chapter 3. Discovering; developing ; experimenting.

Unknowingly, I had given my undeveloped baby muscles a very intense workout, so that, within a few days, they started to become relatively strong for such a small baby. As an extra bonus, this early training also yielded me a huge advantage throughout the next years of my bodily development. Even after several years from now, my excessively trained muscles were still relatively strong for such a young boy! Feeling dead tired but also absolutely wonderful, I closed my eyes and immediately fell asleep...

"My dear son, what have you done? Did you have a bad dream, or did you have a nasty cramp and couldn't get rid of it? All your pillows are spread out all over your place! Why didn't you call me or start crying? I would have helped you..."

Waking up from a happy dream, I first needed a moment to realize where I was now. Then, I started to smile broadly at recognizing the familiar face and voice. My beloved Dad hovered over me; but he looked worried, while he reached towards me and felt my forehead to check for a fever. Then, he tried to look at my tongue...

Oh my, what had I done? Of course, it had never been my intent to make my parents feel worried about me! I had only been playing with my still way too unwilling limbs; and also discovered many new interesting possibilities. Only, I never thought that my parents would misunderstand what I had been trying to do, to develop my untrained muscles and discover even more unknown potentials. What should I do now? How could I tell my Dad I was okay and had only been training my still way too unwilling muscles? Would he understand my thoughts, as our Wise Woman had done so easily?

While offering him my broadest smile, I told my Dad in my mind:

'Please, Dad, don't worry any more. I am only very curious; and, perhaps, my baby brain is a little bit too bright for its own good...'

Much to my happiness, my Dad seemed to understand at least some words of what I tried to tell him, because he started to look much happier and even smiled back at me! Had he really picked up my thoughts? And, would he also be able to pick up a picture of what I wanted him to do? Well, let's try it out...

While I again concentrated on my Dad's mind, this time, I started to send him a picture of him taking me out of my bed and putting me on his lap. Would he really pick it up?

Very much to my delight, within a second, my Dad lifted me out of my bed and took me to our couch in our living room! There, he sat down, took me onto his lap, and folded his safe arms around my body.

Yesss; that was exactly what I had wanted my Dad to do! Had he really picked up my thoughts and my picture? Happily, I nestled into his strong arms, feeling very pleased to have him as my new Dad. While I tried to melt even more into his aura full of love and safety, I also wriggled my baby body backwards, to deepen our bodily contact even more. Again, it felt wonderful to sit on my Dad's lap, feel his tender caring love engulfing me, and be cradled in his strong arms.

However, after a few minutes of doing nothing, my too energetic brain started to feel a bit impatient. Although I cherished my Dad's close togetherness very much, I also wanted to do something more productive and interesting! Therefore, I opened my eyes and restarted playing with my arms and legs, because I wanted to train my muscles some more. This morning, my Mom had played with a couple of very interesting things at the ends of my arms and legs. My Mom had called them 'hands' and 'feet'; and the tiny thingies at their ends were 'fingers' and 'toes'. Now, I wanted to find out how to steer their muscles and what useful things I could do with them.

First, I clapped both hands together, as my Mom had taught me to do; and I felt elated when they really produced an audible sound! Then, I had lots of fun entangling my tiny 'fingers' into each other and pulling at them, to release them with some difficulty. With an audible 'snap' sound, my two hands left each other; while, at the same time, my two arms suddenly opened up and spread out to the left and to the right. They bounced against my Dad's enveloping arms, but my Dad didn't seem to mind at all and only smiled broadly at seeing my childish efforts to play with my hands and fingers.

After some more playing with my hands and all those wriggling little fingers, I suddenly fell silent, because my bright brain restarted to think. What would happen if I tried to entangle my fingers around one of my colored pillows, to grab it and pull at it? Would the pillow snap loose; or would I be able to hold onto it and pull it towards me? Such a newly found ability could be very useful for manipulating my pile of colored pillows even more!

Quickly, I made a mental note to try my newest idea out, first thing after my Dad or my Mom brought me back to my sleeping den to have my next nap.

Chapter 3. Discovering; developing ; experimenting.

Now that I had discovered what useful things I could do with my hands and fingers, I started to concentrate on my legs, by bringing them together and trying to entangle my 'toes' of both feet into each other. Much to my surprise, my toes turned out to be almost useless, compared to my much stronger and certainly more flexible fingers!

Soon, I concluded that my hands and fingers were useful for grabbing and pulling at things; but my feet and toes were only for 'walking' and kicking my pillows around. Therefore, from now on, I would concentrate mainly on my hands and on all those flexible fingers that I could use to try to grab my pillows and pull them towards me.

Yesterday, after bathing me, my Mom had dried my 'two' hands and my 'two' feet. Then, she had counted my 'ten' little fingers and 'ten' toes while kissing them one by one, making me squirm and jiggle with the funny feeling. Immediately after she stopped, I had pushed my hands and feet towards her again, to make her perform the same counting a second time. At the same time, I had repeated the names of all ten numerals in my mind, because I wanted to remember them to use them for a next time. Although my undeveloped baby brain couldn't count yet, my Shaman inside already seemed to understand the real meaning of counting and using numbers. Of course, my bright baby brain immediately agreed and just continued to repeat all those numbers until it knew all of them by heart.

After playing with my two hands and my ten little fingers some more, another interesting thought popped up in my always-curious mind. Would my ten fingers be able to grab one of my feet and pull it closer to my face? Immediately, I bent one of my legs upwards and inwards, so that its foot moved towards my chest and I could see it. Now, I tried to grab my hovering foot with both hands, which turned out to be extremely difficult and demanded quite a lot of muscle coordination. After lots of trying, I finally succeeded in grabbing my still hovering foot, and immediately folded my ten fingers around it to keep it steady. Slowly, I pulled my foot towards my face, while following its movement with my eyes...

Much to my surprise, while my foot approached my face, it magically seemed to grow bigger and bigger! I had never seen such a strange phenomenon before. How could my foot suddenly look bigger than it had been before? Curiously, I pulled my foot even closer to my face, until I saw TWO approaching feet! Feeling shocked, I released both feet; and saw how they neatly refolded into only one foot.

To read all our famous 'Gypsy Series' books, please visit www.gypsyseries.com

Well... obviously, some of those interesting new things could be a little bit too incomprehensible; even for a precocious and extremely fast developing Gypsy baby with a way too bright brain! Therefore, my curious mind just decided to accept this too strange phenomenon without thinking it over too much, at least for now. Soon, I again grabbed one of my still hovering feet and pulled it towards my face, to take an even closer look at those strange phenomena.

Unexpectedly, my 'big toe' touched my lips, making me gasp with the surprisingly pleasant feeling. Remembering how I always loved to suck on my Mom's 'breasts', I opened my mouth wide and pushed my big toe into it. Immediately, I pushed my toe even further into my mouth, while I started to suck on it with all of my might and very much enjoyed the unexpected sensation. Although my big toe didn't resemble my Mom's breast, and it also didn't give me any tasty nourishment, it surely could do as a temporary substitute!

All the time, my Dad had watched my playing, while he kept his safe arms around my squirming little body to help me sit upright and prevent me from falling over. Now and then, he had chuckled at seeing my funny efforts to play with my tiny fingers and toes; but he didn't intervene and just let me discover my own things. That is, until he saw me grabbing my foot and sucking on my big toe with all of my might while getting a blissful smile on my beaming face! This time, my Dad started to bellow with laughter. Almost hiccupping from fun, he nearly let me slip out of his arms; but he rescued me at the last moment and just in time pulled me back into his safe embrace.

My Dad's unexpected reaction took me by surprise, because I nearly fell down and he could rescue me only at the last moment. Unfortunately, my still inexperienced baby brain didn't understand what could have happened. Therefore, I first let my big toe flip out of my mouth with a loud 'plop'. Then, I looked up at my Dad with a shocked face, and started to cry.

Immediately, my Dad apologized for his clumsy behavior, looking a bit ashamed but also still chuckling:

"Sorry, my dear son! Of course, I am not laughing at you; but I just cannot help chuckling because you were such a funny sight..."

4. Talking to my Dad; and what is Real Love.

While I listened to my Dad's apology and tried to understand what he told me, something VERY important dawned on me. In sudden wonder, I stared at my Dad's moving mouth and even stopped crying. Much to my own surprise, my bright baby brain was already able to understand quite a lot of my Dad's words, even without sensing their energy! This was a MAJOR discovery!

Until now, my 'sixth senses' had always translated the energy of the spoken words, so that my little baby brain could understand what people meant. Or, in case my sixth senses couldn't translate some too difficult words, I just concentrated on people's minds and easily read their thoughts or their expectations.

Now, all of a sudden, my extremely bright brain seemed to recognize nearly all of my Dad's spoken words, and it was relatively easy for me to put them together into a meaningful sentence! Feeling on cloud nine, I tried to tell my Dad about my important discovery...

Alas, 'understanding a person' and 'talking to a person' turned out to be two totally different abilities; because, again, the only things that left my mouth were small air bubbles and a lot of saliva. Obviously, I still had to learn quite a lot more, before I would be able to have a real conversation with my Dad.

All the time, my Dad had stared at me as if he tried to understand what I could be saying, while he looked at my quickly opening and closing mouth in obvious marvel. After I stopped my idle tries to talk, he hesitatingly asked me:

"My dear son; are you really trying to TALK to me? What do you want to tell me, with your wise eyes? Ultimately, your baby body is only three weeks old! Yet, it looks like you already understand every single word that I am saying, as if you are a Very Wise Old Soul. What do you think; could I be right, or am I talking nonsense?"

Again, my bright baby brain understood every single word that my surprised looking Dad told me, even without using my 'sixth senses. From now on, I really was able to understand my Dad!

Feeling elated and very happy with my newest discovery, I smiled broadly at my Dad, while I nodded my wobbly head up and down vigorously. At the same time, I tried to project a picture of a happy looking little Prince Harold into my Dad's brain, hoping he would be able to pick up at least some of its energy. While projecting my happy picture into my Dad's brain, I also told him in my mind:

'Dad, you are absolutely right, and my extremely clever brain really understands all of your words! I am so happy...'

Much to my delight, my Dad's eyes suddenly brightened considerably. Clearly, he had again picked up at least some of my projected energy! Had he also received my projected picture? First, he took a few tissues from our table and cleaned my again drooling mouth. Then, he refolded his strong arms around my baby body and pulled me into an enormous bear hug. Although, in his over-enthusiasm, he almost suffocated me and involuntarily nearly crushed my tiny ribs, I didn't mind at all and just waited until I was able to breathe again.

With a still very proud face, my broadly smiling Dad asked me:

"My dear son, were you really projecting your words into my mind and sending me your pictures, although both your baby body and your still undeveloped baby brain should be way too young to be able to do such difficult things? My so precocious and extremely clever son, who are you in reality? With all respect, you could easily be an upcoming Shaman, or perhaps our new Wise Man. Have our Ancestors kept your soul awake, so that you could bring your Cosmic Powers into your earthly life? From the first day on, I've thought I could sense your energy looking at us and probing our energy fields, from within your Mom's womb... Therefore, from this moment on, I will start talking to you as if you already understand everything that I am telling you. I only hope I am doing the right thing, without overloading your still developing brain too much..."

YESSS! Much to my happiness, my Dad suddenly decided to talk to me according to the REAL development of my 'wise old soul'. This was a major step forward in our father-son relation! Again, I tried to look as enthusiastic as I could, to encourage my Dad even more, while telling him in my mind that he was absolutely correct and doing the right things by seeing me as a 'wise old soul' and treating me accordingly. At the same time, I projected another picture of a happy looking little Harold into his mind, hoping he would pick it up again and feel encouraged even more.

Chapter 4. Talking to my Dad; and what is Real Love.

By using my inherited Shaman abilities, I contacted my Dad's enveloping aura and sensed how, for a few seconds, he still tried to deny my baritone voice in his brain and the second picture that suddenly showed up in his mind. Then, he started to smile even broader, while he looked at me with an enormous amount of love and with quite a lot more respect! Obviously, my Dad had now accepted my special status as a Very Wise Old Soul.

Again, I nodded my wobbly head vigorously, while sending my Dad another picture of myself as a 'wise old man' with an enormous beard. Would he be able to pick this up as well?

Two seconds later, I started to chuckle with laughter and almost hiccupped from sudden fun, because my broadly smiling Dad sent me a funny picture back of his bearded 'wise old son', this time also adorned with an enormous mustache! Until now, I never knew that my Dad would be able to use at least some of those powerful 'Shaman abilities' that I seemed to possess in abundance...

Since that remarkable day, my Dad always kept his promise; and he really started to talk to me as if I were a grownup! Because I soon understood every single word that he told me, it also helped me tremendously in developing my already bright brain even faster. We also started to read each other's facial expressions, and that bonded us even more. Now and then, we had a silent communication, without using any words, making my Mom a little bit jealous because she couldn't understand what we were doing.

Of course, my Dad had already told my Mom about his sudden experiences and his promise to talk to me as if I were a grownup; but he couldn't convince her. She just didn't believe him, told him her little baby boy was still way too young to be able to understand anything important, and stubbornly continued to baby-talk to me.

Although, time and again, I concentrated on my Mom's mind and tried to send her my thoughts and my pictures, she just didn't pick them up. Obviously, she didn't have any of the useful 'Shaman abilities' that my beloved Dad could use from time to time, and that I seemed to possess abundantly.

Again, my Mom started to use her silly baby-words, while she changed my soiled diaper, washed me, dried me, and powdered my sensitive parts. Of course, I wasn't really mad at her; but I hated being treated as a little baby and therefore responded indignantly.

To read all our famous 'Gypsy Series' books, please visit www.gypsyseries.com

Why didn't my Mom accept that I was a 'very old soul' and only temporarily living in my tiny baby body? Just wait until I am a couple months older and able to speak properly...

Again, my Mom started to laugh at seeing my indignant face, while she kissed my wrinkling baby nose and told me she loved her little boy anyway. Again, I tried to talk to my Mom, this time also forcefully projecting my words into her brain:

"Mom, please stop acting ignorant; because, within a few months, you will be very surprised, and that is a promise!"

Unexpectedly, my Mom started to look distracted, while she took a tissue and absent-mindedly removed my excessive saliva and little air bubbles that again showed up around my mumbling mouth. Obviously, this time, she had felt at least some of my projected energy, but didn't know what to do with it. Could it be because I was a man, my Dad was a man, but my Mom was a woman and therefore reacted different from my Dad and me? Involuntarily, I started to laugh, but immediately suppressed my insolent chuckling.

Women... they will never understand us men.

After I woke up from my next nap, I faintly remembered a beautiful dream wherein I had returned into our Timeless Eternal Realm and immediately felt At Home. Now that I was awake, my Inside still felt very strange; as if 'I' consisted of two different entities that had to live together in such a tiny baby-body with all its annoying impediments and restrictions. My first entity felt like a newborn baby that played with its tiny arms and legs, while discovering the outside world, and wanting to feel safe and loved on a cozy lap or in two strong arms.

At the same time, my second entity felt like being VERY old and wise beyond my most daring imaginations, waiting until I would be able to use my inherited Cosmic Powers to help our so terribly confused Planet Earth and make it a much better place to live on.

Still feeling confused, my tiny baby brain tried to make sense of my entangled feelings. Who was 'I' in reality, and why was 'I' here; trying to behave as a little baby but feeling much older and wise beyond my earthly years, and sometimes remembering our Timeless Eternal Realm where I still felt AT HOME with a deep longing to be there again? Fortunately, my remembrances soon faded away, and I stopped thinking and just restarted playing with my arms and legs.

Chapter 4. Talking to my Dad; and what is Real Love.

Happily, I first pulled my colored pillows towards my body by grabbing them with my fingers, and then kicked at them with both legs at the same time, to make them jump up high into the air. Again, I grabbed the same pillows and pulled them next to my body, unless they already disappeared towards the floor and I couldn't find them any more. For quite some time, I just went on and on, giving my muscles another thorough workout, until I started to feel too tired and closed my eyes to take a quick nap before I restarted again.

For many weeks, I went on discovering more and more useful abilities; while my steadily growing baby body became stronger and stronger due to my arduous training and stubborn nature. At last, my neck muscles were strong enough to lift my head, which allowed me to look around for a couple of seconds. Finally, I was able to look around more or less effortlessly, certainly after I first kicked my pile of colored pillows out of the way and onto the floor. Unfortunately, my Mom always immediately restacked them around me.

Women...

Now and then, my inherited Shaman abilities sensed a few curious visitors who approached our caravan and wanted to see me. Around ten seconds later, our visitors knocked on our front door and politely asked to be allowed to see their little Prince with his bright blue eyes and his always-happy smile. Again, many visitors reacted stunned at seeing such extremely fast development for such a tiny boy!

Sometimes, they wanted to take me out of my pillows and cuddle me, while letting me sit on their laps on our couch in our living room. Well, I didn't mind at all. Much to my onlookers' surprise, I seemed to understand everything that they told me, because I always responded correctly to their spoken words. Otherwise, I just read their thoughts and thus knew exactly how they expected me to react...

As a little baby, I always loved being taken out of my pillows and cuddled on a cozy lap; or held in two warm and safe arms. Therefore, I always started to smile broadly at my visitors; and my happy face and sparkling bright blue eyes caused them to smile back at me and 'love' me even more!

My extremely bright brain had already found out that smiling caused my visitors to 'love' me a lot more than crying did. When I started to cry, mostly to develop my still growing lungs, they seemed to feel uneasy and soon returned me to my Mom or Dad.

Therefore, every time I wanted my visitors to take me out of my pillows and onto their cozy laps, I immediately offered them my broadest smile! Perhaps, I was really acting a little bit 'manipulative'; although, at that time, I didn't even know the word...

Of course, my bright brain already understood the vast difference between the kind of 'love' that our visitors showed me, and REAL Love. REAL Love was what radiated from my parents, Michail, my grandmother, and a couple of others who really adored me. Their Real Love always made me feel all warm and mushy inside; and, with them, I felt absolutely safe and cared for. With them, I could cry whenever I felt the urge to expand my lungs or train my deep baritone voice, without any fear of being rejected.

From the first day on, I always hated being belittled or treated as a little baby. Didn't my visitors know that I was a 'very old soul', temporarily living in this tiny baby body, waiting until I would be big enough to become a grownup? They didn't need to use those silly baby words, because my inherited Shaman abilities were able to sense what they thought anyway! Just wait, until I've learned how to use my deep baritone voice to tell them the truth...

Again, one of those visitors took me into her arms and started using the silly baby words that always made me angry. Soon, I felt too frustrated, stopped smiling, stared at her, and tried to send her a message... My visitor didn't understand why I suddenly didn't smile any more; and she reacted rather surprised:

"Look at the little sweetheart. Why doesn't he smile any more? Maybe, he has pooped his diaper? Hey, you little teeny-weeny; now give me a proper smile! Come on, goo-goo, ga-ga..."

Thanks to this silly visitor, I suddenly knew how I could teach all my visitors a lesson, to prove they didn't really love me. Therefore, I just pooped my diaper, this time on purpose!

Within a few seconds, many distracted visitors sniffed the air, handed me back to my Mom, and didn't 'love' me anymore.

See? Those visitors didn't REALLY love me.

My smiling Mom took over, cleaned my smelly bottom, attached another diaper, and kissed my wrinkling little nose.

See? My Mom did love me, always, and with REAL love!

A few weeks later, I unexpectedly found out that I really was a special child; with extremely strong muscles and a surprisingly deep baritone voice for such a tiny baby! A 'gadjo doctor' visited our Gypsy community; and my parents asked him to come over and check my bodily development. Immediately when the friendly doctor entered our caravan, I liked him at first sight and happily let him check my eyes, probe his fingers into my belly, listen to my lungs, and stare into my throat with a little flash light. He also asked me to move my arms and legs up and down, try to sit upright, take a few wobbly steps while he held my hands, and I had to follow his slowly moving finger first with both eyes and then with one covered eye at a time.

Then, the doctor asked me a couple of easy questions; and I had to answer them by nodding or shaking my head. After the doctor had examined me thoroughly, he ruffled my unruly blond hair and told my still anxiously waiting parents:

"Your son turns out to be an extremely mature and absolutely healthy child! Although his tiny body may be a bit too small for his age, his muscles are surprisingly strong and his mind is already very bright. He also has very large vocal cords that give him a deep and sonorous sounding baritone voice. I am relatively sure that, within a few years, he will turn into a low bass. Mentally, your son is very precocious, and he gives me a gut feeling that he already understands everything that I am saying, although he is only a few months old. Your son certainly is a VERY special child..."

My happy looking parents thanked the gadjo doctor abundantly for his professional help. Finally, they could be sure that everything was all right with their extremely precocious son; and they didn't need to worry any more about my too low voice, my too strong muscles, and my too fast mental development.

All the time, I smiled broadly at the gadjo doctor; to let him know I understood everything he told my parents, and that I absolutely agreed with every single word! Of course, I already knew I had a surprisingly deep baritone voice; because many visitors had reacted a bit funny at hearing such an unexpected 'grownup' sound coming from such a tiny baby. Then, they always told my proud parents I was a very special boy with a beautiful voice!

A few days later, I accidentally found out that I seemed to use at least two different kinds of crying.

The first kind of crying, I seemed to use when I felt bored and wanted to have my parents' immediate attention. Then, my parents smiled at me while they told each other:

"Listen to our little Harold. He is developing his lungs."

Another kind of crying, I used when I felt hungry, had soiled my diaper, or didn't feel well. Then, immediately, my parents were there for me; to look after me, clean my smelly bottom, or call for our Wise Woman to heal me and give me some sour tasting medicine.

How did my parents know the difference? Although I tried out several different ways of crying, I just couldn't find the proper way to catch their attention. At last, I started to feel frustrated and cried from anger, because I couldn't find a workable way to 'manipulate' them.

Again, my parents only smiled at me, while they told each other:

"Listen to our little Harold! He sounds angry or frustrated, but that helps him develop his lungs."

Grrrr!

From the first day when I was born, I had been able to sense all the different energies that radiated from the people who visited our caravan. Soon, I was even able to recognize them by their specific auras! Within a few days, my inside could clearly distinguish my Dad's energy from my Mom's, from my Grandmother's, or from Michail's. Many times, I felt their surrounding auras preceding them, some time before they planned to pay us a visit. Then, I sensed their outstretching energy field entering our caravan at least ten seconds before they actually knocked on our door.

At first, my parents couldn't understand why I suddenly became excited, at least ten seconds before somebody knocked on our door. However, very soon, they got used to my strange 'abilities' and just accepted them. Often, my Dad or my Mom went to the door, to open it and let our stunned looking visitors in, ten seconds before they actually reached our caravan.

Of course, many visitors reacted surprised and asked:

"How did you know I was on my way to pay you a visit?"

"Little Harold told us, by getting excited. We think he has some sort of clairvoyant ability."

"That is very special! Do you think he will become a Wise Man?"

Chapter 4. Talking to my Dad; and what is Real Love.

"It will certainly be of great help when he is our new King."

I always felt ecstatic when the man I liked most, besides my own Dad, planned to visit us. Michail was a HUGE and truly impressive man; always wearing his inseparable fur coat, unless the weather was extremely hot. His powerful energy and Real Love always filled our entire caravan and engulfed everybody inside, including me. Therefore, I always LOVED to sit on my Big Friend's enormous lap and feel his strong arms around my tiny baby body!

Again, I felt Michail's preceding energy enter our caravan, at least ten seconds before he actually knocked on our door. Of course, I immediately started to fidget in my pillows on our couch, while at the same time trying to make enthusiastic sounds!

My Mom saw my sudden excitement, smiled knowingly, and already opened our caravan door in advance. Then, she welcomed my broadly smiling Big Friend:

"Hi, Michail, come in and take a seat! Didn't you bring your betrothed with you?"

My Big Friend shook his head, while he sat down on our couch that moaned under his heavy weight. Of course, he didn't feel surprised at all, knowing that my 'Shaman abilities' always worked flawlessly. He even seemed to be very proud of his so special little friend with his strange but also very useful 'sixth senses'.

In the meantime, at the other end of our couch, I still fidgeted in between my pillows and tried to catch Michail's attention.

My Mom smiled at seeing my eager face, lifted me from my pile of pillows, and put me onto Michail's enormous lap.

Yes, that was exactly what I wanted!

Michail folded his enormous arms around my tiny baby body and 'gently' crushed my small ribs against his chest. Happily, I let myself melt into his powerful aura, while I very much enjoyed the safe feeling of his strong arms around me. I loved my Big Friend with all my heart, mind and soul, and with REAL love!

Michail started to chuckle at seeing my beaming face and sparkling blue eyes; and bent over to kiss my forehead. His huge mustache tickled my nose and made me sneeze, but I loved even that!

Now and then, he brought Felicia, his girlfriend; and, then, I had to sit on her lap too. However, SHE didn't radiate the powerful Real Love I so cherished from my Big Friend.

Mostly, I first offered Felicia a tiny smile, and then started to fidget on her lap while staring intently at Michail. That always helped. Felicia felt a bit disconcerted; and soon put me onto Michail's lap. My Big Friend certainly didn't disapprove; and I had what I wanted!

Perhaps, I really acted a little bit 'manipulative'?

Hmm...

5. Sitting upright; seeing my possible future.

When my Mom returned from her kitchen, Michail laid me back in between my pile of pillows, to be able to drink his coffee. However, that was not to my liking! I wanted to sit on my Big Friend's enormous lap and have his strong arms around me quite a lot more!

Feeling frustrated, I first kicked my pile of pillows out of the way, because I wanted to free my path towards my chuckling Big Friend. Soon, all my colored pillows had disappeared onto the floor. Now, I only had to move my body towards my coffee-drinking Big Friend, who looked at my ministrations with curious eyes.

Lying on my back, I first wiggled my body around by using both my arms and my legs, as I had taught myself while playing around in my bed. Soon, my head pointed towards Michail; and I firmly planted my feet against the seat of our couch and started to kick myself backwards towards my Big Friend. Slowly, my body wobbled backwards, although I now couldn't see anymore where I went, and my baby brain didn't seem to understand anything about using 'symmetry'. Therefore, after some more forceful kicks, my head unexpectedly bumped against the backside of our couch!

Feeling surprised, I stopped my efforts and started to think this new situation over. What could have happened to my suddenly halting head? Tentatively, I tilted my stuck head and pushed myself backwards again, while I used my neck muscles to wobble my head back and forth. Much to my happiness, my body started to move again, although my head seemed to slide upwards and my shoulders followed suit! This was a totally new sensation to me. What would happen if I just went on pushing both my head and my shoulders upwards against the backside of our couch?

This time, I also planted my hands next to my body and started to push and kick both my hands and my feet at the same time, because my gut feeling told me I could be on the verge of doing an important discovery. Groaning with the effort, I could feel how first my head and then my shoulders slid upwards against the backside of our couch.

Fortunately, my thoroughly trained neck muscles were already strong enough to wiggle both my head and my shoulders upwards without injuring my neck, although my tiny baby body wasn't even three months old and still a bit too small for its age.

Totally unexpectedly, and much to my surprise, my baby body suddenly sat UPRIGHT against the backside of our couch, so that I was able to look around in our living room, just like all the others around me were doing! Yesss, this was what I had wanted to do all the time; but, up to now, my undeveloped baby muscles had been too small to be able to push my entire body upright. Now, all of a sudden, I was sitting upright; and I had done it all by myself, without any help from anybody else! With a proud face, I smiled at my surprised onlookers, as if saying:

'Do you see that? I am sitting upright, just like you, and I have done it all by myself!'

Of course, the same moment I turned my head around, I lost my balance and fell back onto our couch. Well, not feeling fazed at all, I just wiggled my body around until again my head pointed towards the backside, put my hands and feet against our couch, and simply kicked and wrestled upright again. Then, I did it again, and again...

Every time, wrestling upright was a bit easier; until I discovered how I could turn my head and look around without ever losing my balance. Within five minutes, I had taught myself how to sit upright, all by myself and without any help from anybody!

My proud looking Dad had been staring at my ministrations as if he couldn't believe his own eyes. Michail had a broad smile on his face, and he seemed to be very proud of his little friend; while my stunned looking Mom exclaimed:

"LOOK AT THAT! Our little Harold sits upright for the first time, and he has done it all by himself, although he is not even three months old! Janov, you are right, and Harold really is a very special child! Now, it's time to bring him to our Wise Woman, to let her read his past lives and his possible future. I am right back..."

Hurriedly, my Mom left our caravan, clearly to tell my Grandma, our Wise Woman, and everybody else in our camp, about her little baby boy's extraordinary and extremely early achievement! In the meantime, I started to train myself even more in sitting upright.

Chapter 5. Sitting upright; seeing my possible future.

Time and again, I let myself fall down on our couch, wiggled my head towards its backside, and wrestled upright again; until I could sit upright at lightning speed and almost effortlessly. All the time, both my Dad and Michail stared at my unexpected achievements with sparkling dark brown eyes and proudly beaming faces!

Soon, my Mom returned into our caravan, followed by several others. All of them wanted to have a first look at their so extremely early little Crown Prince, who really had to be the fastest developing child ever. Clearly, I had become their day's hero!

More and more surprised looking people showed up and waited outside, until it was their turn to enter our caravan and take a quick look at their proudly sitting little Prince. Again, many stunned visitors assured my parents I had to be the fastest developing baby that had ever existed! Now, they were even more curious about what our Wise Woman had to tell about my past lives and my possible future...

The next morning, my Mom tried to dress me into a small green-and-golden garment that once belonged to my Dad when he was still little. Wearing such a garment for the first time felt very strange; as, up to now, my baby body wasn't used to wearing any clothes other than my diaper. Of course, I started to protest fiercely, by groaning and kicking around while plucking angrily at the itchy sleeves. I wanted my Mom to remove the musty smelling thing immediately!

For the first time, my parents didn't listen to my complaints. They only told me to be quiet and get used to wearing our official Royal garments. Today, we HAD to wear our own Royal colors; because my parents were our Gypsy King and Queen, and I was their newborn Crown Prince and only Heir to the Throne!

Chuckling at seeing my angry little tantrum, my Mom went on helping my Dad with dressing into his own similarly colored garment. In the meantime, I stubbornly tried to get rid of the strange pieces of clothing that I already started to loathe. Unfortunately, my untrained fingers didn't know how to unbuckle all those weird looking buttons. Why didn't my parents listen to me and help me out of this musty smelling thing I absolutely didn't want to wear? Feeling betrayed, I glared at my Dad, trying to let my eyes shoot burning daggers...

At last, my frustrated looking Dad shook his head, pulled me into his strong arms, and tried to explain:

"My dear son; all three of us HAVE to wear our Royal garments today, because our subjects want to SEE their Beloved Leaders and their newborn Crown Prince! Could you please stop being angry, and try to behave as the proud Gypsy King that you once will be? Please, don't disappoint your already waiting subjects..."

Suddenly feeling very surprised, I looked up at my Dad, while my brain tried to digest this new information. Then, the real importance of wearing our Royal garments started to dawn upon me. For the first time, I understood that being our Crown Prince was not only a lot of fun, but also brought a lot of responsibilities! Although my baby brain still couldn't grasp the full extent of this important revelation, my Inner Self told me, loud and clear, that I had been a rather important Leader before. Therefore, in my Inside, I already knew how a real Aristocrat should behave. Even a tiny one like me...

Quickly, I suppressed my silly anger, by regulating my breath and forcefully shutting down my emotions. Next, I produced a huge smile, while forcing myself to be the happy looking little Crown Prince that my parents and my beloved subjects wanted to see. Still feeling a little bit guilty, I sighed and whispered:

"Sowwy..."

My suddenly shocked looking Mom stared at me and almost gasped from disbelief, while she exclaimed:

"Janov, you are right again! Our little Harold DOES understand you! Just look at him. He suddenly switches from anger to a smile, just like that! How in the world is that possible, for such a tiny child? And, did I really hear him whisper something that sounds like 'sorry'? I still cannot believe my own ears..."

Shaking her head in utter amazement, my Mom stared at me with a totally new expression on her face. Well, I was already sure that my astonished Mom would have to get used to enduring many more of those unexpected surprises. After all, I WAS a special child!

A few seconds later, I sensed the powerful aura of my Big Friend, obviously planning to join us. Immediately, I started to fidget in my Dad's arms while trying to make enthusiastic sounds. My Dad smiled knowingly at seeing my sudden excitement, while he went to our front door and opened it to let our Vice King enter.

Michail, this time clad in his neatest clothes, looked us over from head to foot while he chuckled:

Chapter 5. Sitting upright; seeing my possible future.

"Well, I suppose I've entered the wrong caravan! The people I'm looking for usually don't dress this refined."

While Michail stealthily winked at my already broadly smiling face, my chuckling Dad responded:

"Well; I almost forgot how YOU look without your inseparable fur coat. But, today, you look great."

After Michail ruffled my unruly blond hair, he reopened our front door and politely guided us outside. Together, we went to our faintly glowing campfire and sat down on our own Royal wooden bench; and I looked around at all our colorful caravans in sudden surprise.

Vaguely, I remembered the second day of my life, when my Dad had taken me to this same circle of wooden benches. Then, everything around us had been covered in blinding snow, while I was wrapped in a warm plaid blanket that left only my face free. Now, nearly three months later, all the white snow was gone; and this colorful world differed quite a lot from the first one I had seen! Today was only the second time I was outside, and I looked in sudden surprise and total awe at all those abundant colors around me.

Today, my Dad didn't throw me high into the air; but he only sat me on his lap and folded his safe arms around my tiny baby body. I always loved that feeling, which reminded me of my Mom's warm and cozy womb I had been living in for nine months. Feeling safe and protected in my Dad's strong arms, I looked at all the colorful people that showed up in the circle of caravans around our campfire.

Several smiling people approached us, greeted my proud parents and Michail, and ruffled my unruly blond hair, before sitting down on their wooden benches. Many suntanned young children were frolicking around or chasing after each other around our faintly glowing campfire, now and then curiously staring at their little Crown Prince. Every time I smiled at them, they smiled back at me immediately!

Sitting together on our own Royal wooden bench, my parents and I waited until all the grownups around us sat down, this time wearing their most beautifully colored garments. Only their suntanned young children didn't wear anything at all, except for a few really young kids that only wore diapers. Soon, all the frolicking children stopped their playing and climbed onto one of the many inviting laps, obviously wanting to be cuddled and feel loved just like I always did.

My Big Friend, Michail, sat next to us on our own Royal bench. Only, this time, he seemed to be way too caught up with his girlfriend, Felicia. Much to my disappointment, they were too busy whispering, kissing, and smiling at each other, to pay any proper attention to ME.

Feeling abandoned, I tried to catch Michail's attention, by fidgeting and trying to make enthusiastic sounds that only created a lot of saliva around my bubbling mouth. However, this time, my Big Friend didn't even see me. All the time, Felicia and he went on whispering and kissing, as if I didn't exist to them any more...

Involuntarily, I started to dislike the woman who so easily caught Michail's attention. Why was SHE having all the fun with my Big Friend, while that always had been MY privilege? Clearly, I was starting to feel a bit 'jealous' of Felicia; although, at that time, I didn't even know the word. Feeling more and more abandoned, I again started to fidget while trying to make audible sounds...

Until my frustrated looking Mom turned towards me, took a tissue, and angrily cleaned my drooling mouth. Then, she admonished me:

"Now, please, sit still and behave as a real Crown Prince!"

Feeling surprised, I looked at my Mom and nearly started to cry from my suddenly welling feelings of shame. However, because I also wanted to behave as a real Crown Prince, I quickly suppressed my upcoming emotions. Ultimately, I was already sure I had been a real Aristocrat before, and therefore I had to live up to that standard again! While heaving a heartfelt sigh, I tried to show that I really could be an obedient child, and therefore whispered:

"Yes Mum..."

The sudden expression of total disbelief on my Mom's stunned face was priceless!

When everybody was seated, our two violin players rose from their benches and started to play beautiful Gypsy melodies full of sadness and longing. The yearning sounds tore at my heartstrings; so that I felt like crying but desperately tried to repress my upcoming sobs. I absolutely didn't want to be a nuisance to the others around me, or to disturb our heartwarming atmosphere!

My Dad looked at me, saw my welling tears, and gently wiped them away. Then, he rubbed my stomach to relieve my tension; while I again regulated my breath and repressed my upcoming emotions.

Fortunately, that helped. My sobbing faded away; and I looked at my Dad and sent him my love and my thanks. Now, I saw that my Dad had tears in his eyes too, and I loved him even more! Again, I was sure that my Dad and I were kindred souls.

A few minutes later, our violin players let their music fade away, returned to their wooden benches, and sat down. Now, my Grandmother rose from her own wooden bench, clearly to greet us and make her announcements. First, she looked around the circle, making eye contact with everybody, until her eyes rested on me. She smiled at me; and I recognized her, smiled back at her, and longingly stretched my tiny arms out towards her...

Several surprised onlookers reacted astonished and exclaimed:

"Wow, look at that! Our Prince already responds to his Grandmother, although he is not even three months old! What an extremely special child is he; and look at those bright blue eyes! They feel like staring straight into your soul, just like our Wise Woman always does. Our newborn Crown Prince certainly is a Very Wise Old Soul..."

After all the surprised looking people had calmed down again, my Grandmother announced:

"Today, our newborn Crown Prince, Harold Janovski Romani, shows up in our circle for the second time; this time to let our Wise Woman read his past lives and his possible future, as we always do when a member or our Royal Family sits upright for the first time. His father, our beloved King Janov Nikkinsky Romani, has already proven to be 'one of us'; meaning he has been a Gypsy before in at least one of his past lives. His mother, our beloved Queen Maria Soren, also has proven to be 'one of us' before she married my son. Once we are sure that our newborn Prince is 'one of us' too; he will have the status of Royal Crown Prince, and we will raise him accordingly. Now, my little Prince and beloved grandson, our Wise Woman will look into your past lives and your possible future; and she will share her relevant findings with us. So be it."

My Grandmother bowed towards me, turned around, and sat down again on her wooden bench. Now, my Dad rose from our own Royal bench while carrying me in his arms. First, he bowed towards his beloved Mother and previous Queen, to show her his love and respect. Next, he carried me to our Wise Woman and handed me to her.

The Wise Woman sat me down on her lap; while staring at me with her piercing dark brown eyes as if she looked directly into my soul. The intensity of her piercing stare made me feel uneasy, so that I nearly started to cry from sudden discomfort. I didn't want to be left with our Wise Woman! I wanted to sit on my Dad's lap and feel safe in his strong arms! Where was my Dad?

Fortunately, before I could start crying, the Wise Woman quickly turned me around on her lap so that I sat across her legs. Gently, she covered my eyes with one hand, while she put her other hand against the back of my wobbly head. Then, she started to hum, producing a strangely sonorous and monotonous sound.

Immediately, an intense energy started to radiate from her hands, numbing my baby body and making me feel drowsy. At that same moment, my Inside felt totally at ease and safe; because I suddenly recognized her powerful Shaman energy and knew what it was going to do to me. I recognized the intense energy that engulfed me; and I was sure I had used this same kind of energy myself many times before. In my former incarnation as a powerful Shaman and Mystic Mage, I had cured and healed many ill people; by helping them remember their past lives and healing their Karmic traumas. Now, our Wise Woman was helping me remember my own past lives, to be able to look into them and share her findings.

Soon, my Inner Awareness left my human body and entered our Timeless Eternal Realm, where I immediately felt AT HOME. Here was where I belonged in reality; and to where I would return after I first redeemed some nasty Karma, performed my Earthly duties, and readied my Important Tasks on Earth. Now that my awareness was freed from the impediments of my material environment, I again remembered who I was in reality, and why my Cosmic Friends had chosen ME to descend towards our Planet Earth and become the next Gypsy Leader. I also sensed many Beloved Ancestors and Spirit Friends around me; but they only sent me their greetings while telling me to go on. Another time, we would talk; but, today, I was here only to let our Wise Woman look at my past lives and my possible future.

After I had greeted my Beloved Ancestors and Eternal Friends, the Wise Woman changed her humming, so that I drifted into a much deeper trance. Soon, I left our Timeless Eternal Realm and propelled backwards along my timeline, until I entered my last past life on earth and remembered my former 'trapper Dad' who also was my Eternal Soul Mate. In this past life, my Mom had died in childbirth.

Chapter 5. Sitting upright; seeing my possible future.

Therefore, my trapper Dad had raised his son all alone, now and then helped by our nearest neighbor and closest friend who lived half a mile away in the same dangerous forest with its steep ravines and foaming rapids. From a very young age, my trapper Dad had taken me outside and taught me how to set traps, skin animals, and spice their tasty meat using carefully selected herbs. I grew up happy and carefree; until a hungry grizzly bear killed me, my former trapper Dad, and our closest friend. My Inside was sure we would meet each other and be very close friends again in our present lives, after first my parents and I had redeemed some old and very nasty Karma.

Soon, the Wise Woman changed her humming again; making me propel even deeper backwards along my timeline, until I entered another past life. In that past life, as a 'preacher', I had hunted down several so-called 'witches', to burn them on stakes and thus 'save their souls from burning in hell for all eternity'. Now, according to our universal Law of Karma, 'an eye for an eye and a tooth for a tooth', I first had to endure the same ordeal, to clean my Soul and redeem my former sins. This Cosmic Law is not for punishment; but it forces us to gain much more Love and Compassion for our previous 'victims', thus enabling us to better ourselves. Unlike my burnt victims, I would prevail; but the extremely profound experience would make me much stronger and certainly quite a lot humbler.

Again, the Wise Woman changed her humming; making me propel even deeper backwards along my timeline, until I entered another past life where I had been a real Aristocrat! Immediately, I recognized my former 'trapper Dad' and Eternal Soul Mate. In this past life, he was our Beloved 'Gypsy Monarch Harold the Great', while I was our Vice King and his very best friend. Working closely together, we had founded our modern Gypsy way of living, filling it with much more Love, Gratitude, Understanding, and Compassion. I also recognized this same secluded community with its surrounding mountains; proving I had been living in this same secluded place at least once before. Then, I had been our Beloved Vice King; while now, after I had grown up some more, I would be our next King and the Beloved Leader of all forty million Gypsies on Earth.

Suddenly, the Wise Woman changed her humming to a higher pitch that propelled me forward towards my 'possible future'. During my first six earthly years, I would grow up healthy and prosperously; while my 'wise old soul' would develop in lots of Real Love, to prepare itself for its Important Task on our Planet Earth.

To read all our famous 'Gypsy Series' books, please visit www.gypsyseries.com

A few months after my sixth birthday, I would first redeem my old Karma; helped by a nice man and his young son who once had been my Dearest Friends and again would be my devoted Helpers.

A few months after my eighth birthday, according to my Cosmic Plan, I would finally meet the man who once had been my former 'trapper Dad' and also was my Eternal Soul Mate and our beloved 'Gypsy Monarch Harold the Great' that I was named after. He would adopt me and be my new Dad, to help me grow up until I would become our next Gypsy Leader. Working closely together, we would write several books about our peaceful and lovable Gypsy way of living; and our 'Gypsy Series' books would be read all over the world!

At last, as a grownup, I would marry a nice Gypsy girl and raise my own little Gypsy Prince, to help him follow in our footsteps.

All the time, all our Beloved Ancestors, Cosmic Helpers, and Spirit Friends would be around us and help us from within their own timeless Eternal Realm. I could always reckon on them; and they could always reckon on me.

6. Daddy, Mommy, Harry luvyou deawly too.

The Wise Woman let her humming fade away, until her strange sound stopped completely. Almost immediately, my Inner Awareness returned into my body; where my human brain restarted thinking and already wiped out my trance experiences. I felt as if I woke up from a strange dream, making me feel confused, while my still drowsy body started to tremble all over. Fortunately, our Wise Woman asked my Dad to take care of me, because she had to recover first.

My Dad carried me back to our Royal bench, where he sat me on his lap and folded his safe arms around my trembling body. He filled me with his powerful energy while rubbing my upset stomach; until I sighed, burped, and started to feel better. All the memories from my strange 'dream' faded away, until I couldn't remember anything of what had happened during my induced trance. Soon, I started to look around again with curious eyes, and fidgeted enthusiastically when Michail finally looked back at me and smiled at me.

After our Wise Woman had recovered from her trance and first drank some water, she explained:

"Our little Crown Prince absolutely is 'one of us'; because, in one of his former incarnations, he has been our own beloved Vice King! He also was the dearest friend of our beloved 'Gypsy Monarch Harold the Great'; therefore, it is a good thing that he carries the first name of his deceased Great-Grandfather. After his sixth birthday, he has to redeem some very nasty Karma first; but he will prevail, helped by many Beloved Ancestors and powerful Spirit Friends. Then, he will meet the next incarnation of his Great-Grandfather; and, working closely together, they will start writing many 'Gypsy Series' books that will be read all over the world. Finally, he will marry a Gypsy girl and raise his own little Gypsy Prince to follow in his footsteps. Therefore, my beloved Royal Crown Prince, you are welcome again in our Gypsy community; and, from now on, we will raise you according to your officially recognized Royal status."

Immediately, our violin players rose from their wooden benches and started to play joyful Gypsy melodies full of hope and glory.

At the same time, all our subjects rose to their feet and approached my parents; to congratulate them with their now officially recognized Royal Crown Prince. Many people also congratulated ME, by touching my hands, kissing my forehead, or ruffling my unruly blond hair. At first, I loved all their well-meant attention very much. However, after some time, I started to feel too tired, and tentatively closed my eyes to shut everybody out for a moment. Immediately, I tumbled into a deep and sound sleep, probably because I was dead tired from living through all those emotional sensations. Being deep asleep, I didn't even feel my Dad or my Mom putting me to bed.

A couple hours later, I woke up in my own small sleeping den, opened my eyes, and curiously looked around. Obviously, my Mom or Dad had brought me home, undressed me, and laid me in between my pillows while I was still asleep. Smilingly, I realized that I now felt much happier, without wearing my too itching Royal garment. Inwardly, I hoped I never had to wear those musty smelling things again! Unfortunately, my wet diaper now started to feel itchy, so that I wanted to ask my Mom to replace it.

Because I felt totally happy and absolutely didn't feel like crying, I decided to try to CALL my busy Mom who seemed to be working in our kitchen, according to the sounds of cutlery and rattling pans. Ultimately, I had already been able to pronounce the words 'sorry' and 'yes Mum'. Now, I only had to make my voice a bit louder, to be heard by my busy Mom! Happily, I started to try to make audible sounds; by willing my baby throat and lips to form the word 'Mom'...

Only, very much to my frustration, this time, my mouth didn't produce any audible sounds at all! How come? What was I doing wrong? Again, I tried to speak through my throat and my lips, this time even more forcefully; but, again, my mouth didn't produce any audible sounds. I only had to swallow a lot of excessive saliva. What the heck could I be doing wrong? I was absolutely sure I HAD spoken the audible words 'sowwy' and 'yes Mum', because my stunned looking Mom had heard me; although, at that time, I had merely whispered those words. What should I do now?

Feeling more and more frustrated, I tried to find out how I could have whispered those words, just a few hours ago. Clearly, I was now doing something wrong, but what? With a deep sigh, I started some heavy thinking. What could I be doing wrong now, that I had been doing correct before? Perhaps, replaying my whispering in my mind would help me find out what exactly I had done?

Aad Aandacht is a Dutch psychotherapist who loves writing 'books with a message'

Chapter 6. Daddy, Mommy, Harry luvyou deawly too.

Immediately, I closed my eyes and tried to remember how I had been able to whisper the audible words 'sowwy' and 'yes Mum', by using both my mouth and my throat. Step by step, I replayed all the events in my mind; until I suddenly found out what could have happened. I was relatively sure I had mumbled both words while, at the same time, I had heaved a sigh from frustration because I had felt guilty! And, I also knew that 'sighing' meant 'breathing out'. Therefore, I immediately took a deep breath, and again let my throat and mouth form the word 'Mom' while I breathed out with a deep sigh.

YESSS! Very much to my delight, this time, my clumsy efforts worked. My mouth really succeeded in making a whispering sound that resembled the word 'Mhhommm'! Only, my whispering wasn't loud enough for my busy Mom to hear me from our kitchen. How were other people doing that, talking with a much louder voice without any whispering at all? Again, I started some heavy thinking, to find out where other people's loud sounds were coming from.

Soon, I thought I could have found a workable solution. Obviously, I had to use my 'vocal cords' as well, next to my throat and lips, to bring my sonorous baritone voice into my whispered words. Only, how in the world would I be able to do THAT? Up to now, I had only been able to produce my crying sound; next to sort of a 'humming' sound that always made my parents smile at each other...

After some more thinking, I finally decided that the only audible sound coming from my vocal cords that would be loud enough for my Mom to hear me from our kitchen, would be crying! Up to now, my crying had always alarmed my parents, even if they were outside and could hear me only through the open front door. Therefore, I was relatively sure that crying would set my vocal cords into enough action to be heard by my busy Mom in our kitchen, certainly with my extremely large vocal cords and deep baritone voice.

Now that I knew what I had to do, I only had to cry loud enough; while, at the same time, my throat and lips had to form the audible word 'Mom'... Okay, let's try it out immediately! Happily, I inhaled a deep breath first. Then, while trying to form the word 'Mom' with both my throat and my mouth, I forcefully exhaled and CRIED...

Well; after hearing my own very loud but also pathetic sounding result that still echoed through our caravan, I almost started to laugh at myself! This rather hilarious noise sounded more like some deadly wounded animal in distress...

Within a split second, my worried looking Mom stormed into my sleeping den. Immediately, she dived towards me, scooped me into her arms, and started to look my squirming body over from head to foot. Of course, she couldn't find anything to be worried about, although she again looked me over for a second time and even for a third time. Then, she finally saw my sparkling bright blue eyes and broadly smiling face! At first, she looked rather confused, until she sniffed the air around me. With a suddenly understanding but still rather choked voice, she admonished me:

"What the heck did you do, although you only soiled your diaper? For a moment, I thought you had fallen out of bed and broken all your bones... Please, Harold, never ever utter such a terrible scream again! Now, come here, and let Mommy change your diaper and feed you."

Well, this was exactly what I had wanted my 'Mommy' to do. At least, she would now change my still itching diaper and feed me her delicious nourishment from her breasts! However, at the same time, I also felt sorry for unintentionally alarming her like this; although I still didn't know how else I could have trained myself to use my voice properly. Clearly, I had to find another way of expressing myself, other than trying to cry and talk at the same time...

While my 'Mommy' took me to our living room to change my itching diaper, I decided to try to repeat her new word that I hadn't heard before. In my still inexperienced baby ears, her new name, 'Mommy', sounded much friendlier than her old name 'Mom' had sounded! Therefore, I took another deep breath, breathed out, and tentatively whispered my Mom's new word:

"Mhhhommmmy... Mhhommmy..."

My suddenly stunned looking Mom nearly let me slip out of her enveloping arms, while she stared at me in total astonishment! Fortunately, she could rescue me just in time, by quickly putting me down in between my pile of pillows on our couch. Still staring at my mumbling baby mouth in total bewilderment, she exclaimed:

"Harold, you REALLY can talk! My dear son, you ARE a very special child! Just wait until your Daddy hears you."

Immediately, I started to try out my Dad's newest name, 'Daddy', by whispering both new names:

"Dhhadddy... Mhhommmy... Dhadddy... Mhommy..."

Every time I repeated my new words, they sounded slightly better; until they started to sound like my Mom had spoken them, but still without the deep baritone voice from my large vocal cords. How would I be able to mix both sounds together, without again alarming my still trembling Mommy? Would 'humming' be able to do the trick? Well, let's try it out! I had already been 'humming' before; when I had felt totally at ease and wanted to expand my still growing lungs without making a crying sound. So far, both my Mom and my Dad always started to smile at hearing my happy humming...

While my Mommy changed my itching diaper, I tentatively started to hum, as I had done before when I felt totally at ease and didn't want to cry. Only, this time, I also used my throat and my mouth to speak. Much to my delight, my vocal cords reacted to my attempts and suddenly produced a soft but absolutely audible baritone voice! YESSS! At last, I had discovered how to talk more or less properly, although I first had to practice a lot more to say my words correctly. Happily, I started to repeat both new words, over and again, while trying to say them louder and louder:

"Mhommmy, Dhadddy, Mhommy, Dhadddy..."

All the time, my Mom stared at my talking mouth with a huge smile on her now proud looking face, while she washed and dried me, powdered my sensitive parts, and put a fresh diaper on my wiggling little bottom. For a moment, I had to stop talking; because my Mom took me onto her lap to feed me with her yummy nourishment from her breasts. Hungrily, I drank and drank, until my stomach was filled to the brim and I had to burp the excessive air out.

At last, my Mom laid me down on our couch in between my huge pile of pillows. Of course, I first kicked my pillows onto the floor, because I wanted to have more freedom! Then, I wrestled my body around and pushed myself up; until I sat upright and leaned against the backside of our couch. From here, I could overlook our living room and follow my busy Mom with my always-curious eyes wherever she went, until she again disappeared into her kitchen.

All the time, I continued to train myself to speak both new words even more loudly and properly. Stubbornly, I went on and on, until my words sounded more or less as my Mom had pronounced them. Feeling relatively satisfied, I just continued to concentrate on saying my words both louder and as correctly as possible...

Half an hour later, I suddenly sensed a very well-known aura that approached our caravan and clearly planned to be home early. Immediately, I started to hop up and down from sheer happiness. I almost fell off our couch, but could regain my balance at the last moment. Within ten seconds from now, the man I loved most in the world, would enter our caravan! Enthusiastically, I exclaimed:

"Daddy home!"

My Mom looked at me with a surprised face, while she asked me:

"Really? Is Daddy already coming home, this early? I still don't know how you always are so sure..."

Ten seconds later, our front door opened, and my Dad entered our caravan. He shucked his shoes, entered our living room, and first kissed my beaming Mom. Then, he came over to me, smiling broadly at seeing my brightly sparkling eyes and over-enthusiastic face. Offering him my happiest smile, I started to repeat my new word:

"Daddy, Daddy, Daddy!"

This time, my Dad looked totally perplexed! Nearly stumbling over his own feet, he stopped abruptly. Slowly, he opened and closed his mouth, as some caught fish that craved for more oxygen. Then, he stumbled towards me while he stuttered:

"My dear son, are you really calling me 'Daddy'? Has your Mom taught you how to say this word?"

Enthusiastically, I bobbed my head up and down, to let my Dad know I really copied the new word from my Mom. Then, I started to repeat all my words, trying to speak them as correctly as possible:

"Daddy, Mommy; Daddy, Mommy, Hawol... ...Hadol... ...Harol..., Harol...th..., Harol...p..., Harol...k..."

Then, I fell silent, feeling utterly frustrated. Why didn't my mouth want to speak my own name correctly? Now that I finally could speak some words, I also wanted to pronounce my own name! Only, my untrained mouth and tongue just couldn't couple the sound 'Harol' to its immediately following 'd' without making me splutter... This was VERY annoying! Feeling severely disappointed, I tried it again; but, again, the name that left my mouth didn't sound as it should be. Clearly, my untrained mouth wasn't able to pronounce my own name, 'Harold', with 'd' at its end, without breaking my tongue over it.

Chapter 6. Daddy, Mommy, Harry luvyou deawly too.

What should I do now? Of course, I stubbornly wanted to be able to say my own name correctly! Again, I tried to say 'Harold'; but, again, my untrained tongue refused to pronounce the too difficult 'd' at the end of my name. Now, I fell silent, while my bright brain took over and started to think. Obviously, I had to train my too unwilling tongue some more first, to be able to say my own name correctly.

Only, couldn't there be an easier way to pronounce my own name, at least for the time being? I just WANTED to be able to tell everybody my name, now that I could speak a few words! After some more heavy thinking, my built-in little 'brainiac' suddenly came up with what could be a workable solution, at least for now. My untrained mouth and tongue had already been able to pronounce the new words 'Daddy' and 'Mommy' without any difficulties; so... yes, why not?

With a naughty smile, I looked at my parents and asked them:

"Mommy, Daddy... I Harry?"

For several seconds, total silence fell over our living room. Then, my extremely proud looking Dad raced towards me and scooped me into his strong arms. Enthusiastically, he started to cuddle me, in the process nearly crushing my tiny ribs. Well, I certainly didn't mind at all, although my worried looking Mom seemed to fear for my life and desperately tried to take me over from my Dad's arms.

Her worried action seemed to calm my Dad down considerably, because he looked a little bit guilty, next to still looking very proud. With a slightly trembling voice, he told me:

"Harold, my dear son, from the first day when your Mom told me she was pregnant, I already knew you would be one out of a million! How old are you in reality? According to our calendar, you should be not even three months old. Yet, you are already understanding every single word that I am telling you, you are already sitting upright, and now you are even talking to us and coming up with a clever solution for pronouncing your own too difficult name. From now on, I am totally convinced that you are the fastest developing child ever! And, my precious 'Harry', both your Mommy and I love you dearly!"

Without thinking, I answered my proud looking parents:

"Daddy, Mommy, Harry luvyou deawly too!"

This time, my Mom nearly started to cry from happiness, while she approached me and took me over from my proud looking Dad.

For quite some time, my Mom stared into my eyes, as if trying to understand who or what her little baby boy could be in reality. Then, she shook her head, as if denying her own upcoming thoughts. At last, she just sat me down against the backside of our couch, where I could sit upright and look around in our living room.

My Mom went back to her kitchen to prepare dinner; while my Dad slumped down next to me and scooped me into his strong arms. This time, he was a lot more careful not to crush my tiny ribs too much, although I still didn't mind at all. Feeling totally safe in my Dad's enveloping arms, I looked up at him and smiled broadly at seeing his sparkling dark brown eyes full of love and happiness.

My Dad and I absolutely were kindred souls!

7. Restricted; I am teaching myself crawling.

A few weeks later, I woke up from my morning nap on our couch, and first produced a heartfelt yawn. Then, as usual, I kicked my pile of pillows out of the way to have some more freedom, and to be able to sit upright and look around properly. A moment later, all my pillows were on the floor, except for one stubborn pillow that shoved just out of my reach. Well, who was the boss here? Of course, I wanted to kick that obstinate thing towards the floor as well!

Happily, I wiggled my tiny body around so that my legs pointed towards the unruly pillow, stretched out at full length, and kicked at it. Alas, the pillow went even further away. Teasingly, it shoved just out of my reach, instead of following its friends to the floor.

Now, I became angry at the pigheaded pillow that didn't obey me. The persistent thing HAD to listen to my will! Stubbornly, I wrung the upper half of my body towards it; while, at the same time, forcefully kicking my legs against our couch. Now, I only had to flail my arms to roll over onto my stomach, as I had done many times before. Now lying prone, I tried to wriggle my body forward to reach the mischievous pillow. Unfortunately, my little baby body only jiggled from left to right; but it did not move forward.

What should I do now? I absolutely wanted to kick that scalawag pillow towards where it belonged! Of course, I could just turn around until I was on my back again, and then kick my body backwards towards the pillow. Only, then, I couldn't see where I went...

Feeling frustrated, I decided to try out something different I had never done before. Still lying prone, I pushed my arms up against our couch while stretched them at full length. Slowly, the upper half of my body rose up from our couch, supported by my outstretched arms. Now, I only had to lift my head, to be able to look around.

Hey! Looking around like this was even more fun than sitting upright had been! Again, I had discovered something new, and I had done it all on my own. Now, I only had to bend my two arms, to lower my baby body back onto our couch and lie prone again...

Suddenly, my clever brainiac brain restarted to think. What would happen to my body, if I bent only ONE arm? Of course, I had to try it out, and it turned out to be even more fun than I had anticipated! Immediately after I bent only one arm, my entire body rolled around along its axis, so that I was lying on my back again. At the same time, I had also rolled a couple of inches towards my obstinate pillow!

Well, that unruly pillow could wait until later. Again, I turned back onto my stomach, pushed myself up, and rolled around. Feeling elated with my newest discovery, I rolled around and around...

Only, because I totally forgot to look at where I went, my happily rolling body suddenly fell off our couch and towards the ground, as if following my obedient pillows. With a loud yelp, I tumbled upside down and bumped my head on our carpeted floor.

OUCH! That hurt! Feeling both frustrated and a bit angry, because my over-enthusiasm had betrayed me like this, I started to cry...

Immediately, my worried looking Mom showed up from our kitchen and raced towards me. Quickly, she squatted down and scooped me up from the floor, to look me over for any damage. Only, I had already gritted my teeth and stopped crying. Of course, falling off our couch had been my own fault, for not paying enough attention to where I was rolling. Now, I had to pay the price for this valuable lesson, with a painfully swelling lump on my head.

Well... although my lump was painful, I was already sure I would survive. Therefore, I just smiled broadly at my worried looking Mom, to let her know I was okay and wanted to go on with my interesting experiments as soon as possible.

However, instead of putting me back onto our couch, my Mom started to look around our living room. Why did she do that? Feeling a bit uneasy, I tuned in into her mind to read her thoughts. Then, I felt severely shocked! Much to my dismay, I suddenly sensed that my Mom was thinking about restricting my freedom, to prevent me from falling again or having any other accidents...

Only, I didn't WANT to be restricted by my worried looking Mom! I had planned to experiment with moving around on our couch quite a lot more! And, of course, I still wanted to kick that scalawag pillow to the floor. Besides, would my pillows get headaches and swelling lumps too, from falling off our couch and bumping onto the floor? As far as I knew, they never yelped...

Now let's get back to where I was. How could I convince my still worried looking Mom I would be a lot more careful from now on, because I had learned my lesson the hard way? Of course, I could try to tell her what I was planning to do and that she didn't need to worry about me any more. However, I was also sure she again wouldn't pick up my thoughts or pictures. She never did. Perhaps, as an alternative, I could try to manipulate her motherly feelings for me? Hmm...

I looked up at my Mom and offered her my biggest smile, while I told her the words I had practiced many times:

"Mommy, Harry luvv you deawly and verry musj!"

Immediately, my Mom got tears in her bright blue eyes, while she answered me with a choking voice:

"My dear Harry, I love you dearly too; very, very much! Only, apart from that, I still want to protect you from falling off our couch again. What shall I do now, to restrict your movements..."

Of course, I really meant what I had said. I still loved my Mommy dearly, and with REAL love! Only, I absolutely loathed her idea of protecting me, if that also meant restricting me from experimenting. How could I convince my cautious Mom to let me keep my freedom?

Feeling rather desperate, I decided to try to force my thoughts into my Mom's too insensitive brain. Perhaps, I would be able to reach her brain easier if I first brought our heads together?

Tentatively, I put my arms around my Mom's neck and pushed my face against her warm cheek. Then, I tried to send my pleading thoughts directly into her too insensitive brain. Hoping she would pick up at least some of my projected energy, I begged:

'Please, Mom, don't restrict me, because I NEED to experiment; and I promise I will be a lot more careful from now on!'

For quite some time, my Mom only stared at me with a surprised face; until, at last, she hesitatingly responded:

"Will you really be a lot more careful from now on? I don't want to send my precious Harry baby to a hospital with a broken neck..."

YESSS! This time, my Mom had really picked up some of my projected thoughts! At least, she had understood the last part of them, because she had correctly answered my projected question!

In response to her answer, I nodded my head vigorously; while I tried to send her a picture of a happy 'precious Harry baby' that was safely playing on our couch. My Mom could count on me!

Surprisingly, this time, my Mom only sat me upright against the backside of our couch, while she told me:

"Okay, I will trust you that you really are a lot more careful from now on. However, I also want you to move around quite a lot safer. Therefore, please, sit still until I am ready, and be patient until I have prepared our room for your crawling around."

First, my Mom dragged our table out of the way, clearly to create some more free space on our carpeted floor. Then, all my colored pillows went back onto our couch, next to where I was sitting. One by one, she piled them up on top of the unruly one. Now, she picked me up from where I was sitting and put me down onto our floor, which fortunately had a thick rug and was spotlessly clean.

Very much to my delight, my Mom turned out to have a really good idea! Feeling elated, I immediately restarted my interesting experiments. Again, I started to roll around and around; but, now, I first looked carefully at where I was and to where I was going. I didn't want to get a second lump on my still painful head!

After lots of rolling around and having very much fun, I started to feel a little bit too tired and therefore decided to try out something even more difficult. Although my body had rolled across the floor at a reasonable speed, it still was a rather impractical way of moving, and a rather tiring way as well. Therefore, I now wanted to try out something more practical that also felt more natural.

After again rolling onto my stomach, I first folded both arms and legs under my body. As if it came to me naturally, I planted both my hands and my knees onto the floor and pushed myself up. Suddenly, I sat on all fours, looking up at my still watching Mom! My body only wobbled a little bit; but I succeeded in keeping my balance.

Because my arms were much longer than my thighs were, I sat almost upright and could look around with ease. Again, I had discovered something new and usable that turned out to be lots of fun. And, again, I had done it all by myself! Now, I only had to find out how I would be able to move around properly... Because it also came to me naturally, I suddenly started to shift both my arms and my legs back and forth, hoping to move forward.

Chapter 7. Restricted; I am teaching myself crawling.

Unfortunately, I lost my balance and tumbled onto my back. What could I have done wrong? Feeling a little bit frustrated, I tried to think it out. Only, even after some very heavy thinking, I still didn't understand what I had been doing wrong. Therefore, I decided to go on with exactly the same experiment, at least for now.

Again, I rolled onto my stomach, folded my arms and legs under my body, and pushed myself up on all fours. However, this time, I carefully placed only one arm forward while trying to keep my balance. Next, I placed my other arm forward; and it felt natural to let one knee follow, and then the other one...

YES! Very much to my happiness, this time, my body had moved forward at least a couple of inches, and with surprising ease! Plus, I was still on all fours and keeping my balance! Now, I only had to train myself in moving my arms and legs faster and rhythmically.

Less than half an hour later, I was racing around our living room at an astonishing speed. This was the real work! This time, I was really crawling around on our carpeted floor, and again I had discovered everything all by myself! Again, I had achieved what I had been trying to do all the time, but up to now didn't know how to do it.

Feeling more and more enthusiastic, I started to crawl faster and faster, at the same time moving my arms and legs even more rhythmically. Only, because I was too over-enthusiastic, I again forgot to look out where I went, although I now could look forward easily...

Soon, the inevitable happened. Unexpectedly, I bumped my still painful head against one of the surrounding walls and stopped in sudden surprise. OUCH, that hurt terribly! The same painful lump on my head that I still had, now hurt even more! Feeling a bit silly, I slumped down on the floor and tumbled onto my back.

Again, I had forgotten the most important rule of playing it safe and be careful with any new things, always and everywhere. Safety first! Again, I just gritted my teeth and paid the painful price for this important lesson. From now on, I HAD to look out where I was crawling, all the time and everywhere! Quickly, I looked up at my wary Mom, while forcing myself to show her a broad smile.

Fortunately, my Mom immediately smiled back at me, obviously feeling reassured by my again beaming face. She also seemed to be very proud of her so extremely fast developing 'little baby boy' who was discovering how to crawl around all on his own!

To read all our famous 'Gypsy Series' books, please visit www.gypsyseries.com

Suddenly, my Shaman inside felt an already very well-known powerful aura that stretched out into our caravan! Did I really sense my Dad's joyful energy, planning to come home? Immediately, I sat on all fours and ready to greet him, while I exclaimed:

"Mommy? Daddy home!"

Ten seconds later, my Dad entered our caravan and shucked his shoes in our hallway. Of course, I was already sitting ready for take-off, impatiently waiting to show off my newly gained ability! The moment my Dad entered our living room, I crawled towards him at lightning speed. I bumped into his legs, and looked up at him with a proudly beaming face and sparkling bright blue eyes.

Looking absolutely stunned, my Dad scooped me off the floor and took me into his strong arms, while he uttered:

"My precious son; again, you surprise me! Are you really crawling around, all on your own and without any help from anybody else? And this is while you are not even four months old! My dear 'Harry', again you are a real super boy; and, again, I am very proud of your extremely fast development! Could you please demonstrate your crawling again while I am looking at you?"

My proud looking Dad first laid me back onto our floor. Then, he sat down on our couch, to enjoy looking at me and at my recently discovered astonishing achievements. Of course, I first rolled around and pushed my arms up, so that I sat on all fours. Then, I demonstrated my newest ability, by adeptly rounding all the corners of our living room, on my way avoiding all those grownup legs-in-my-way.

Then, I saw one of my unruly pillows that had fallen off our couch and onto the floor, and crawled towards it. Spontaneously, I decided to help my Mom with tidying. Therefore, I grabbed the pillow with one hand, and towed it towards my Dad on only one arm and two knees. Reaching the pillow towards my Dad, I asked him:

"Pwease Daddy, pillow up cous?"

Of course, my Dad immediately understood what I wanted him to do. With a broad smile, he took the unruly pillow out of my hand and ceremoniously placed it onto our couch where it belonged. Good Daddy! I am already sure you will be perfectly trainable.

My still extremely surprised looking Dad stared at me for quite some time, until he finally uttered:

"My dear son; I still don't know what to think of your extraordinary achievements, at such an extremely young age. Up to now, I always thought that babies started to crawl around for the first time after they were at least seven months old. And, I was sure that youngsters couldn't talk properly before they were at least a year old. Now, I am looking in marvel at my own little son; who, according to our calendar, is only three months and three weeks old. Yet, much to my surprise, my little son already crawls around our living room at lightning speed, and he even speaks a couple of words! My dear son, who are you in reality? Our Wise Woman told me our Ancestors are with you, and that you have an important task to fulfill on our earth. Is that why you are so precocious and extremely clever? Has it to do with your amazing 'Shaman abilities'? Then, I feel very blessed to have you as my son! I only hope I will be able to educate you properly, without making too many mistakes..."

Because my Shaman inside sensed my Dad's doubts, I first pulled myself up by his trousers, to ask for a warm cuddle. Immediately, my Dad lifted me onto his lap and folded his strong arms around my small frame. Gently, he pulled me against his broad chest, this time trying not to crush my tiny ribs too much.

Feeling perfectly happy; I immediately 'octopushed' my tiny body against my Dad's broad stomach, while trying to melt away in his enveloping warm aura. First, I looked up at him and offered him my most beautiful smile. Then, I told him, while trying to articulate my spoken words as correctly as possible:

"You aw a vewwy good Daddy, and I luvv you deawly!"

At that same moment, I also projected my thoughts directly into my Dad's brain while I spoke to his inside:

"Please, Dad, stop doubting so much. You already ARE a good Daddy, and I am sure I will never find a Dad who is a better parent than you are. I love your dearly; but, please, stop worrying. All our Ancestors and Spirit Friends are with us, and they will never allow you to make any serious mistakes. You only have to listen to your own heart. And, please, let me experiment whenever I feel the urge to develop myself or my upcoming Shaman abilities even more..."

Clearly, my Dad had picked up everything that I projected into his mind, because he smiled back at me respectfully. He really was a good Daddy, and I had meant every single word of what I had said!

For quite some time, we only stared into each other's eyes, while feeling our powerful mutual love radiating between us and warming our souls. That is, until my wet diaper started to feel too itchy; and I asked my Mom while using my normal baritone voice:

"Pwease Mommy, Harry clean diaver?"

Working together, my parents removed my soiled diaper, cleaned my smelly bottom, powdered my sensitive parts without making me sneeze, and my Dad put a fresh diaper on me. After many kisses and cuddles, my Mom laid me in between my pile of pillows; where I fell asleep almost immediately. Vaguely, I heard my parents talk about my extremely fast mental development, my grown-up sounding deep baritone voice, and my already astonishing knowledge of all those difficult words for such a young child...

Several hours later, after I woke up and got another fresh diaper, my Dad and I sat across from each other on our floor, having lots of fun rolling a plastic ball to and fro. Every time our ball escaped behind me, I crawled after it and kicked it back to my patiently waiting Dad. Every time our ball escaped to another place, I pointed at it. Then, I told my chuckling Dad:

"Pwease Daddy, ged ball and give to Harry?"

Much to my delight, my Dad started to behave more and more as a well-trained parent. Obediently, he crawled after our ball, went back to his own place, and again rolled our ball towards me. Most of the time, I caught the ball between my legs, took it in both hands, and threw it back to my patiently waiting Dad. The few times when the naughty ball escaped from my legs, both my Dad and I had lots of fun crawling after it, because we also tried to be there first while bumping into each other on purpose.

At last, after quite some time of playing ball and having lots of fun, my little body started to feel too tired. Therefore, I suddenly left our ball, crawled towards my Dad, and clambered onto his safe lap.

My Dad took me to our couch, where he slumped backwards with his head resting on my pillows. Immediately, I draped myself all over his broad chest and put my little nose into his left armpit. This always was my most favorite place, from our first day on! Now smiling from ear to ear, my chuckling Dad told me:

"You really are my little octopus! Harry, my dear son, I am very, very proud of you, and I love you with all my heart!"

My Dad started to stroke my bare back, and I loved the feeling very much. Happily, I basked in the nice sensation of being close to each other and loving each other dearly. That is, until I became too drowsy and closed my eyes... Within a minute, both my Dad and I were sound asleep on our couch, happily snoring together.

After I woke up again, I crawled down from my Dad's stomach, slid off our coach towards our floor without any help, and happily started to crawl around again. However, now that I was able to move around, nothing in our caravan was safe for me any more! Soon, I disappeared into our interesting kitchen, where I tried to have a closer look and a possible feel at every colorful or blinking thing that caught my attention. Fortunately, my Mom saw me just in time, and swiftly took me back to our much safer living room.

For quite some time, my parents were busy preparing our caravan for my too early moving around. Working together, they placed everything out of my reach that could be opened, put into my mouth, or would be too sharp to handle. Fortunately, much to my happiness, both my Mom and my Dad still loved me dearly, and they never complained about their too adventurous little son.

Now and then, my Dad took me to our front windows, where he sat down on our couch and lifted me on his knee to let me take a look outside. I always loved sitting on my Dad's knee while looking at our glowing campfire and our huge circle of wooden benches around it. Sometimes, a couple of people sat on their benches, softly talking to each other while drinking coffee. Several suntanned children were playing around our campfire or chasing after each other, now and then shouting at each other but always having lots of fun.

Of course, I desperately wanted to join the happily playing kids, to partake in their games. However, my Dad had already explained that I had to wait first until I would be able to walk around properly, before I was allowed to play outside and perhaps join the other kids. I only had to be a little bit more patient... Yeah well, up to now, patience hadn't exactly been my most developed capability. I always wanted to have my want NOW! When would I finally be big enough to walk around and join our happily playing kids outside?

Then, a couple of playing children saw me looking at them from behind our windows, left their games, and enthusiastically waved at me! Suddenly feeling extremely happy, I immediately raised my own hand and waved back at them!

The playing kids had recognized me, and they clearly wanted to be my friends. Now, I wanted to join them outside even more!

Unfortunately, I was still too young and too small to be allowed to do that. Therefore, I again started to think... Couldn't I skip a couple of years, so that I would be old enough to play outside immediately? I so longed to join my playing friends who were again chasing after each other and having lots of fun around our glowing campfire...

8. Walking; and a wandering question mark.

From time to time, my parents had to fulfill a Very Important Task outside our camp, because they were our Gypsy King and Queen. Before leaving our camp, they always asked my Big Friend, Michail, to take care of their little son until they returned home, mostly before the end of the day. I always loved these times, when I could be together with my Big Friend and romp with him or play our games.

Michail was never tired of rolling my plastic ball towards each other; or stacking my pillows until the heap suddenly collapsed. Then, we both shrieked with laughter, and immediately started to stack the huge pile of wobbly pillows again. We always had lots of fun, and Michail never complained or got too bored.

Sometimes, Felicia, his girlfriend, accompanied him. Then, she always sat very close to her boyfriend on our couch while desperately trying to catch all his attention. From the first day we saw each other, I was sure that Felicia didn't like me! Could she be jealous of all the attention my Big Friend and I were paying each other? She never helped me; and always left everything to her boyfriend, even bathing me and changing my diaper. Well, I certainly didn't protest, and always crawled towards Michail when I needed any help. Michail didn't protest either, and always happily did what I had asked for.

One day, Felicia sat on our couch next to Michail, silently sulking and moping because her boyfriend again cuddled and romped with me while I sat on his lap and in his safe arms. For quite some time, I could clearly feel my Big Friend growing more and more irritated. Then, Felicia started to complain about feeling bored...

Suddenly, Michail growled at his still pouting girlfriend:

"Please, Felicia, SHUT UP and leave us alone."

Much to my delight, Felicia really listened to her angry boyfriend! She rose from our couch, stomped out of our caravan, and slammed our front door shut with a loud bang. Fortunately, my Big Friend only laughed at Felicia's silly antics, and then confidentially told me she always made it up to him again, usually after a day or so.

Smiling back at Michail, I secretly thought that Felicia was acting very 'childish'; but I wisely kept my mouth shut and didn't say a word. Now that we were alone, I enjoyed our close togetherness even more, while I happily cuddled up against my Big Friend's broad chest.

Half an hour later, Michail wanted to fetch coffee for himself and some baby drink for me. Therefore, he lifted me off his lap and sat me down on our couch. While my Big Friend entered our kitchen, I crawled past my pile of colored pillows towards our front windows. First, I pulled myself upright. Then, I stretched out at full length and craned my tiny neck, to be able to take a look outside.

Longingly, I stared at all the happily playing children around our campfire who again had lots of fun chasing after each other. Every time I saw them playing outside, I so wanted to join them and partake in their happy games... Unfortunately, I was not allowed to go outside until my wobbly legs would be strong enough to walk around on my own. When would my tiny legs finally be strong enough to let me walk outside and join the other children around our campfire?

Again, a few playing kids saw me staring at them from behind our windows. Immediately, they nudged the others, and then everybody enthusiastically waved at me! Feeling touched by their clearly visible affection, I again lifted my own hand and waved back at my friends. Unfortunately, that caused me to lose my balance. With a loud yelp, I fell backwards onto our couch and from there onto our carpeted floor. Obviously, my wise Dad had been right, and my tiny legs really were too wobbly to keep me upright for a prolonged time.

Fortunately, this time, I didn't bump my head onto our carpeted floor, although Michail immediately returned from our kitchen to find out what I was doing. Feeling reassured, he sat me back on our couch and went back to our kitchen, to fetch his coffee and my baby drink.

After Michail returned to our couch, I again crawled on his lap, to be held and comforted. Sitting together, we sipped our drinks, while my Big Friend helpfully cleaned my dripping mouth and chin with a tissue. After we finished our drinks, he suddenly lifted me from his lap and tried to let me stand upright on our floor, while he continued to hold my hands. Why would my Big Friend do that? By reading his mind, I found out what he wanted me to do, and I felt elated! My Big Friend wanted me to try to WALK, while he kept me upright by holding my hands! YESSS! Walking was what I had wanted to learn all the time, preferably as soon as possible...

Happily, I held on onto Michail's enormous hands with all of my might, while he carefully guided me along our couch while letting me take my own wobbly steps forward. Now and then, he had to pull me upright again, so that I stayed more or less vertical on my still way too wobbly legs. Wow, this was the real work! Finally, I was learning how to walk, with the help of my Big Friend! Feeling thankful, I took the next step that was already less wobbly...

Within a few minutes, helped by my Big Friend, I taught myself how to walk around our living room without wobbling or wandering too much, still safely holding myself up at Michail's enormous hands. For quite some time, I proudly pranced around, so that my still way too wobbly leg muscles could get used to the unusual new sensations and hopefully become a bit stronger. Finally, I was walking around, for the first time in my young life!

From now on, I only had to train myself some more, until I would be able to walk around without any help. Tomorrow, I would ask my Dad or my Mom to help me walk around like this more often, until I could do it all by myself. Feeling grateful, I thanked my Big Friend abundantly; but he just shrugged it off and told me that his own Dad once helped him in exactly the same way...

After a couple weeks of arduous training, at first with a lot of help from my Mom or my Dad, and then all by myself by holding onto our couch or our small table, I finally found out how I could walk around in our living room without ever losing my balance.

Day after day, I had taken my wobbly steps while holding myself up against my Mom's apron or onto my Dad's trousers. Then, I started to walk alone while holding myself up against our couch or table. However, every time I tried to walk without any help, I stumbled over my own feet, lost my balance, and fell down onto our carpeted floor...

Although my parents tried to comfort me, by telling me that my body was still too small to walk on its own; I just didn't believe them and stubbornly went on trying to walk without any help, by pulling myself up against our couch. I WANTED to be able to play outside, just like all the other kids were doing!

Inwardly, I knew I was an extremely fast learner and that my leg muscles were already strong enough, due to my arduous training. I only had to find out how I could use my wobbly legs the right way, without stumbling any more over my own feet-in-the-way...

One day, I finally found out what I could have been doing wrong all the time. Again, I had pulled myself up against our couch and taken a couple of wobbly steps; and, again, I suddenly stumbled and fell down on our carpeted floor. Feeling disappointed, I slumped down and stared at my still happily walking Mom and Dad. What the heck was I doing wrong that they were doing correctly?

Feeling irritated, I decided to take a much closer look at how my parents were walking without ever stumbling. And, finally, I saw what I had been doing wrong all the time. Clearly, my parents didn't step their feet behind each other, but they stepped them NEXT to each other! That was why my own feet always seemed to be in the way while I took the next step! Why had I never seen this before?

Two minutes later, I finally walked around in our living room, all by myself and without any help! Or, to say it more correctly, I finally toddled around, still wavering from left to right, but already feeling very proud of myself. Although I now knew what I had to do, I still had to learn how to keep a proper balance. Trying not to stumble too much, I toddled towards my busy Mom in our kitchen and looked at what she was doing. Then, I again lost my balance and fell down.

From now on, every morning, as soon as my parents took me to our living room, I immediately pulled myself upright on our couch. Determinedly, I started to toddle around, trying to keep my balance while avoiding all those huge obstacles that always were in my way. Within a few days, I started walking faster and faster, without ever grabbling around any more to keep myself upright. Then, one morning, I finally raced around in our living room without ever falling or stumbling! Finally, I could WALK, and even RUN, all on my own!

Again, my stunned looking Mom told me she couldn't believe her own eyes. Again, my very surprised looking Dad told me he was very proud of his so rapidly advancing son. Ultimately, I was not even seven months old; therefore, statistically, my tiny body should be way too young to be able to walk around all on its own...

The next morning, my parents took me outside our caravan, for the third time since I was a little baby, this time to let me discover some more of our secluded Gypsy world. After I first devoured my Mom's 'healthy breakfast', my Mom put a fresh diaper on me. Then, my Dad opened our front door and guided me down the few steps of our caravan. The moment I stepped onto the solid ground, my Dad released me and told me to have fun!

Chapter 8. Walking; and a wandering question mark.

Much to my happiness, a fascinating new world opened up to me that seemed to be full of interesting things and unexpected surprises! For a few minutes, I only stared around at all those colorful caravans and at all those wooden benches that were neatly put in a wide circle around our faintly glowing campfire. Vaguely, I remembered the last time I was here, sitting on my Dad's lap, waiting for our Wise Woman to take a look at my past lives and my possible future.

This time, nearly all the wooden benches were empty; except for a few older people who were drinking coffee while softly talking to each other. Now and then, they smiled at their so extremely early little Crown Prince, and I smiled back at them immediately. Helped by the welcoming atmosphere, I soon started to feel more at ease.

Finally, I started to toddle around, while trying to keep my balance on the rugged ground. Feeling curious as always, I also started to look in, under, and behind all those interesting new things that were calling for my immediate attention. I also started to try out all the interesting things that possibly could move, open, or have a peculiar taste.

All the time, my worried looking Mom followed me around, while keeping a close eye at everything I did. Now and then, she stopped me from pulling burning branches from our campfire, eating tasty looking mud, or putting living ants into my mouth.

Near the end of the morning, several suntanned young children showed up who had been playing their games around our caravans. When they recognized their little Prince, they immediately surrounded me and reacted enthusiastic! They even tried to talk to me...

Only, this time, I was way too occupied to let myself be distracted by my subjects. I only waved a hand towards them to acknowledge them; and immediately went on, already toddling towards the next interesting object that was calling for my attention. A next time, I would take some more time to talk to them and perhaps partake in their games; but, today, I was too busy! The kids chuckled, turned around, and restarted playing their usual games of 'hide and seek'.

Then, the inevitable happened. For only a few seconds, my Mom turned around, to answer my Dad who had asked her a question. At exactly that same moment, I left my parents, toddled towards our faintly glowing campfire, and curiously grabbed a burning branch. Feeling fascinated, I stared at its beautifully glowing end with all those playful little flames that tried to enchant me...

Never before had I seen such a wonderful and strangely appealing plaything! Fortunately, I didn't put the burning branch into my mouth to taste it, as I had tried to do with all the other interesting things. Tentatively, as if my Inside warned me in advance to be extremely careful, I only touched its beautifully glowing end...

A split second later, I burst out into a VERY loud and VERY angry ROAR; while my deep and sonorous baritone voice reverberated through our entire camp and even chased a couple of angrily twittering birds away. OUCH! That hurt TERRIBLY!

Feeling utterly betrayed by the unexpectedly searing pain, I threw the burning branch far away with another loud roar!

Immediately, everybody in our camp came storming towards me, alarmed by my loudly roaring baritone voice. All of them crowded around me and wanted to know what had happened to their so loudly screaming little Crown Prince. One of the alerted children took the still burning branch from the wooden steps to one of our wooden caravans, and quickly put it back onto our campfire before it burned our entire camp down! In the meantime, my parents looked at my already reddening hand with worried and guilty faces.

Only, I had already gritted my teeth and stopped growling; because this had been my own fault, for again being too incautious and not playing it safe until I could be sure there was no danger involved...

Curiously, everybody followed my guilty looking parents and me towards our caravan. In our kitchen, my Mom first submerged my painful hand in lots of cold water, until the burning sensation slowly lessened. Next, she took me to our Wise Woman, who put some soothing balsam onto my reddening burns. She also brewed a sour tasting tea and let me drink it, to dull the pain and let me sleep better.

Although I didn't get any blisters, the pain held on for several agonizing hours. All the time, my Mom held me on her lap and whispered soothing words into my ear, until I finally calmed down and fell asleep. This time, my lesson had been a VERY clear one. I HAD to be quite a lot more careful with all these unknown things, until I knew exactly what terrible harm they could do to innocent people!

The next morning, I forgot my painful experience and just went on exploring my new world, albeit acting a LOT more careful. Again, I started to take a closer look at all those very interesting things that were calling for my immediate attention.

However, from now on, I only looked at them, instead of touching them and trying to put them into my mouth, as I had done before. This time, I had really learned my extremely important lesson of being careful always and everywhere.

For quite some time, my worried looking Mom kept on following me wherever I went, albeit now even more closely. Until, at long last, she saw that I really acted a lot more careful than I had done before; and, finally, she started to relax somewhat. That is, until I climbed the few wooden steps to one of our neighbor caravans while pulling myself up by its rickety handrail. Unexpectedly, I stumbled, grabbled around, and tumbled down with a loud yelp and a dull thump!

Of course, I started to cry; not from the tiny bit of pain, but merely from the sudden surprise. My again worried looking Mom tried to comfort me, but I was already on my way towards another interesting object that had caught my immediate attention. This time, my Dad laughed at my worried Mom, while he admonished her:

"Our son has to learn from his experiences, and I am sure he is clever enough not to make the same mistake twice."

Two minutes later, I fell off the wooden steps to the next caravan and landed upside down. This time, I got a painful lump on my head; but who cares. I still had FUN, just gritted my teeth, and was already on my way to another interesting object. My disappointed looking Dad only shook his head, but wisely kept his mouth shut...

Near the end of my first day outside, I started to feel too hungry and tired, and therefore asked my Mom to feed me and put me to bed. My Mom looked again at my burnt hand, but both the pain and the reddishness were nearly gone. Yet, I still had to drink another cup of sour tea, to make me sleep deeper. Okay, I would be able to live with that. After feeding me, my Mom put a fresh diaper on me, kissed my wrinkling little nose, and put me to bed in my small sleeping den.

That night, I slept like a log, but I also dreamed of many beautifully glowing branches with their playfully dancing little flames. This time, they didn't singe me any more, because I had learned my important lesson and already acted a lot more careful around them. Although the burning flames and I would never become real friends, yet, we promised to respect each other always and everywhere. Apart from that, those playfully dancing flames were still enchanting...

The next morning, the reddishness had already disappeared from my hand; and all the pain was gone. After eating my Mom's healthy breakfast and getting my fresh diaper, I went outside and immediately resumed my exploring. Again, I looked in and under every single interesting thing, albeit still a lot more carefully.

Because, from now on, nothing extraordinary happened; my Mom slowly released her excessive wariness. At last, she just sat down on our wooden bench, next to my Dad; and they only looked at me from time to time, to see if everything was still all right with me.

Finally, both my Mom and my Dad saw they could trust me not to do any more dangerous things; and they decided in unison to give me some more freedom. From now on, I could toddle around all on my own, although my parents or a couple older grownups still stealthily kept a little bit of an eye on my ministrations.

A few days later, my Dad and Michail were sitting on our Royal wooden bench, talking and drinking coffee, while I toddled around them and stealthily listened in. Hesitatingly, my Dad told my Big Friend about his promise to talk to his baby son as if already I were a grownup. My Dad felt very relieved when my Big Friend only smiled at him and answered he wasn't surprised at all. From my first day as a little baby, I had been extremely precocious and very eager to learn. Therefore, my parents could expect that I would be extremely early with speaking and understanding as well. Michail even suggested that my Dad and he should try to teach me some extra words, to help my speaking develop even faster...

Feeling VERY enthusiastic, I immediately stormed towards our Royal bench and sat down next to them, to start with my first lesson!

From this day on, both Michail and my Dad were helping me with speaking and understanding all those difficult words, now and then correcting me if necessary, and letting me use the too difficult words in several different sentences. Of course, their assistance helped me tremendously in developing my grammatical knowledge much faster.

Soon, I had developed an impressive and extensive vocabulary for such a tiny kid; and I was able to make myself perfectly clear. I also seemed to have an astonishingly good memory for languages and never forgot any new words that anybody taught me. Within a few days, several other people started to teach me as well. Happily, they joined us on our Royal bench; and all their grammatical lessons and linguistic examples were helping me even more.

Chapter 8. Walking; and a wandering question mark.

Day after day, I sat ready on our bench, to learn and to be taught all those difficult words and their meaning. Within a few weeks, I even started to ask the people around me my OWN difficult questions, and they surely couldn't get away with only some vague half-reply!

With a slightly frustrated voice, one of my tormented teachers exclaimed that I had to be our youngest Gypsy 'linguistic prodigy' ever! Of course, I felt very proud of my new honorary title; and I was even able to pronounce its difficult words correctly.

However, nothing in the world comes without a price. After a few weeks, my tormented teachers started to complain that I had changed into a 'wandering question mark'! Of course, they were right; because my extremely bright brain just couldn't stop badgering them and asking them all those burning questions. The words I loved best and used most, were 'why' and 'what', closely followed by 'how come'.

My curiosity was totally insatiable, and my 'built-in little brainiac' wanted to understand absolutely everything. Slowly, I drove all the people in our camp to despair with my almost impossible questions:

"Why are my Mom and I having bright blue eyes, and how come all the others in our camp are having dark brown eyes?"

"That is because your Mom comes from a far away country that is called Sweden. A few years ago, before you were born, your Dad brought her here and married her."

"What is a 'far away country that is called Sweden'? Why did my Dad bring my Mom here to marry her? How come I look like my Mom and not like my Dad?"

"Well... of course, we are only simple people, and therefore we simply don't know ALL those answers. Please, go ask your Mom or your Dad your next questions. Perhaps, THEY will be able to give you the proper answers that you are looking for."

Feeling a bit angry, and also a little bit rejected, I turned around and trotted towards my parents, to ask them my burning questions.

My Mom started to tell me about several 'other countries', where people were living under different circumstances. Of course, I now felt even more curious and immediately wanted to know:

"When are we going to those 'other countries'? I want to see them all, and with my own eyes!"

"Well, I suppose you may join us to a few other countries when you first have grown up some more and are old enough to travel."

"Why am I not old enough to travel now? You always tell me I am already a big boy!"

This time, my Mom didn't answer any more and only laughed at seeing my eager face; but my wise Dad shook his head and told me I had to be more patient. My time would surely come...

Well; up to now, 'patience' had never been my strongest quality, and I just wanted to travel to those 'other countries' NOW!

My Dad tried to ruffle my unruly blond hair; but I felt too angry, turned around, and retreated to another bench. Why were my parents always telling me I had to wait until I would be old enough? I was already very bright and able to understand everything they told me; so why did I have to wait for so long? Just wait, until I am old enough to travel to those 'other countries' all by myself...

9. My first birthday; exploring Mother Nature.

Unnoticed, time went by; until, halfway through our again cold and snowy winter, I finally celebrated my FIRST birthday, on March the third. Because our camp was very poor, certainly during a cold winter when our grownups couldn't do any work to earn some money in the outside 'gadjo' world, no child ever got any expensive birthday presents. However, our parents always managed to create a really special day for us; thus, we DID celebrate our birthdays, abundantly.

I had been living forward to my first birthday for many weeks; while impatiently counting the remaining days on my fingers and toes, initially adding those of my chuckling parents. Fortunately, I could already count, because my Mom had taught me how to count my own ten fingers and ten toes that made twenty together...

Teasingly slowly, I needed less and less fingers; until I no longer needed to add those of my Mom and Dad. Now, finally, only one little finger remained to count the last day; and I went to bed feeling full of anticipation. Tomorrow would be my first birthday!

Alas, my long-awaited first birthday turned out to be a disaster, because I woke up with a nasty fever and felt awful. That morning, I crawled out of my bed, wavered towards my parents, and started to cry from disappointment. Why had my shivering body chosen exactly this day, to make me ill and ruin my first Official Feast?

While I was asleep, my parents had decorated our living room with many beautifully colored balloons and festoons. However, I couldn't care less, and just crawled in between my pillows on our couch; coughing, shivering, and sniffling.

My Dad took me onto his lap, rubbed my upset stomach, and helped me blow my running nose. Soon, I asked him to lay me back in between my pillows on our couch, because my trembling body felt too dizzy and feverish. I even didn't want to taste my nice looking birthday cake with one burning little candle, but only wanted to drink lots of water. In the meantime, my Mom left our caravan and went to our Wise Woman, to ask her for advice.

Soon, our Wise Woman showed up in our caravan, felt my forehead, looked at my tongue, and told my parents I had gotten a nasty flu. This week, I was the fourth child in a row that got the same illness, and she was sure that many more kids would follow. Fortunately, all the sniffling kids would recover within a week; and they would soon be their happy selves again. She brought me some bitter tasting tea, and trotted towards the next sniffling child.

As usual, our Wise Woman turned out to be right. Within a week, the nasty fever left me, and I immediately felt much better. Now, I could really enjoy our still decorated living room! For the second time, my parents and all our close friends congratulated me with my first birthday. I even got another delicious birthday cake my Grandma had baked especially for me, decorated with one burning candle!

While everybody sang, "He is a jolly good fellow", I had to blow out my candle and do my first secret 'birthday wish' for the upcoming year. Only, I absolutely didn't know what to wish for, because I was only one year old and had never done such a thing before. Feeling a little bit shy, I whispered into my Dad's ear:

"Sorry Dad, but I am only one year old and never did such a thing before. Therefore, I don't know what to wish for..."

Fortunately, my Dad didn't laugh at me for being dumb; but he continued to look serious while he suggested:

"Well; I suppose you could wish for an excellent health during the upcoming year."

Yesss! As usual, my wise Dad had offered me a marvelous idea! Feeling elated, I puckered my lips, blew out my burning candle, and silently wished for an excellent health during the upcoming year for ALL of us. Then, my Mom helped me cut the first piece of birthday cake before she adeptly cut the rest; and my Grandma's cake turned out to taste more than delicious.

That evening, after all my visitors had left our caravan and went home, I helped my parents pop the balloons, remove the colored festoons, and tidy our living room and our kitchen, until everything in our caravan started looking 'normal' again. Now, I only had to wait until my second birthday showed up and I would be two years old. Therefore, I asked my Dad:

"Dad, could you please tell me how many fingers and toes I have to count until my second birthday shows up?"

Aad Aandacht is a Dutch psychotherapist who loves writing 'books with a message'

Chapter 9. My first birthday; exploring Mother Nature.

"Yes, of course, three-hundred-and-fifty-eight! That is seventeen people's fingers and toes, and then eighteen more..."

Oops... Slumping down on our couch, I tried to imagine seventeen people sitting in a long row on our wooden benches, while I walked along them and in the meantime counted all their fingers and toes, and then eighteen more... Well, obviously, until my next birthday showed up, I still had to wait for an extremely looooong time!

Chuckling, I asked my silently waiting Dad:

"Dad, you've already taught me to count to twenty; but that is only my own ten fingers and ten toes. Therefore, could you please help me count all those extra fingers from everyone else, every day, until only my own twenty fingers and toes remain?"

Chuckling back at me, my wise Dad responded:

"Then, I suppose I could better teach you how to count beyond twenty! Show me your twenty fingers and toes, and I will add mine to them. Now, adding my thumb counts number twenty-one..."

A few minutes later, I already grasped the meaning of counting to nine-hundred-and-ninety-nine, without making any errors due to my excellent memory. Obviously, I really was a remarkable boy with an extremely bright brain, although I was only one year and seven days old and still a tad too small for my age. Only summing up beyond one thousand was still a bit too difficult for me.

A few months later, SPRING suddenly showed up in our valley! The hitherto freezing mountain air became much warmer, while the remaining snow first turned into mud and then quickly disappeared into nowhere. From now on, my parents would allow me to play outside again; while, during our freezing cold winter, I had to stay inside from fear of getting a frozen nose and ears. Only our older children had been allowed to play outside, clad in their thick winter outfits with leather boots and warm mitten.

Immediately after the bright sun had warmed the air sufficiently, all our children disappeared into their caravans, shucked their warm winter clothes, and returned clad only in their 'birthday suits', to enjoy the warming sun on their bare skins and get their golden tans back as soon as possible. Of course, I wanted to join them and feel the warming sun on my own bare skin, and therefore asked my Mom and Dad to put on a fresh diaper and help me go outside...

Much to my surprise, my Dad told me I was now clever enough to explore our secluded camp without any supervision at all. Last year, I had proven to be an always prudent and very mature little 'brainiac'. Therefore, from now on, I didn't need my parents' permission any more; and I was allowed to leave our caravan and go outside whenever I wanted! Only, before I went outside, my Dad first explained a couple of very important rules I should remember all the time while playing outside. My Dad and I sat down on our couch, next to each other, while I listened intently to what he told me.

The first very important rule was that I always had to think at least twice, before I planned to do anything that didn't feel good. And, of course, I always had to restrain from doing anything that could be too dangerous or harmful. If I wasn't absolutely sure, I had to ask my Dad, my Mom, Michail, or any other responsible grownup for their advice first. This was the most important rule, and I had to obey this rule always and everywhere, just to play it safe.

Many years ago, our Ancestors had set a second very important rule, because a few flocks of gray wolves were living in the mountains and dense forests around our camp. Sometimes, during a quiet evening, we could hear their howling; sounding from far away, especially when the moon was full. Although, up to now, no lone or stray wolf ever approached our camp or attacked any young children, one could never know. Therefore, to play it as safe as possible and be absolutely sure, all our youngsters had to wait until their bodies were strong enough to fight an attacking hungry wolf, before their parents allowed them to enter our surrounding woods or dense forests.

Of course, measuring the muscle strength and fighting capabilities of each single kid would be a way too tedious task. Therefore, our Ancestors had looked for a more easy way; and they had set a much simpler but satisfactory rule which said: 'All our young children have to stay inside our secluded camp and its surrounding bushes, until they no longer need to wear a diaper and are staying dry during both day and night.' That way, our parents could be sure that even their youngest kids had at least some basic bodily control, in case anything unexpected or too dangerous happened to them.

To say it briefly; I was allowed to play in and around our camp and enter our surrounding bushes; but I always had to stay far away from our surrounding woods and forests. The winding paths across our surrounding bushes that were leading outside our camp, were strictly forbidden; until I was experienced enough to fend for myself.

Even after I stayed dry all day and night, I had to join an older and more experienced kid first, until I was a trained trapper and no longer needed supervision. That way, all our kids would always be as safe as possible while scouring our woods and dense forests.

My Dad also told me a third very important rule I always should remember, in case I ever entered our forbidden woods. If I ever happened to meet a hungry wolf or any other dangerous predator with sharp teeth, I immediately had to grab a long and sturdy branch. Then, I had to push that branch into the open mouth of the predator, using all the muscle strength I could bring forth. Hopefully, the predator would fight the branch instead of me, or run away from the pain.

All the time, I had listened intently and open-mouthed; now and then shuddering at the thought of being attacked by a nasty predator with an open mouth and sharp teeth. Now, I solemnly promised my parents I would always obey our important rules; and I would be very careful. My parents could count on me, always and everywhere!

After kissing my parents and telling them I loved them, I finally opened the front door of our caravan and went outside. Slowly, I descended the few steps that led to the ground, while I immediately enjoyed the warming feeling of the bright sun on my bare skin very much! When could I finally shuck my diaper during the day and go completely naked, just like all the other happily playing kids around me were doing? My Dad once told me that most Gypsy toddlers became dry during the day only after they became four years old; and they stayed completely dry around being five or six years old...

During my second spring and summer, my toddler body continued to grow up steadily, healthy, and prosperously. Every day, I trotted outside as soon as I had devoured my Mom's healthy breakfast and put on a clean diaper. Happily, I strolled around in our camp, stared at what the other children were doing, or tried to 'help' my Dad or Michail. Now and then, I still badgered our grownups by bombarding them with my thousand-and-one questions. Fortunately, everybody seemed to like their over-curious little Crown Prince very much, and they always took all their time for me.

During the first few days, I had tried to play with the other kids, because I wanted to partake in their usual games of 'hide and seek'. However, an older kid explained that I was too young and had to wait until I no longer needed my diaper during the day...

Of course, I tried to convince them otherwise, using all my brainy persuasiveness; but they still didn't let me join them. The mere fact that I was early in my mental development or extremely bright for my age, or our Beloved Royal Crown Prince, didn't make any difference to them. I HAD to wait until my parents allowed me to be clad solely in my 'birthday suit' during the day. Until that time, I had to play with my fellow 'toddlers' in our camp, until I could leave my diaper at home and go naked, just like all the other sun-tanned kids always did during our long and warm summer.

Feeling disappointed, I left the kids and stomped home; where I crawled onto my Dad's lap to be held and comforted. I didn't WANT to play with my 'fellow toddlers', because most of them still behaved like 'little babies' and were no fun at all! The only things my fellow toddlers seemed to be good at, were sucking on their thumbs and playing with mud and small pebbles. Besides, I had already found out that most little toddlers in our camp couldn't even talk properly...

After I calmed down, my Dad again explained that most 'toddlers' in our camp had to wait until they were four years old before they became 'dry' during the day. After they needed their diaper only during the night, they were called 'diaper kids' and could join our naked 'diaper group' and partake in their kid games in and around our secluded camp. Then, our 'diaper kids' had to wait until they were five or six years old, before they definitively shucked their diaper and stayed dry during the entire day and night. Being called 'older kids', they were allowed to join our group of older children who always left our camp and scoured our outstretched woods to catch small animals and roast them over our campfire to eat their tasty meat.

Of course, my Dad's wise words made me think again... Because I was only one-and-a-half year old, I still had to wait for - counting on three fingers and two half-fingers - another two-and-a-half years before I became a 'diaper kid'. Couldn't I force my 'toddler' body to grow up faster and warn me in advance before it had to urinate or defecate? My bright 'brainiac' brain was already growing extremely fast; so, why couldn't my steadily growing body be able to follow my fast brain and become dry during the day a few years earlier?

Much to my disappointment, my Dad only laughed at hearing my heated arguments; and he told me again to be more patient. My time would surely come... Yeah, well, I was sure I had heard those 'wise words' many times before! Only, ultimately, I didn't even WANT to be impatient, or to feel restricted by my little toddler-body.

Although I was still a tad too small for my age, even my deep baritone voice already sounded like a grownup. Didn't that fact make me quite a lot more special? If only my tiny toddler body would listen to my heated arguments and start doing what I so badly wanted it to do, by growing up faster and staying dry during the day...

Now that I thought some more about it, being 'precocious' and a 'brainiac' only seemed to make my life a LOT more difficult than the seemingly easier lives of my little 'fellow toddlers' were. THEY didn't seem to have so many problems with waiting until they grew up, whilst playing with their mud and small pebbles...

Suddenly, I started to laugh at my silly self-induced misery, kissed my wise Dad, and just went outside again. For a few seconds, I stared longingly at our 'diaper kids' who again played their usual games of 'hide and seek' around our caravans. Then, I definitively stopped my stupid self-pity and again forced myself to smile.

Pretending I was one of those little 'toddlers', I gathered a handful of small pebbles and sat down on our wooden bench. One by one, I threw my pebbles into our faintly glowing campfire, trying to hit a specific burning log. Every time I hit the log, a beautiful shower of tiny sparkles appeared around it, spreading out into many different directions. After some more training, I was able to hit the log very accurately, exactly at the place where I wanted the sparkles to show up. Now that I had reached my goal and couldn't do any better, I started to feel bored, threw my pebbles away, and left our campfire.

After again looking longingly at the still happily playing 'diaper kids', I brusquely turned around and trotted towards our surrounding bushes, because I wanted to look at our interesting forest fauna and abundantly growing vegetation. Only, I was still a little bit afraid of unexpectedly meeting some hungry wolf or other dangerous predator! Therefore, I first looked around until I found a sturdy branch with a sharp point; and took it in both slightly trembling hands, to be able to defend myself if ever necessary.

Chuckling at my own silly fears, I left our camp and entered our surrounding bushes, where I first looked around warily. Fortunately, no nasty predator with open mouth and sharp teeth showed up, and nothing dangerous happened. Soon, my excessive wariness left me; and I already started to feel more at ease while exploring our beautiful and extremely interesting Mother Nature.

Almost immediately, I saw one of the mysterious paths that led towards our surrounding woods and dense forests. Longingly, I stared along the winding path that seemed to disappear into nowhere. When would I finally be allowed to enter it and catch my own small animals to roast them over our campfire? Every morning, our group of 'older kids' left our camp and followed these paths, to set up traps and catch marmots and other edible critters. I always longed to follow them; but I had to stay behind until I became a 'real big boy' and no longer needed a diaper at all. Only then would they allow me to join them...

Of course, as an obedient child, I just stayed where I was and only stared along the mysterious path, because I didn't want to disappoint my parents or to forfeit their valuable trust in me. To be honest, I also didn't want to take any risk of being attacked by some nasty predator with sharp teeth. Although I understood what I had to do, I wasn't sure whether my small arm muscles would be strong enough to push a sturdy branch into such an open predator mouth...

Again, I laughed at my own silly fears, while I dropped my branch and just stepped into the many thick bushes that surrounded our camp. Almost immediately, I became VERY interested in the abundantly flourishing vegetation around me. Feeling totally in awe, I squatted down and stared at all those beautifully colored flowers that were attached to small branches adorned with green leaves or little needles.

My wise Dad once told me that, after the flowers wilted, their remainders started to grow and finally became much bigger fruits, seeds, or pods. Other plants didn't have any flowers but just sprouted out of Mother Earth, like 'mushrooms' and 'ferns'. Of course, my brainiac brain started to think again. Why had our Supreme Being created such an abundant diversity? Could there be a hidden meaning behind our interesting Mother Nature? Would my Mom be able to give me any answers? Cautiously, I started to touch several flowers, leaves, and colored pods, while sensing their surrounding energy auras...

Half an hour later, I brought home some very interesting plants, to ask my Mom my questions about them. Of course, I was already sure my plants were harmless, because I had 'sensed' their energy in advance. The harmful plants had immediately warned me to be careful, by making me feel nervous or queasy; while the harmless plants were making me feel good. Obviously, my Shaman inside had discovered another very useful 'sixth sense'; which warned me in advance in case some unknown plant could be poisonous or dangerous...

Much to my surprise, my Mom reacted rather warily at seeing my nicely smelling plants. She called them 'weeds'; and warned me not to touch any of them ever again, because they could be poisonous and make me ill. With a sour face, she threw my 'weeds' into our trashcan; and I had to wash my hands thoroughly before she allowed me to go outside again, with another warning not to touch them ever again...

Of course, as an obedient child, I didn't want to object; but my own 'intuition' already told me my Mom knew next to nothing about my nicely smelling and good-feeling 'weeds'! She only wanted to play it safe and protect me from any harm. Therefore, I just kissed her, thanked her for her warning, and trotted outside again.

Although my 'intuition' or 'sixth senses' tried to tell me otherwise, my Mom's warnings had made me doubt and feel a little bit guilty. Therefore, I decided to be a lot more careful. From now on, I would not touch any interesting 'weeds' any more, but only look at them. Why didn't I listen to my own 'Inner Wisdom' any more, although it never betrayed me? Maybe, our wise Mother Nature had intended to teach me another very important lesson first...

Half an hour later, I squatted down to have a closer look at some beautifully colored flower. Suddenly, an insect left the flower and landed on my unclad thigh. I tried to brush the unknown beast off; but I did it too wildly, and the angry insect stung me before it ran away and disappeared into the surrounding bushes.

Involuntarily, I yelped from the unexpected pain! Feeling shocked and betrayed by Mother Nature, I stared at a rapidly reddening stitch that started to swell and itch terribly. What should I do now? Should I run back to our caravan to let my Mom have a look at the more and more swelling stitch? However, I didn't want to act too 'childish', by immediately toddling home and crying for my Mommy...

Very much to my own surprise, I suddenly started to feel like a 'little trapper boy'. Even more surprisingly, I also knew exactly what I had to do! Could my own 'Inner Wisdom' have recognized this insect and was it now telling me, loud and clear, how to cure its stitch?

Still feeling extremely surprised about my unexpected knowledge, I looked around until I found a dark brown 'weed'. For a split second, my wary mind hesitated again, because my cautious Mom had strictly warned me not to touch any unknown weeds or other plants any more... Only, this was an emergency!

Therefore, I just took a few of the tiny brown leaves, squashed them, and smeared the foul smelling juice onto the more and more nasty looking swelling. Within ten seconds, the itching went away and the nasty swelling already started to diminish!

How the heck did I suddenly know exactly what I had to do to cure my nasty stitch after that unknown insect stung me? And, why had I suddenly 'remembered' being some 'little trapper boy'? Could I have remembered one of my own 'past lives'? Inwardly, I made a mental note to ask our Wise Woman about my unexpected memories, as soon as I saw her. Perhaps, she also could tell me some more about what my Dad and Michail always called my 'Shaman abilities'?

Fortunately, as a direct result from my unexpected experiences, I immediately restarted to trust my own 'sixth senses'. From now on, I would only listen to my own 'Inner Wisdom' and 'Shaman abilities', instead of to my silly fears and to my Mom's ungrounded wariness...

Before I left the brown weed, I thanked it in my mind for curing me. Much to my surprise, I thought I heard a faint 'you are welcome my human friend' in my inside, but wasn't absolutely sure.

Apart from that, being thankful certainly felt great!

10. A metamorphosing little caterpillar friend.

The next morning, soon after I reentered our surrounding bushes, I saw a couple of small birds that were feeding their tiny offspring in their cleverly hidden nest. Immediately, I stood still and tried to observe them. All the time, both small parents were flying back and forth, bringing their tiny kids many insects and other 'tasty' vermin.

At first, they seemed to be afraid of me; until I 'tuned in' into their tiny bird-minds and 'told' them I only wanted to be their friend. From then on, they always trusted me; even when I nearly put my nose into their small nest to have a closer look at what they were doing. Within a few days, they also started to greet me whenever I showed up, by flying towards me while twittering loudly!

Unexpectedly, I found a huge caterpillar in a thick shrub that was eating leaf after leaf and therefore growing fatter and fatter. Now THAT was an interesting insect! Immediately, I wanted to know quite a lot more about it. For example, why was it eating only leaves and never leaving its own shrub? From now on, every morning, I first went to my always-eating caterpillar to observe it, until my curious brain started to produce too many questions. Would my wise Dad be able to answer my burning questions about this strange animal?

For a second, I hesitated before I touched it and took it home. Could this caterpillar be poisonous and make me ill? Or, would it try to bite me, just like that angry insect had stung me? Fortunately, my seemingly built-in 'little trapper boy' showed up in my inside and already knew the answer. I could touch this particular insect and take it home without any fear! Happily, I thanked my 'little trapper boy' in my mind, but he didn't answer. Now, I plucked the always-eating beast from its leaf, trotted home, and showed it to my Dad.

My Dad started to laugh when I showed him the still wriggling caterpillar in my hand; but he also told me:

"You better bring your caterpillar back to where you found it, and leave it alone until it spins itself into a cocoon. Next spring, it will wake up again and leave its cocoon as a beautiful butterfly."

Immediately, I had at least a zillion questions about this extremely interesting phenomenon! Would really my always-eating caterpillar become a beautiful butterfly, after it first cocooned itself?

My Dad explained that, near the end of summer, my caterpillar would stop eating and spin a sturdy cocoon around its fattened body, to protect itself. During our cold winter, it would be asleep in its safe place; while its appearance would 'metamorphose' into a beautiful butterfly. Soon after next spring showed up, its cocoon would burst open and a beautiful butterfly would show up and flap away, to find a mate and start making new little caterpillars!

Of course, I decided to see my caterpillar grow up, spin itself into a sturdy cocoon, and then 'metamorphose' into a beautiful butterfly! Wow, our Mother Nature seemed to be full of unexpected surprises! Happily, I thanked my Dad for his advice. Then, I brought my still wriggling caterpillar back to its own shrub, where it immediately started to eat again as if nothing special had happened.

From now on, every morning, I first went to my eating caterpillar, to stare at it and wait until it would start to spin itself into a cocoon. All the time, I hoped that no birds of prey would see it and eat it, or bring it to their always-hungry offspring to have a feast meal. Of course, I had already told my little bird friends to leave my caterpillar alone, even after their children grew up and started to fly around and feed themselves. Fortunately, they really listened to me and never did any harm to my always-eating caterpillar.

A few months later, just before fall set in, my caterpillar suddenly stopped eating, spun some silky filament, and attached itself to a rigid branch. Now that it hung upside down, it also started to spin a silky cocoon around its fattened body! Of course, I sat glued to the strange spectacle during the entire day. Only reluctantly, I left my place to eat my Mom's healthy food and have my itchy diaper replaced. Then, I immediately returned to my still spinning caterpillar, to go on watching its slowly proceeding 'metamorphosing' process.

After three days of arduous work, the silky cocoon seemed to be ready; because my caterpillar stopped moving and just hung upside down. From now on, its cocoon became darker and darker; until, at last, I could no longer see its inside. Now, according to my Dad, I only had to wait until next spring showed up; which would be a few months after I celebrated my second birthday...

Chapter 10. A metamorphosing little caterpillar friend.

A few weeks later, an icy cold winter wind started to blow, coming down from our surrounding snowy mountaintops. That morning, several little snowflakes were whirling outside our caravan windows; and I stared at them in fascination! Immediately after I had eaten my healthy breakfast and donned a clean diaper, I jumped up to go outside and play with the little bit of whirling snow. Only, my Mom told me to stay at home because of the suddenly cold weather...

Of course, I protested fiercely, because I wanted to go outside anyway! No cold winter weather or wary Mom could ever stop me from taking another look at what my metamorphosing caterpillar had done during the night. What if some nasty predator had found its cocoon and eaten its inside? Besides, up to now, every single morning, I had left our caravan and studied our beautiful Mother Nature. Now, all of a sudden, I had to stay at home only because the outside weather could be a little bit too cold? No way!

Feeling determined not to let any cold weather or wary Mom spoil my day, I stomped towards our front door, to go outside and have a closer look at the whirling snowflakes. Although my Mom still tried to tell me something important, my wise Dad only chuckled at seeing my little tantrum. He even opened our front door to let me through...

Because I was stubbornly determined and still didn't listen to my too wary Mom, I just trotted outside and jumped off the few steps into the already melting snow. Well, again, my wise Dad turned out to be absolutely right! Within a few seconds, I got goose bumps all over my arms and legs, while the too cold mountain wind almost choked my throat. My unclad body started to shiver, so that I hastily retreated inside and quickly attached myself to my chuckling Dad, to feel warm again. From our living room, I heard my Mom mutter about her little son being too 'pigheaded'... Pigheaded? Who? Me?

After the cold snowflakes on my shivering body had melted away, I left my Dad and clambered onto our couch in our nicely warmed living room. From there, I stared outside at the chilly weather and already lessening whirling snowflakes. I also stared at our steadily growing group of 'older children', who were waiting for the last lazy ones to show up. This time, they were clad in beautifully colored garments, to protect them from the winter cold. Soon, they lined up and disappeared into the winding paths, to search for the last edible nuts and any cleverly hidden small animals in hibernation.

To read all our famous 'Gypsy Series' books, please visit www.gypsyseries.com

Only our usual group of younger 'diaper kids' stayed in our camp; this time also clad in brightly colored winter garments. Of course, they were still trying to gather the fallen snowflakes, to make little snowballs out of them and throw them towards each other.

Suddenly, a few diaper kids saw me looking at them and waved at me. One of them even threw a tiny snowball towards our window! Again, I desperately wanted to join my diaper friends and throw my own snowballs... Unfortunately, my still shivering body wasn't clad in a warm winter garment, as all the outside kids were...

Unexpectedly, I got what sounded like a brilliant idea! Quickly, I turned around and asked my still muttering Mom:

"Mom, could you please clad me in some warm winter garment, just like all the other kids are wearing, so that I can join them and play outside and throw my own snowballs?"

Surprisingly, my Mom only stared at me with a sad face, as if she didn't understand my question. At the same time, my wise Dad shook his head, while looking at me as if he felt a bit angry. After what felt like an awkward moment of silence, my Dad uttered:

"My dear son; your Mom and I HAD planned to clad you in a nicely warming garment before you went outside. Only, you didn't want to listen to us and already seemed to have another plan..."

What? Had I really heard this correct? While my parents still stared at me with disappointed faces, my face slowly colored a deep red. This time, I absolutely had been too 'pigheaded'; and I also had been way too impatient for my own good! Clearly, my Mom had asked me to stay home because she wanted to clad me in some warm winter clothes... Again, I had to learn an important lesson; this time about listening first before coming to an incorrect conclusion and throwing such a 'childish' tantrum. Feeling truly ashamed of myself, I bowed my head in submission and mumbled:

"Sorry, Mom and Dad, for thinking you wanted to keep me inside to protect me from the cold winter weather. Therefore, I reacted too childish and refused to listen to you. Please, Mom and Dad, forgive me for being too pigheaded; and I sincerely promise I will do my utmost to change my stubborn behavior from now on..."

My suddenly proudly beaming Dad scooped me into his strong arms and held me very close, while he almost cheered:

Aad Aandacht is a Dutch psychotherapist who loves writing 'books with a message'

"Thank you, my precious son, for letting us see who you really are! Now, both your Mom and I are PROUD of you, because you are willing to change yourself for the best. Let's clad you into the warm jeans, watertight coat, and shiny boots we've already bought in advance, so that you can go outside and join our 'diaper kids'..."

Two minutes later, my Mom had dressed me into the most beautiful clothes that I had ever seen! Vaguely, I remembered the first time when I had to wear my musty smelling Royal garment, a long time ago. Then, I had protested fiercely, wanting my parents to remove the itchy thing immediately. Now, again wearing clothes beside my usual diaper, was a very strange feeling, as if my skin felt too tight and itchy. However, this time, I just accepted it, because I knew I HAD to get used to wearing my warm winter clothes during our cold weather. And, I still wanted to have my daily look at my sleeping caterpillar in its cocoon that hopefully soon would 'metamorphose' into a beautiful butterfly and flap away to make little baby caterpillars.

After my Mom had dressed me, I walked towards our hallway and looked in our oblong wall mirror. Until today, I had always looked at a little toddler with light brown skin, unruly blond hair, and bright blue eyes, wearing only a diaper. Now, I suddenly looked at a little stranger I had never seen before. The new boy was wearing a beautifully colored watertight coat, nice looking dark blue jeans, shining red plastic boots, and a pair of brightly colored warm mitten. I liked the new boy at first sight and winked at him; and the little stranger in our mirror winked back at me immediately!

My Mom started to chuckle at seeing my proudly beaming face, while she asked me:

"Does your beaming face mean you like your new clothes?"

"Oh yes, Mom, I like them very much! Thank you again; and I am still very sorry for being too pigheaded."

"That is okay, and I understand. Now, go play outside in the snow and have fun with the other kids!"

First, I hugged and kissed both my Mom and my Dad. Then, I proudly pranced outside. Would the other kids look at my beautiful new clothes and perhaps feel a little bit jealous? While I halted on the first step, I looked around curiously... Much to my disappointment, the snow had already stopped and most snowflakes had melted away.

All the 'diaper kids' had disappeared; perhaps trying to gather the last tiny bits of snow outside our circle of caravans.

Well, our cold winter weather had just started; and I was sure that, soon enough, much more snow would fall from the still clouded sky, just like it had done last year! Last winter, I had been a one-year-old little toddler who had to stay home because he still wet his diaper during the day and his little nose and ears could be freezing. Now, I was a much bigger boy, nearly two years old, and I still wet my diaper but only if I felt too agitated or forgot to pee in time.

Besides, now that I was wearing my beautiful warm winter clothes, my diaper was cleverly hidden underneath my brand new blue jeans and nobody could see it from the outside...

Still feeling very proud of my new winter clothes, I decided to pay Michail a visit to show them off. Therefore, I trotted to his caravan and climbed the few steps to his front door. Politely, I knocked on his door, expecting that my Big Friend would show up and admire the new boy he hadn't seen before...

However, when the door opened, only Felicia glared at me, with a suddenly distracted face! Obviously not liking the unwelcome disturbance, she grunted under her breath:

"Yes? What do you want?"

"Is Michail inside, please? I want to show him my new clothes..."

"Michail is too busy; so just go home and forget it!"

Fortunately, my Big Friend already showed up, angrily shoved his pouting girlfriend aside, and exclaimed:

"My dear Prince, you look FANTASTIC! Or, are you a brand new boy I haven't seen here before? Who are you?"

"Michail, you are silly! Of course, I am still the same Crown Prince Harold, and only my new clothes are new."

"Yes, of course, and they look GREAT on you! Do you want to come in and drink hot chocolate?"

For a split second, I hesitated. Then, I again saw Felicia's angrily moping face, and quickly answered:

"No, thank you; but another time will be fine. Today, I feel more like staying outside."

Fortunately, Michail seemed to understand my hesitancy, because he told me to have fun outside and come back a next time. By reading my Big Friend's mind, I sensed that, although he absolutely didn't approve of Felicia's behavior, he also didn't want to fight her.

Both Felicia and he disappeared inside; and I turned around and went to our surrounding bushes, to take a quick look at my metamorphosing caterpillar in its cocoon. Surprisingly, I already got used to wearing my new clothes. Although I was wearing them for only a few minutes, they already started to feel nicely warm and cozy! Therefore, from now on, I would nevermore protest if my Mom told me to wait because of the too cold winter weather.

In our surrounding bushes, my dormant caterpillar cocoon was still untouched. My two little bird friends had already disappeared towards a much warmer place, probably taking their offspring with them. Most trees and bushes were already losing their remaining dead leaves; and, this time, Mother Nature looked strangely gloomy.

Because the melancholic surroundings made me feel a little bit depressed, I left our bushes and sauntered back to our faintly glowing campfire. There, I clambered onto one of the wooden benches, next to two parents who were sitting there with their little toddlers. Of course, I had seen both little kids before; but I had always been too busy to pay any attention to them. Now, for the first time, I tried to talk to the little girl and to the slightly older boy.

Well, very soon, 'talking' to both little children turned out to be a disaster! The little girl just sat on her Mom's lap; while sucking on her thumb and looking rather dumb. I asked her a few simple questions; but she only stared at me, sucked even harder, and didn't respond to any of my easy questions. Chuckling inwardly, I secretly thought that this little girl really 'sucked'.

All the time, the slightly older boy had been playing with some small dinky toy, by shoving it around and around on the wooden bench. In the meantime, he was producing several rather silly sounds. Well, I really hoped that talking to this boy would be a bit more entertaining! Tentatively, I asked the playing boy what he was doing, but he only answered to my easy question:

"This is my car! Vroom, vroom..."

Feeling perplexed, I could only stare at my silly 'fellow toddler'. Could this dumb acting young boy really be older than I was?

Although he had to be over two years old, he was still talking and playing like some brainless little baby! I was sure I had never seen such strangely dull and uninterested behavior before! Could both silly acting kids be a little bit 'retarded', as my Dad once told me some uneducated 'gadjo' children seemed to be?

Or, suddenly shivering at the unwelcome thought, could this silly behavior be USUAL behavior for 'normal' toddlers of around two years old? If so, I certainly didn't want to be one of them!

Something important started to dawn in my way too bright brain that involuntarily made me shudder at the unwelcome thought. If both little toddlers were showing 'normal' behavior for being around two years old; then, I REALLY had to be extremely 'precocious' for my age, next to being a way too intelligent little 'brainiac'!

This idea also explained why I always wanted to play with older kids, and never looked at any young toddlers. Although, technically, I still was such a two-year-old little 'toddler' myself; both my inside and my deep baritone voice already felt like being MUCH older than they were! Could my 'very old soul' be in the way, by making me act much more mature than my real age would require?

Now that I had seen those two toddlers, I didn't WANT any more to be such a precocious 'brainiac' or a bright and extremely special 'child prodigy'! Up to now, being such a 'special' child had only brought me lots of extra trouble and misery. Therefore, inwardly, I desperately wanted to be a NORMAL boy, just like all the other kids of about my age seemed to be. Being a 'brainiac', 'impatient', and 'pigheaded', like I always seemed to be, had already made my young life quite a lot more difficult than it should have been! Why couldn't I just sit still on one of our wooden benches and suck on my thumb, or just play with some dinky toy and make silly sounds? Now that I thought about it, I didn't even have a dinky toy...

Feeling more and more depressed, I slid off my wooden bench, greeted both parents and their 'sucking' little toddlers, and sauntered back to my still silently hibernating caterpillar in its sturdy cocoon.

Suddenly, I felt a bit jealous of its extremely easy way of living. Couldn't I spin myself into a sturdy cocoon and hang down for a couple of years, so that I could metamorphose into a more 'normal' child and be just like the 'older kids' when I finally joined them into our surrounding woods to catch my own animals?

Chapter 10. A metamorphosing little caterpillar friend.

The next morning, very much to my delight, our entire Gypsy camp was covered with a very thick blanket of snow! Immediately, I forgot my silly depression, while I almost forced my Mom to put on a fresh diaper and my new winter clothes in a record time.

Teasingly, I told my Mom the words I once heard from my Dad: "Come on, Mom, hurry up! Life is too short to waste it..."

My Mom only chuckled at my teasing antics, while she made me eat her 'healthy breakfast' first. Then, I raced outside and immediately started to roll around and around in the amazingly soft blanket of snow! Soon, my snow-covered body looked like a little snowman with a brightly beaming face and an enormous smile that unzipped from ear to ear. In the meantime, I again remembered being a 'little trapper boy' that always did exactly those same things in the freshly fallen snow, until my 'trapper Dad' called me to eat breakfast. Now, rolling around in the freshly fallen snow again felt marvelous!

After I scrabbled upright, I first brushed the excessive show off my brand new winter clothes. Then, I grabbed a handful of snow, trotted towards a couple of loudly cheering 'diaper kids', and just joined them in their ferocious snowball fight!

Very much to my delight, the 'diaper kids' immediately accepted me as being one of them, because I turned out to be extremely good at fighting our 'enemies'. Although I was the tiniest kid in our group, my lithe body already seemed to know exactly what it had to do, probably because my built-in 'little trapper boy' enjoyed the snow at least as much as I did and therefore helped me dodge the thrown snowballs from our 'enemies'. Almost naturally, I cleverly dodged all of their attempted attacks, so that they nearly couldn't hit me at all!

Then, I started my own counterattacks. Now, my friends found out that I was able to throw my snowballs at our 'enemies' extremely accurately, so that I was able to hit them nearly every time! Suddenly, I felt very happy to have trained myself in advance, by throwing my small pebbles at a burning log in our campfire.

For many hours, I had the time of my life; until my Mom called me and I reluctantly returned to our caravan to eat her healthy lunch. Immediately when my parents allowed me to leave our table, I again raced back outside, to resume our ferocious snowball games of attack and counter-attack.

Clearly, I now 'belonged' to our 'diaper kids'; and they finally accepted me for who I was and for what I could do, instead of for my diaper-clad little body! They even seemed to forget that I was less than two years old; and, of course, they didn't know that I still wore a diaper underneath my blue jeans.

Now that nobody was able to see my diaper, all my new friends seemed to be very happy to have their clever little Crown Prince in their midst, and they totally accepted me as being 'one of us'! To them, I was just the smallest kid in our diaper group; and, only now and then, somebody teasingly called me a 'little runt'.

Unfortunately, during our cold and snowy winter, our diaper kids seldom played their usual games of 'hide and seek', because the freezing winter weather was too cold to sit or lay still for a prolonged time. Again, I had to be 'patient' until next spring arrived, before I would be able to partake in their usual games...

11. Second birthday; and Michail's marriage.

Again, March the third showed up, and I celebrated my SECOND birthday. Again, my parents decorated our living room with colorful festoons and balloons. Again, my Grandma baked a delicious birthday cake, this time decorated with TWO burning candles! All day long, all the people who adored me showed up to congratulate their little Crown Prince with being two years old. After sipping their nicely colored drinks, they disappeared, to make place for even more people who entered our caravan and congratulated me.

Now and then, somebody brought me a small birthday present, making me blush and feel special. I already knew that everybody in our camp was very poor, especially during our cold winters when nobody could find any work in a 'gadjo' town to earn some money.

During the few quieter moments, I always crawled onto my Dad's safe and cozy lap to play 'octopus' against his broad chest and feel even more loved. Of course, I didn't even think about going outside and joining my 'diaper friends' to have another snowball fight. Today, I had to be home, in case any new visitors showed up to congratulate me! Besides, I still hadn't seen my Big Friend, Michail...

Finally, during the afternoon, Michail showed up in our caravan, accompanied by his girlfriend. Much to my surprise, my Big Friend brought me a colored picture book that showed all sorts of beautiful butterflies and their caterpillars! With eyes full of love, he told me that everybody in our camp had collected a little bit of their own spare money, to buy this special birthday present and give it to me!

For several seconds, I just felt too overwhelmed to say anything at all. Had my beloved subjects really collected such a lot of money; and had Michail been to a 'gadjo shop' or a 'market', especially for me, to buy me this beautiful and splendid birthday present? When I woke up from my stupor, I smothered my Big Friend with several big kisses, to thank him for buying me such a beautiful picture book! Next, I also dived towards Felicia and kissed her on her suddenly blushing cheek. Tomorrow, first thing in the morning, I would go outside and thank my other subjects for their beautiful birthday gift!

Happily, I retreated to our couch and started to flip through the beautifully colored book pages that were showing all different kinds of butterflies and their caterpillars. Suddenly, I found a picture in my book that looked EXACTLY like my own caterpillar had been, just before it hung upside down and cocooned itself! In total awe, I stared at the picture next to my caterpillar; showing a huge and majestic butterfly that left its already opened cocoon while spreading its enormous wings! With a choked voice and shuddering from my suddenly welling emotions, I asked my Big Friend to read the accompanying description to me, while I followed the words with my finger.

From the description, I learned that my metamorphosed caterpillar butterfly is called an 'Admiral'; and this enormous flying insect is one of the most beautiful butterflies on earth! Soon after spring showed up, my little caterpillar friend would metamorphose into what had to be the Absolute King of Beautiful Butterflies! I nearly started to cry from sheer happiness, while I kissed my broadly smiling Big Friend again. Then, I dived towards Felicia and again kissed her fiercely blushing cheek. This splendid picture book was the most valuable birthday present that I could ever think of! Starting tomorrow, my Dad or my Mom could help me reading the accompanying descriptions, until I would be able to read them all by myself.

Near the end of the day, our two violin players showed up and started to play our beautiful Gypsy melodies full of joy and happiness. Now, it was time to blow my two burning candles and to do my secret birthday wish for the upcoming year. Only, even after quite a lot of deep thinking, I just couldn't come up with any wish at all. I already felt totally happy, and I already possessed everything that I wanted; so what else could I wish for, to have during the upcoming year?

After some more heavy thinking, I finally decided to wish again for a long and happy life full of Love and Gratitude, for ALL of us. While whispering my birthday wish, I blew my two burning candles, everybody clapped, my parents kissed me, and I was sure I had wished for exactly the right thing!

Now, I only had to wait for another two years, until I finally would be four years old and become dry during the night, so that I could join the 'older kids' into our mysterious woods. Or, would my tiny body decide to be a bit earlier, perhaps because of its extremely early bright brain? I absolutely hoped so...

Chapter 11. Second birthday; and Michail's marriage.

A few weeks after my second birthday, I was playing outside with my 'diaper friends', of course still clad in my beautiful winter clothes, when I suddenly felt an urgent 'call of nature'! Of course, I had felt this same call many times before, but the feeling had always been too late to act upon it. Now, for the first time, I felt an urge to defecate just BEFORE I pooped my still dry diaper! Hurriedly, I raced home, dived into our lavatory, jerked my clothes and diaper down, and let myself go with a deep sigh of satisfaction. FINALLY, my body had started to warn me in advance, although I was only two years old.

After I had defecated and urinated, I first took some toilet paper and meticulously cleaned my bottom. Then, I washed my hands and dried them, before I reattached my diaper and pulled my blue jeans up. Being very proud of myself, I raced to our living room and jumped onto my Dad's lap at full speed. Enthusiastically, I exclaimed:

"DAD and MOM; this time, I have pooped and peed all by myself, and my diaper is still dry! Finally, my little toddler body is growing up and I am becoming a REAL 'diaper kid'!"

Of course, my parents congratulated me abundantly with my early achievement; while my proud looking Dad folded his strong arms around my body and held me very close. Chuckling at seeing my over-enthusiastic face, my Dad told me:

"My dear 'Harry' son; again, you are making me proud with being extremely early! Only, are you sure your body will stay dry during the day from now on, or could this be a one-time happening?"

"Dad; I am absolutely sure that, from now on, I will stay dry during the day, because I can feel it in my Inside. From now on, my body will always warn me, every time I have to poop or pee."

"Okay, I believe you. From now on, you really are our Big Boy!"

Smilingly, I wrestled in between my Mom and Dad on our couch, and very much enjoyed the happy feeling of being sandwiched in between the two people I loved most in the entire world. Both parents put their arms around me and around each other, and we continued our group-cuddle for quite some time. It felt marvelous, to be a little growing-up kid in our Gypsy community, and to be cuddled in between my lovable parents on our couch. That is, until I grew a little bit too impatient and wrestled free from our shared sandwich. Then, I asked my Mom to help me shuck my still dry diaper...

Only, my always-wary Mom immediately restarted to doubt again, because she hesitatingly asked me:

"Are you really sure you don't need your diaper any more during the day? What if your body doesn't warn you in time and you unintentionally soil your new blue jeans? Ultimately, you are only two years old; and I also don't want to clean you up and wash your clothes only because you are too stubborn to wear a diaper anymore."

Feeling absolutely sure about my newest achievement, I answered:

"Mom, you really can believe me, because my Inside is absolutely sure, and I can feel it in my guts as well. Please, trust me on this. From now on, I will need to wear a diaper only during the night when I am in a deep sleep and my inside cannot wake me up in time."

Finally, my Mom surrendered; and she helped me shuck my still dry diaper underneath my warm winter clothes. Immediately, without the extra clothing around my belly and bottom, I felt much freer. Still feeling extremely happy, I raced outside to rejoin my playing 'diaper friends'. Although I felt very happy to finally be a REAL 'diaper kid', I decided NOT to tell anybody about my 'little-kid-achievement'. My little 'diaper playmates' just didn't have to know...

Fortunately, from now on, my way too early body never betrayed me during the day; so that I never disappointed my Mom's trust in me. I always immediately went to our small lavatory when I had to go; and I needed to wear my diaper only during the night. Now, I only had to be patient until I didn't need any diaper at all and was allowed to join the 'older kids' into our woods; hopefully very soon...

Finally, SPRING showed up. Immediately, the outside air became much warmer and all the snow disappeared. Happily, I trotted outside without wearing any clothes at all, and joined my OWN group of 'diaper kids'! Finally, I could join them completely naked, for the first time since my birth, although my body was only two years and a few months old. Happily, we frolicked around, chased after each other, and enjoyed the warming sun on our bare skins. Soon, our bodies would lose their paleness and regain their golden tans.

Suddenly, I thought of my still metamorphosing caterpillar in its enveloping cocoon. During our cold winter, it had only slept and slept, obviously waiting until spring would show up. According to my book, it was now time for my beautiful 'King Admiral' butterfly to wake up, leave its cocoon, and find a mate to make new baby caterpillars!

Chapter 11. Second birthday; and Michail's marriage.

Immediately, I was in a tremendous hurry, left my playing group of 'diaper friends', and raced into our surrounding bushes, to take a quick look at my cocooned caterpillar friend. Would it finally leave its dangling cocoon and become a beautiful butterfly?

Alas... The dangling cocoon was still hanging upside down from its branch, slowly moving in the steadily warming breeze. Nothing seemed to have changed; and my metamorphosing caterpillar inside was still asleep. Or, could it be frozen to death during our too cold winter? Feeling disappointed, I returned to my still playing friends. Only, I now felt nervous all day, fidgeted around, and almost couldn't wait to have a first look at my metamorphosed 'King Admiral' butterfly. That is, IF it had survived our cold winter and really would wake up from its hibernation as a beautiful butterfly...

From now on, every morning, immediately after eating my Mom's healthy breakfast, I stormed outside and towards my sleeping cocoon, hoping its butterfly would show up today. Impatiently, I stared at the silently dangling thing, as if trying to urge its sleeping inside with my thoughts to leave its shelter and greet me NOW.

For several days, nothing happened; and, slowly, I started to feel more and more disappointed; until, at last, I started to lose all interest. Maybe, both my Dad and my beautiful picture book were wrong; and my caterpillar had really frozen to death during our cold winter...

Feeling severely disappointed, I finally decided to live with the facts. Tomorrow, I would take my dead cocoon from its branch and ceremonially bury it in Mother Earth. Then, I would forget all about it, and just go on with my life as if nothing had happened.

The next morning, I was still deep asleep when some warm and soulful voice called my name! Feeling surprised, I woke up and sat upright, while rubbing the sand out of my eyes. Had really somebody called my name and woken me up? I looked around and listened, but everybody else in our caravan was still asleep and snoring. Perhaps, I had only dreamt about some stranger calling my name? Then, again, a warm and soulful voice in my inside told me:

"Please, my young friend, wake up and go greet your butterfly!"

This time, my Inside recognized the well-known warm voice of our Beloved King of Ancestors; one of my dearest Cosmic Friends who was still living in our Timeless Eternal Realm! Was my dear Ancestor Friend really trying to help me meet my butterfly?

To read all our famous 'Gypsy Series' books, please visit www.gypsyseries.com

Hastily, I jumped out of bed, chucked my diaper, and first raced to our bathroom to wash up. Then, I left our caravan and sprinted towards our surrounding bushes, shivering from the sudden morning cold on my bare skin. Would finally my beautiful King Admiral Butterfly reveal itself to me, so that I could see it and greet it?

In our surrounding bushes, I stared at the lazily dangling cocoon in utmost surprise. Much to my happiness, the top of my cocoon was already OPENING! Clearly, my Beloved Ancestor Friend had been absolutely right. Something unbelievable and wonderful was happening! Teasingly slowly, my cocoon opened its top. Little by little, my totally metamorphosed caterpillar friend showed up, this time looking like some strange and almost unearthly creature.

While I hopped up and down from sheer enthusiasm, I stared at the strange looking creature that slowly showed up. In total awe, I stared at the unbelievable spectacle of seeing my beautiful King Admiral butterfly reveal itself to my surprised eyes.

First, it put two tall antennas up into the air and felt around, as if testing its environment. Then, it unfolded two enormous butterfly wings that were decorated with many beautiful red, gold, and blue colors. Gasping at the unbelievable spectacle in absolute rapt, I nearly forgot to breathe from my involuntarily welling emotions. This enormous and splendid looking animal, which once had been my little caterpillar friend, was the Absolute King of Butterflies!

In total awe, I stared at my beautiful King Admiral friend, which for several months had been my caterpillar friend. I never thought it would be able to transform into something this wonderful and unearthly magnificent! Would my newborn friend allow me to touch it, as a greeting? Tentatively, I stretched my hand out towards it...

At that same moment, the body of my huge King Butterfly shuddered as if it rearranged its enormous wings. After a few tentative flaps, it rose majestically up into the air. Then, it landed exactly on my outstretched hand! Sitting on my hand, my butterfly friend turned around and stared at me with two enormous eyes full of tiny facets...

Now, I was sure it recognized me and wanted to greet me! Feeling deeply thrilled and unable to speak from my again welling emotions, I stared back at the enormous butterfly on my hand. This was the most honoring thing that I had ever felt! Slowly, almost reverently, I bowed my head towards my butterfly, in an attempt to greet my beautiful butterfly Friend King Admiral for the first time.

Chapter 11. Second birthday; and Michail's marriage.

At the same time, I thanked it in my mind for being my little caterpillar friend for so many months, and for letting me see its wonderful transformation. Would it really understand my human thoughts?

Much to my surprise, my staring butterfly Friend suddenly rose high onto its thin legs and slowly performed a deep bow towards me! Then, it spread its enormous wings out at full width and flapped a couple of times, as if waving farewell to me. For several seconds, we again stared into each other's eyes. Then, my beautiful King Admiral butterfly friend flapped its wings, rose high into the air, turned around, and slowly flapped away; leaving me totally in awe and feeling deeply grateful. It HAD understood my human thoughts!

After my beautiful King Admiral Friend flapped away and slowly disappeared behind the treetops, I sat down on an old stump while supporting my head with my hands. Almost sobbing from my totally overwhelming emotions, I wiped the welling tears out of my eyes. I already MISSED my caterpillar friend! Ultimately, it had been my little friend for many months, until it transformed into an enormous butterfly, greeted me, and flapped away to find a mate.

Secretly, I hoped I would be able to find a new little caterpillar friend. Would our Beloved King of Ancestors still be around me? Silently, I thanked Him in my mind, for waking me just in time to greet my beautiful King Admiral butterfly. Again, I heard His warm and soulful voice in my inside, responding to my thanks:

"You are very welcome, my young friend! Within a short time, we will meet again and talk some more. However, for now, you have to return to your parents and forget everything about me."

For a moment, I started to doubt. Could I have made my Friend's warm voice up, perhaps because my too clever brain expected to hear His answer? I wasn't absolutely sure... Nevertheless, thanking my Beloved Ancestor Friend felt great! Still feeling thankful and humble, I slowly rose from my old stump and sauntered home.

At home, I immediately woke my still snoring Mom and Dad. Impatiently, I waited until they had rubbed the sand out of their eyes. When they stopped yawning and were ready to listen to me, I had an unbelievable and truly amazing story to tell! Enthusiastically, I told them everything about my going outside and watching my beautiful King Admiral butterfly reveal itself to me, land on my hand, bow towards me, and finally flap away to find a mate.

Surprisingly, I had totally forgotten everything about my Beloved King of Ancestors Friend and his soulful voice in my inside...

A few weeks later, Michail finally decided to marry Felicia, after a long time of being 'engaged'. Therefore, we organized a Big Feast, while everybody in our camp contributed some nice looking goodies or tasty snacks. Soon, many filled platters showed up; to be set out onto the hastily arranged circle of wooden tables. Of course, I too raced around the circle and tried to 'help' everybody wherever I could!

At last, all our wooden tables were covered with many copiously filled platters and cups of brightly colored lemonade. Only, first, we had to sit down on our wooden benches, to listen to my Grandmother marrying the happy pair. All the kids left their games and crawled onto one of the inviting laps, to be cuddled and feel loved.

This time, I sat on the lap of Pietro, our technical man; because a small girl had already occupied my Dad's lap and another girl sat on my Mom's lap. However, I wasn't jealous at all. Live and let live!

My Grandmother married the happy pair by ceremoniously binding their hands together with two colored ropes, symbolizing they wanted to be a couple. Next, she blessed them in the name of our Beloved Ancestors and our Highest Supreme Being. Now, the happy bride and groom embraced and kissed each other, to seal their vows. To end the ceremony, Michail and Felicia freed each other from their colored ropes, knotted them together, and threw them into our faintly glowing campfire. While both brightly flaring ropes ascended towards our highest Supreme Being, they were now a married couple!

My Grandmother returned to her own Royal wooden bench and looked around with a happy face; while our violin players started to play beautiful songs full of love and happiness. Now, everybody else rose from their benches and queued up, to congratulate the newly married couple. Of course, I too stepped into the forming queue, next to Pietro, and waited until it would be my turn.

For a moment, I hesitated... Should I congratulate only Michail, or his new spouse as well? How would Felicia react if I congratulated her too? I was still sure she didn't like me at all... Then, it was my turn, and I just stepped towards them. With my politest face, I congratulated both my Big Friend AND his new missus, and wished them all the good luck in the world! Totally unexpectedly, Felicia embraced me and offered me a tiny kiss on my cheek, her first one ever!

Chapter 11. Second birthday; and Michail's marriage.

Suddenly feeling confused, I forgot to kiss Felicia back. I never thought she would ever like me, not even the tiniest bit...

Michail started to laugh at seeing my confused face, and teasingly ruffled my unruly blond hair; while I wiped the unexpected kiss from my cheek and slowly turned around. I needed a moment for myself, to regain my posture and to get rid of my strange feelings.

Then, I sauntered towards the arranged circle of tables, to partake in our Big Feast. Enthusiastically, I started to wander from table to table, on my way tasting several nice goodies and colored snacks. Yummy! Those snacks tasted much better than the so-called 'healthy meals' my Mom always cooked! Still munching, I already sauntered towards the next table.

Several other kids had joined me along the tables, while carefully choosing what kind of snacks they wanted to taste. After they stopped, I just went on and popped some more tasty snacks into my mouth. Unexpectedly, one of the older boys, Misha, warned me:

"You better don't eat too many snacks at once, because they might upset your stomach and make you throw up!"

Only, being 'pigheaded' as I was, I just laughed at Misha's warning while teasingly popping the next tasty looking pastry into my mouth. Why would I listen to this older kid? As a Big Boy, I was now my own boss and certainly mature enough to decide for myself!

Half an hour later, I suddenly raced to our surrounding bushes, to let my upset stomach throw up all the eaten goodies! Of course, my always-wary Mom followed me immediately. First, she waited until I had emptied my upset stomach, before she cleaned my dirty face with some water and a few tufts of grass. Then, she wanted to take me to our Wise Woman, because she thought I could be ill.

However, I assured my Mom that everything was still okay with me. I had only eaten too many snacks, and I wanted to stay outside and have fun for the remainder of the day, or until my body would start feeling too tired. Shaking her head, my Mom returned to our own bench and sat down next to my already chuckling Dad.

In the meantime, the group of older kids approached me again, and Misha teased their too pigheaded little Crown Prince:

"We DID warn you not to eat too many snacks! Clearly, you are still too little to walk around on your own..."

To read all our famous 'Gypsy Series' books, please visit www.gypsyseries.com

Feeling offended, I glared at Misha's smiling face and rebuked:

"You are only jealous of my bright brain, because I am the fastest developing child in our community."

"Well, you surely are the fastest puking child in our community!"

This time, my angry brain just couldn't come up with any caustic response or witty remark. Not knowing how to respond to Misha's teasing, I quickly turned around and stomped away. Feeling frustrated, I trotted to our own Royal caravan and kicked it a couple of times.

Fortunately, the kicking helped; and my flaring anger subsided and soon went away. Of course, Misha and his friends had been right; but I just didn't want to admit it.

Pigheaded? Who? Me?

Hmm...

I returned to the still snickering kids, and humbly offered them my well-meant excuses. Although they suddenly blushed and reacted a little bit timid, they also accepted my apologies. Misha even told me they didn't really mean it, and only wanted to have some fun with their too stubborn little Prince.

Yeah, well... Obviously, I still had to learn quite a lot more, before the older kids really accepted me. Fortunately, Misha smiled at me and ruffled my unruly blond hair, to let me know he understood and that everything was still okay! Together, we strolled back towards the tables, to drink lemonade and try to find any leftover snacks...

12. 'Black magic'; and Felicia gets twin sons.

Next to our big tree, a couple of 'diaper kids' had already started to gather the others, to play their usual games of 'hide and seek' around our caravans. Yesss! This was exactly what I had been waiting for all the time! Finally, I would be able to partake in the games I had stared at so many times while sitting on my wooden bench.

Of course, now that I no longer needed a diaper during the day and was clad just like all the other kids were, wearing only our already nicely tanning 'birthday suits', I now BELONGED to our 'diaper kids'! Therefore, I just joined their steadily growing group; and they immediately accepted me as being 'one of us'.

Before we started, a more experienced kid first gathered the few 'newcomers', and explained their simple but very important playing rules. During our games of hide and seek, every hider should hide only within the appointed borders; and nobody was allowed to go away or enter any of our caravans without warning the others first. Anyone who didn't obey our important rules without a solid reason would be excluded from our group and banned for life...

Yeah, well, the more experienced kid had been smiling all the time, and therefore didn't seem to be too serious about his silly threat. By reciting a funny 'dipping rhyme', we first chose a kid who would be our first seeker. He had to stand next to our big tree while closing his eyes and slowly counting to twenty, before he reopened his eyes, left the tree, and started looking for his hidden friends.

Soon, our seeker closed his eyes and started to count to twenty. Immediately, everybody else swarmed out around our wooden benches and caravans, to find a good hiding place and duck away. Because I had never played this game before, I first looked around at what the others were doing. Then, I saw a small but usable hole at the base of one of the surrounding shrubs, and wriggled my tiny body into it. Quickly, I covered the still visible parts of my arms and legs with some fallen leaves and a little bit of forest litter. While trying to duck into my hole as deeply as I could, I regulated my breath to calm down, forced my body to lie absolutely still, and waited...

Finally, I was playing my first game of 'hide and seek'! From my hiding place, I looked at our seeker who already started to look around. Almost immediately, he tagged the first kid who clumsily tried to hide behind one of the open cartwheels. Then, he tagged one of our girls and another small boy who hid together behind a wooden table. Patiently, I waited, until it would be my turn to be found and tagged. When would our experienced seeker see and tag ME?

After several minutes, our experienced seeker had found and tagged all the other hiding kids, except for their 'littlest runt'. Much to my surprise, even after quite some time of searching and looking around everywhere, our more and more frustrated looking seeker just couldn't find me! At last, he stopped searching and asked the others:

"Are you sure our little Prince understands our rules? Perhaps, our 'littlest runt' hides outside the appointed borders, or he secretly entered one of our caravans. Ultimately, he is the smallest kid in our group. How old is that tiny baby anyway?"

One of the other kids started to chuckle, while he responded:

"Unfortunately for you, I have seen where our little Prince hides; and he isn't doing anything wrong! Clearly, that 'tiny baby' is hiding way too good for you and your clumsy efforts to find him."

"Yeah well... Sorry for being too 'clumsy', but I give up because our tiny Prince is hiding TOO good for me."

Immediately, all the other kids started searching for me, except for the few ones who had seen me hiding and therefore already knew where I was. Everybody else went scurrying through our bushes, crawling under our wooden benches, and seeking under and even on top of our surrounding caravans. In the meantime, I frequently bit my tongue and held my breath, while trying not to snicker out loud at all their clumsy efforts to find me...

At last, one of the searching girls found me accidentally, because she suddenly stumbled across one of my covered legs. Triumphantly, I showed up and wiped the fallen leaves and forest litter from my painfully stiffening body. Immediately, all the other kids started to crowd around me! They congratulated me, high-fived me, and told me I was a surprisingly good hider for such a 'little runt'. Was I sure I was playing their game of hide and seek for the first time? Much to my own surprise, everybody around me wanted to be my 'friend', even our still frustrated looking seeker...

Chapter 12. 'Black magic'; and Felicia gets twin sons.

Because I had won our first game of hide and seek; I now could decide to be our next seeker or appoint somebody else. Of course, I happily went to our big tree and closed my eyes! Fortunately, my parents had already taught me how I could use all my fingers twice to count to twenty. Therefore, I touched my ten fingers, one by one, while counting out loud; and then I did it a second time while counting from eleven to twenty. After arriving at twenty, I reopened my eyes, left our big tree, and started to look around.

Very soon, I found our first hider. Only, because I didn't know his name, I just touched our big tree while pointing at him and shouting "you there!" With a sour face, the tagged boy showed up and told me his name so that I could remember it for a next time. Fortunately, I had an excellent memory and never forgot any new names or faces.

In no time, I had found all the other hiding kids and tagged them; because my Shaman abilities helped me tremendously by sensing their surrounding energy fields, so that I already knew in which direction they where hiding, and only had to look for their auras...

Again, all my friends high-fived me, and told me their 'littlest runt' turned out to be an excellent seeker as well! Now, everybody wanted to be my friend even more... Well, I would be able to live with that. I appointed the next seeker, and we went on with our games.

From this day on, playing 'hide and seek' absolutely was my most favorite game! My 'small runt' body was able to crawl into the tiniest hole; and I always could lie or sit perfectly still for a very long time, by regulating my breath to stay calm. Nearly every time, our seeker couldn't find me, and he had to ask the others to help him. The few times when I was our seeker, I always found my friends almost immediately, by using my Shaman abilities to trace their hiding auras.

Much to my surprise, I suddenly found out that my Shaman inside also switched on some strange but very useful 'ability' that seemed to blur the vision of whoever was searching for me! That way, our seeker always totally overlooked my hiding place, unless he or she accidentally stumbled upon my cleverly hidden body!

Vaguely, I remembered I had developed this useful ability in one of my past lives, where I had been a 'little trapper boy' and had trained myself in sneaking towards some wary prey, to catch it before it saw me and fled away into the dense undergrowth.

Hilariously, in my present life, my Shaman inside didn't seem to know the difference between a wary forest prey and my desperately searching new friends who suddenly couldn't see me any more...

All day long, we continued to play our games of hide and seek, until darkness set in and our parents called us to our caravans, to eat dinner and go to bed. Of course, before we trotted home to wash up, fill our hungry stomachs, and get some sleep, we first promised to restart our games first thing in the next morning, immediately after we woke up and had filled our hungry stomachs!

Much to my dismay, the next morning, my worried parents first took me to our Wise Woman, to let her have a professional look at my too slow bodily growth. My bright brain was developing extremely fast; but my little body stayed too small and just didn't grow enough. Compared to all the other two-and-a-half-year-old 'toddlers' in our camp, I still was and stayed the shortest one.

Yet, my muscles were much stronger than most other children of around my age; and I always won our wrestling contests with ease. Therefore, my new friends didn't tease me too much with my tiny body; except for sometimes calling me a 'little runt'.

After our Wise Woman invited my parents and me in, she sat me down next to her on her couch. First, she looked me over from head to foot, while staring at my small body with her piercing eyes. Then, she asked my parents and me several annoying questions about my eating habits and bowel movements. Fortunately, none of our answers seemed to disturb her or sound too strange.

Finally, she asked us to be silent, because she wanted to consult our Beloved Ancestors and surrounding Spirit Friends about me. She closed her eyes and quickly sank into a deep trance; obviously to ask my Ancestor Friends and Spirit Guides for advice...

A few minutes later, our Wise Woman came out of her trance and first drank some water to recover. Then, she told my parents and me not to worry any more about my bodily development. Our Spirit Guides had told her that my little body didn't grow enough because my extremely bright brain was developing too fast and therefore demanded too much of my energy! Fortunately, I would still continue to grow up in excellent health; and one of our Beloved Ancestors had foretold that my size would catch up with my age soon after I had reached puberty. Until then, I would probably stay a bit shorter than most other kids of around my age...

Chapter 12. 'Black magic'; and Felicia gets twin sons.

Well; I was sure I would be able to live with that! Happily, my parents and I thanked our Wise Woman for her professional advice.

Immediately after I returned from visiting our Wise Woman, all my 'diaper friends' crowded around me. Of course, they wanted to know what had happened to their little Prince; and when would I finally grow up some more and no longer be our 'littlest runt'? Proudly, I told my new friends that my size would catch up with my age soon after I reached puberty!

In the meantime, our 'older kids' showed up from our surrounding woods; and one of them, Misha, listened to me and then thought that I would first have a 'growth spurt', as every normal and healthy kid went through from time to time. I only had to be patient...

Thank you very much, Misha; but 'patience' wasn't exactly my strongest quality! Yet, I decided to keep Misha's prediction in mind. That evening, I helped my Mom put a visible mark on our doorpost, exactly at where the top of my head was. That way, I would always be able to estimate my growth; and I could look out for my first 'growth spurt', whatever that was.

The next morning, I decided to find out what could be happening to me while my Shaman abilities accidentally blurred the vision of our next seeker. Therefore, I squatted down behind an open cartwheel without hiding at all. Much to my surprise, I soon found out that I could switch my abilities on and off on purpose, by using my will as a switch. I also found out that I could deceive my friends by just concentrating on them. I only had to tune in into their minds, access their visionary brains, and wipe out my own picture. That way, my friends always overlooked me totally, even when I was in plain sight!

For around an hour, I had the fun of my life; as nobody was able to find and tag me any more, unless I generously allowed them to see me again. Then, my fun slowly disappeared, because I started to feel like an outcast. Wasn't I cheating terribly by deliberately using my powerful Shaman abilities on my unsuspicious friends? Yet, my 'pigheaded' streak refused to give up its unexpected fun by playing 'normal' again. Clearly, it just wanted to WIN all the time...

At last, my strange 'abilities' were becoming too obvious; and a few kids plainly refused to play hide and seek any more, because even our Natural Trappers couldn't find their hiding littlest runt any more!

Now that I had been winning all our games, their former fun was gone; and they soon started to mope and angrily walked away.

Surprisingly, nobody around me ever found out how I had been able to disappear completely from their vision; although, every time anybody looked at the place where I was hiding, I concentrated on them and blanked their minds or wiped out my own picture.

Only our Wise Woman seemed to know what I was doing, because she stared straight at me with her piercing eyes while shaking her head. Then, she called me towards her! Invitingly, she patted the bench next to her, until I hesitantly sat down and listened to her. With a serious voice, she bent over to me and whispered:

"Please, my young friend; be very careful with your powerful Shaman abilities! Always listen to your own heart first, before using any magic tricks. You are quickly developing into a surprisingly strong Shaman; but, unintentionally, you could harm your friends by using some dangerous kind of 'black magic' with your exceptional powers."

Suddenly feeling strange and nonplussed, I responded:

"How do YOU know what I have been doing? I am absolutely sure I never told anybody! And, how could I ever harm my friends? I am only wiping out my own picture or blurring their vision, so that they suddenly cannot see me any more..."

"Well, to be honest, I once did the same things when I was about your age! Fortunately, reading thoughts or blurring someone's vision is relatively harmless. However, your steadily developing Shaman powers could easily go too far and cause some serious damage, like a lasting headache or a nasty eye cataract. Therefore, I am warning you in advance not to use any kind of 'black magic', before it is too late."

Oh my, what had I done... Of course, I already knew that our 'own heart' always connects us to our Supreme Being; and it only acts out of Pure Love and never does any harm to anybody. Therefore, my own heart would never allow me to use any 'black magic', but it would always tell me to act solely out of Pure Love and Compassion.

Besides, my Most Important Task on Earth was bringing much more Love and Light to the people around me; and I had to use my 'special abilities' accordingly! Until now, I never thought I could be a serious DANGER to the people around me! I loved everybody in our camp dearly; and I absolutely didn't want to cause anybody any harm at all. What the heck had I been doing, albeit unwittingly...

Chapter 12. 'Black magic'; and Felicia gets twin sons.

Feeling severely shocked, I immediately decided to be a lot more careful with my strange 'gifts'! From now on, I would always listen to my own heart first, before again using any of my quickly developing Shaman powers. I never knew that using my powerful Shaman abilities also could work against me, by harming my innocent victims...

Our Wise Woman seemed to have picked up my thoughts, because she started to smile broadly. Suddenly, she hugged me fiercely and told me she would be very happy to be my 'special friend' and 'personal advisor'! From now on, I would always be welcome in her caravan; and I could always ask her any important questions that bothered me or required an immediate answer.

Still feeling very strange, I returned her hug, left her caravan, and sauntered into our surrounding bushes. For quite some time, I sat down on my old stump, while trying to 'listen to my own heart'.

Slowly, I started to understand that cheating had NOT been a proper way of playing games with my friends, unless our rules explicitly allowed me to do so. Unintentionally, I had broken my friends' valuable trust in me, by manipulating their minds and visions without their consent. How could I ever make this up to my friends?

Feeling truly ashamed, I decided to stop using all of my developing 'Shaman abilities'! From now on, I would play 'hide and seek' with my friends only by cleverly hiding or searching, without any more cheating by wiping my own picture or blurring their visions.

The next morning, my surprised friends found out that, overnight, their searching capabilities had become much stronger! All at once, they were able to find their 'littlest runt' much more easily, although I still was one of the best hiders and seekers in our camp.

Not surprisingly, my friends restarted to play our games with much more enthusiasm; only now and then teasing me because they could find me too easily! Even the hitherto moping kids forgot about their jealousy, returned to our group, and rejoined us to partake in our games of hide and seek again.

Today, I found out that playing without cheating could be a LOT more fun than always winning had been. Again, I had learned a valuable lesson, and again I had bettered myself. Fortunately, everybody in our 'diaper group' still wanted to be my friend, because I still was and stayed their best hider and seeker.

Once a month, my Mom measured my new length, while I stood upright against our doorpost and she marked the top of my head by using my beautiful picture book. Much to her and my delight, the new mark always was a tiny bit higher, showing that I really had been growing up some! Yet, I still stayed the 'tiniest runt' in our group of diaper kids. Now and then, I stared at the advancing marks and hoped to keep on growing until I was at least as tall as my Dad was. Only, when would I finally have my first 'growth spurt', as Misha had predicted? I couldn't wait to grow up and proudly show it to Misha...

Again, summer turned into fall; and fall turned into another cold winter, forcing us to wear our warm winter clothes. Again, as soon as the snow showed up, my 'diaper friends' and I rolled around and around in the thick blanket of snow until we looked like little snowmen. Again, we started to fight each other and had several ferocious snowball fights. That is, until we felt too tired to go on and just slumped down in the thick blanket of snow, until it was time to go home, eat dinner, and go to bed.

That winter, I celebrated my THIRD birthday, this time with THREE burning candles on my tasty birthday cake. Everybody visited our caravan and congratulated me with being THREE years old. Unfortunately, this year, nobody bought me a birthday present.

From now on, I only had to wait for one more year; until I would be four years old and, hopefully, become 'totally dry' and therefore an 'older boy'! Then, I would finally be allowed to join our group of 'older kids' into our woods; to set up my own traps and catch my own animals to roast them over our campfire and eat their tasty meat.

I had already been extremely early in my bodily development, by becoming dry during the day while I was only two years old. Now, I hoped and prayed that I would be extremely early again in becoming 'totally dry'. Well, only time would tell...

A few months later, my parents had to visit another Gypsy community, to perform their Royal duties as our Beloved King and Queen. As usual, they asked Michail to look after me while they were away. Of course, I was very happy to have my Big Friend around for the whole day! Only, much to my disappointment, Michail also brought his missus, Felicia, to accompany him; and, all the time, they sat next to each other on our couch. Feeling neglected and a little bit jealous, I climbed onto Michail's lap and tried to catch his attention...

Chapter 12. 'Black magic'; and Felicia gets twin sons.

Fortunately, my Big Friend still didn't seem to mind, romped with me, and patiently answered all my questions; like 'how come our sun shows up every day and disappears every night'.

Now and then, I secretly peeked at Felicia's belly, while I started to feel more and more curious. Using my Inner Eye, I could clearly see two tiny boys that cozily floated around in their shared womb! Therefore, I was certain that Felicia was pregnant; but why did she carry TWO tiny infants in her belly?

Vaguely, I remembered how crammed my Moms womb had been with only me in it. Wouldn't Felicia's womb, with TWO baby boys in it, be way too crowded for both of them? In our camp, nobody else had twins, and nobody ever told me they existed...

At last, I started to feel too curious, and suddenly blurted out:

"Felicia, why do you carry TWO babies in your stomach?"

All of a sudden, total silence fell over our living room; so that my bright brain started to doubt. Could my Inner Eye be wrong, or had I asked Felicia a too improper question? Yet, I still saw those two tiny fetuses, brotherly floating around in her womb...

Unexpectedly, Felicia jumped up from our couch, while she glared at me as if she saw some dangerous alien from another planet. For a moment, she still tried to calm down and respond to my improper question, while her face grew redder and redder with rage. Then, she shouted, while staring at me with fire-shooting eyes:

"How in the world do YOU know that I'm pregnant? Even Michail doesn't know yet, because I wasn't sure and didn't want to tell him until I would be certain. You REALLY are a little freak! And, why do you want me to carry TWO children? I don't want to have twins! One little crybaby will be more than enough, thank you very much."

At hearing Felicia's unexpected outburst, I felt severely shocked and nearly started to cry from frustration. Had I really done such a terrible thing? When I stealthily looked at her belly again, I was still sure she was carrying two tiny infants in her womb, and both of them were boys. Within a couple of months, my Big Friend and his missus would be the proud parents of TWO healthy baby boys!

Only, why didn't Felicia look much happier? Didn't she like little children? That would be truly sad...

Suddenly, my Inner Eye saw a nasty dark cloud along Felicia's timeline that surrounded her but not her two babies. Both boys would be born healthy; but something terrible was going to happen to their mother, and both children would grow up without having a Mom!

Now feeling horrible, I refused to see any more nasty predictions and angrily shut my 'Shaman gifts' down. I didn't even answer Michail's worried questions; but only buried my teary face into his broad chest and started to sob uncontrollably. Having such extremely powerful 'Shaman abilities' was not always fun...

After only eight months of pregnancy, Felicia suddenly gave birth to two tiny baby boys. Although they were twins, they didn't resemble each other. The first-born baby, Michi, was somewhat taller than his shorter twin brother, Movi, who was a bit chubbier.

Unfortunately, their mother started to bleed after labor; and it didn't stop. This time, even our Wise Woman couldn't help her. In a tremendous hurry, Michail rushed his bleeding missus to a 'gadjo' hospital; where Felicia died before the gadjo doctors could help her.

Fortunately, for all of us, Felicia didn't die in our camp, because our Gypsy belief forbade us to live in the same place where one of us had died. Therefore, we would have had to leave our secluded camp and move on to some other place. That is why all Gypsies were living in their mobile caravans, always ready to move on if necessary.

After Michail returned home, he was inconsolable! He blamed himself for Felicia's death and cried all the time. Day after day, he visited our caravan; but the only things he did was sit on our couch, stare into empty space, and sniffle. My worried parents tried to talk to my Big Friend, but all their efforts to console him were in vain.

Of course, I too tried to talk to him; but my Big Friend didn't even see me! Yet, I too wanted to pull him out of his grief and make him care for his little sons. I was sure both boys missed their Daddy terribly and that they needed him at least as much as I needed my own Dad. How could I help my Big Friend out of his misery?

After some heavy thinking, I decided to do something really drastically, to pull my Big Friend out of his stupor. Therefore, I balled my fists, suddenly stormed towards him, and forcefully punched his stomach while using all the power my small but relatively strong arms could bring forth! Immediately, Michail flinched, coughed, gasped for breath, and stared at me in total confusion...

Chapter 12. 'Black magic'; and Felicia gets twin sons.

Now that I finally had his undivided attention, I told my Big Friend, while using my sternest deep baritone voice:

"Michail, please go get your two sons and start being their Daddy! I am sure your sons need you and that they already miss you terribly. Now that their mother is dead, you are the only person in the world they have. Please, take up your responsibilities and start being the Daddy they need. Of course, it is okay to feel sad; but don't punish your sons for what they cannot help. Now, please, stop moping, stand up, find out where your sons are, and GO GET THEM!"

For quite some time, Michail only stared at my heated face and still blazing eyes; obviously feeling totally bewildered. Then, finally, some life returned into his eyes, and he heaved a couple deep sighs of frustration. Slowly, he stretched his arms out as if wanting to grab me.

For a second, I was afraid that my Big Friend would be mad at me for punching him, and tell me to leave him alone... Then, he pulled me onto his lap, folded his enormous arms around my tiny frame, and started to cry his heart out! However, this time, his desperate crying sounded totally different from what he had done so far. It was now clear that my Big Friend no longer pitied himself.

After crying his heart out, my Big Friend suddenly unfolded his strong arms from around my nearly crushed ribs. He kissed my wrinkling little nose, lifted me off his huge lap, sat me down onto my Dad's lap, and took a couple of tissues from our table. Then, he left our caravan and trotted away, without saying a word.

For quite some time, both my Mom and my Dad only stared at me, but I saw lots of pure love and adoration in their proud looking eyes. Obviously, they thought I had been doing exactly the right things, although I still doubted. Hadn't I been too harsh to my Big Friend, after he lost his wife and suddenly became a widower?

Finally, my proud looking Dad exclaimed:

"My so precious and lovable son; today, you have PROVEN to be a real Royal Prince! Both your Mom and I are VERY proud of you, because you were the only one who knew exactly what to do, to help Michail out of his sad stupor. My precious son; thank you very, very much, for being the loving and caring Very Old Soul that you are and always will be..."

Exactly at that moment, Michail returned into our caravan. Still looking a bit ashamed, he ducked his head to pass our doorpost and stepped into our living room. Only, he now carried his two tiny sons in his arms, carefully wrapped up in colorful blankets!

He laid both tiny babies down in between my old pillows; while he smiled at us with a look of regret but also with a lot more pride in his still teary but again beaming eyes that now radiated Pure Love.

My motherly looking Mom immediately doted over both babies; and she started to remove their smelly diapers, clean them up, and powder their sensitive parts. Next, she cooked some milky baby food and fed both tiny babies with it; until they were filled to the brim, burped, and spilled at least half of their food onto our couch.

Suddenly chuckling inwardly, I secretly thought that I wasn't the only fastest puking kid in our community!

After my Mom put both tiny boys back in between my pillows, I tried to play with them; but, much to my disappointment, they were still way too small to have any real fun with.

13. Four years old; discovering tasty 'spices'.

Again, summer turned into fall; and fall turned into another cold winter. Finally, my parents and I celebrated my FOURTH birthday! For many months, I had looked forward to being FOUR years old; because, all the time, I had hoped that my growing body would finally stop wetting my bed at night and become completely dry. Then, I would finally be allowed to join the 'older kids' into our surrounding woods and catch my own small animals! I also still hadn't had my first 'growth spurt' as Misha once predicted, although my Mom and I had measured my slowly increasing length every month.

When I was still a 'toddler', my Dad once told me that most Gypsy children became 'dry' during the day at being around four years old; and they didn't need their diapers any more and became 'totally dry' around five or six years old. Well, at only two years old, my body had already been extremely early by becoming dry during the day; therefore, I hoped it would be extremely early again by becoming totally dry. Then, our strict camp rules would finally allow me to join our 'older kids' into our surrounding woods, to set my own traps and catch my own small animals to roast them over our campfire!

Today, my Grandma had decorated my tasty birthday cake with FOUR burning candles; and, this time, I knew exactly what my 'secret birthday wish' would be! After my visitors congratulated me, and our violin players showed up to play their beautiful Gypsy melodies; I blew my four candles and closed my eyes, while everybody around me cheered and clapped. Secretly, I wished that I very soon would be completely dry! Now, I only had to wait.

Would my secret birthday wish come true? Or, was a 'birthday wish' only some superstitious nonsense that was found out to mislead easy-believing kids like me? Only time would tell...

Alas... Within a few months after celebrating my fourth birthday, I had to admit that month after month had passed by, and I still needed a diaper during the night! Obviously, wishing such a secret 'birthday wish' REALLY was only superstitious nonsense, as I already suspected it would be.

From now on, every year, I would just blow my birthday candles, without having any more stupid 'secret wishes' ever again. From now on, our 'littlest runt' was no longer a silly 'believer'!

Morning after morning, I woke up being soaking wet and feeling utterly betrayed by my still too immature little body. Why couldn't my tiny frame magically grow up a lot faster, as my extremely bright brain always seemed to do? I was growing TIRED of all that waiting while nothing spectacular happened!

Of course, I also still waited until I would have my first 'growth spurt' and finally grow a lot taller. Compared to other 'diaper kids' of around the same age, I still was and stayed our 'tiniest runt', although my clever brainiac brain was quite a lot more mature and my sonorous baritone voice already sounded quite a lot older...

As month after month passed by and still nothing spectacular happened, I slowly started to feel a bit depressed. I also I started to hate living in this too small body that still refused to do what I wanted it to do. Couldn't I cocoon myself, just like my little caterpillar friend had done; to pop up when I would be old enough to stay dry all day and night? I still desperately wanted to join our 'older kids' into our woods, to set my own traps and catch my own animals.

Unfortunately, our strict Gypsy rules forbade me to join them until I would be a 'real big boy' and 'totally dry'. Of course, I had already asked my Dad, my Mom, and even Michail about growing up faster. However, all of them only told me to wait and be more patient. My time would surely come... Grrrrrr!

Every morning when I woke up, I first rubbed the sand out of my eyes. Then, I shucked my wet and therefore acid smelling diaper, took a warm shower, wolfed my Mom's healthy breakfast down, and gulped a glass of milk. At last, I trotted outside, to sit on our wooden bench. From there, I stared longingly at our slowly queuing group of 'older kids', who left our camp and disappeared into our woods.

I already knew they went looking for interesting animal prints and edible nuts, to bring them home and divide them among us kids. They also set up traps and caught small animals in their snares, to roast them over our campfire and eat them. Every time our group of older kids disappeared into our surrounding woods, I felt more jealous; and I started to mope more and more about my misfortune of being too little. When would it finally be MY turn to enter our woods and have fun setting my own traps and catching my own small animals?

Near the end of the day, when our older kids returned from our woods, I always immediately joined them and listened to their stories. However, next to listening to them, I also wanted to SEE what they had been doing, with my OWN eyes!

When our older kids returned from our surrounding woods, they mostly were in a cheerful mood. During summer, they always carried several caught animals; and, now and then, a few baskets filled with edible nuts and delicious fruits. After they divided the nuts and fruits among us; they immediately started to skin and clean out their caught animals in our small butchery near our parking lot.

First, they smeared the animal meat with a little bit of salt and some squashed yellow plant leaves they called 'spice'. Then, they started to roast their prepared animals on wooden stakes over our brightly stoked campfire, to savor them when they were ready.

Day after day, I listened to their interesting stories, while they were preparing their caught animals. For example, they told me about chasing a small pig through the woods; or catching a rat, which always caused lots of laughter because nobody in our camp ever wanted to eat a roasted rat. Next to listening to them, I also dreamed about joining them into our woods and setting my own traps. I so desperately wanted to be one of them and 'spice' my own roasting animals with their yellow leaves and a little bit of salt...

However, until now, they didn't even let me HELP them! Unfortunately, our strict rules forbade me to help them until I had set my own trap and caught my own animal first. But, I couldn't set a trap and catch my first animal, because I wasn't allowed to join them into our surrounding woods. And, I wasn't allowed to join them into our woods, because I still needed a diaper at night... Grrrrrr!

This morning, again, our older kids disappeared into our woods; while I almost burst out in tears. Again feeling too small, depressed, and truly sad, I sauntered around our faintly glowing campfire, visited Michail's caravan and his tiny baby boys, and badgered a couple of grownups with my impossible questions. That is, until they told me to leave them alone and go pester my diaper friends.

Reluctantly, I went to my 'diaper friends'. Only, today, they suddenly were way too small to be my real friends! Of course, they were again playing their usual games of hide and seek; but, this time, they suddenly seemed to act way too 'childish' to have any real fun with.

Obviously, my steadily developing brainiac brain was becoming too bright for them, or too precocious for my own good. Although I was only four years old; in my inside, I already felt a lot older and certainly much wiser. I knew that my bright brain was developing extremely fast; but why couldn't my immature little body follow my fast brain? Wasn't there some 'magic way' to force my too small body to grow faster, or to train it to listen to what I wanted it to do?

Would our Wise Woman, or maybe Michail, know some magic way to let me grow up faster and stay dry all day and night? I asked Michail about it; but my Big Friend only started to laugh at seeing my sour face, while he told me:

"My dear Prince, be happy to be such a small boy, and enjoy your early youth for as long as you can. Way too soon, you will be an old man like me; and, then, you will regret your missed chances."

"But, I WANT to be like you! I HATE being too little, and I cannot wait to grow up and join our older kids into our woods. I want to enjoy my early youth NOW; by joining the older kids and set my own traps and roast my own animals over our campfire."

"Well, you might be a tad too intelligent for your own good. Ultimately, you are only four years old. Yet, I can talk to you as if you are a grownup; and you already understand everything that I am telling you, sometimes outwitting me with your clever answers. This is not a common behavior for a boy your age. Most four-year-old kids are still sucking on their thumbs or playing with mud and pebbles. Therefore, please, stay the young child that you are for as long as you can."

Still feeling frustrated, depressed, and angry, I left my Big Friend's caravan. Outside, I went to our big tree and forcefully kicked and pummeled it. For quite some time, I raged and muttered, while trying to kick my anger and frustration away; until I finally started to feel a little bit better and thanked the big tree for helping me get rid of my childish anger. A few 'diaper friends' had chuckled at seeing my muttering and kicking, but they wisely kept some distance from me. They already knew how caustic I could be when I was angry...

Of course, my Big Friend had been right; but that didn't make my waiting any easier. Ultimately, I didn't even WANT to be such an intelligent 'brainiac'! I wanted to be just like any other four-year-old kid and feel happy with my early youth. I was sure that being 'normal' would make my frustrated life quite a lot easier! I only didn't know how to change my too clever way of thinking...

Chapter 13. Four years old; discovering tasty 'spices'.

Again, I strolled into our surrounding bushes, this time without looking for any big caterpillars. They would only remind me of my bigger friends, who now were setting their traps and catching their small animals. Sitting on my old stump, I put my head in my hands and started to think. Yesterday, I had asked one of the 'older kids', Misha, about the yellow 'spice' they always smeared onto their roasting animals, next to using a little bit of salt and some oil. Misha had answered all my questions; and also explained that the yellow plant they always used to spice their food, was called an 'herb', and they used only its tasty yellow leaves.

Then, Misha added a couple of interesting facts! His friends and he were sure there had to be many more useful 'herbs' among our abundant vegetation; but none of them knew how to recognize them or how to use them on their food. Only our Wise Woman knew everything about 'herbs'; and she always gathered her 'healing herbs' from our woods. Then, she used them for example to cure illnesses, or to smear them onto nasty animal stitches and inflamed wounds.

Suddenly, I started to understand what I had done instinctively, after that nasty insect stung me and I had smeared some brownish juice onto its itching swelling! Without knowing what I did, instinctively, I had 'healed' myself; by using the leaves of what I now was sure had to be such a 'healing herb'! Was I REALLY becoming a 'Wise Boy', to recite the words my wise Dad once teased me with? Or, perhaps, I was already turning into an 'upcoming Healer', next to being a 'powerful Shaman' and having been a 'little trapper boy'...

Near the end of the day, I again returned to my wooden bench and sat down. Here, I always waited until our older kids showed up and started to prepare their caught animals. Much to my happiness, this time, after they had spiced and roasted their caught animals, Misha suddenly shared a small chunk of his own roasted marmot with me! Of course, Misha already knew how eagerly I wanted to join him into our surrounding woods, to catch and roast my own animals. Perhaps, as an older boy, he even pitied me a little bit...

Feeling grateful, I savored the nice tasting chunk of roasted marmot meat, while the other kids smiled at me indulgently. They all seemed to like their eager little Prince very much; and I smiled back at them broadly, because I liked them very much too! After I thanked Misha for his unexpected generosity, I trotted to our own caravan, to wash my hands and eat dinner with my parents.

The next morning, immediately after the older kids disappeared into our surrounding woods, I told my 'diaper friends' I wanted to be left alone. Then, I sauntered towards the bushes where I knew Misha's yellow 'spice herbs' were growing. Soon, I found them; and, feeling curious, I plucked one of the yellow leaves, squashed it, and tasted a little bit of its yellowish juice on my tongue.

Yes, this yellow 'spice' really tasted like the flavor from Michail's roasted marmot! Only, in its pure form, its taste was way too strong and pungent to be pleasing. Of course, I had to smear the yellow juice onto some roasting meat first, together with a little bit of salt.

Suddenly, my inside seemed to REMEMBER this tasty yellow 'spice', as if I had used it many times before! Unexpectedly, I had another vivid recollection of being a 'little trapper boy'; helping my trapper Dad spice our huge chunks of animal meat before roasting or preserving them over our campfire. From a very young age, I always scoured our rocky mountains, dangerous rapids, and outstretched woods, to collect many different types of spicy herbs.

As a little trapper boy, I knew exactly which herb would be poisonous or make me ill; by 'talking' to the herb and 'feeling' its energy. My trapper Dad already knew I had sort of a 'special gift'; and he always relied blindly on my infallible 'sixth sense' of knowing which particular herbs we could use to spice our daily food...

Still feeling extremely surprised, I shook my head to get rid of my unexpected 'memories from a past life'. Then, I started to be VERY curious! Had I really been a little trapper boy in one of my past lives; helping my trapper Dad collect many tasty herbs and spices? Last year, I had 'felt' the energy of all the different plants around me, and sensed whether they could be poisonous or harmful. Could my special 'trapper gifts' still be working, as a heritage from my past life?

Immediately, I started to 'feel' and taste all the different plants around me, to put their information away for later use. I also tried to 'talk' to the foreign plants that my Inside did not remember. Much to my delight, the tasty and nicely smelling herbs still wanted to talk to me; and they even 'told' me on which particular food they could be used best! Again, the dangerous or poisonous herbs made me feel nervous or queasy; and I discarded them immediately.

Feeling more and more enthusiastic, I soon found several useful herbs that I was sure would spice Misha's roasted marmot quite a lot better than his usual 'yellow spice leaves' were doing!

Chapter 13. Four years old; discovering tasty 'spices'.

Near the end of the day, I returned to my wooden bench, to wait for our group of older kids to show up and roast their caught animals. Would Misha again offer me a chunk of his own marmot? Perhaps, after I told him about my newly discovered tasty spices, he would even let help him roast his marmot or other caught mammal...

Or, would Misha be too wary about using any possibly 'dangerous' herbs, and would he refuse to try out my newly discovered plants? Our grownup always told us to play it safe in the first place; and I knew that our Wise Woman had warned the older boys not to experiment with any unknown herbs or mushrooms, because they could be dangerous... Well, let's wait and see. Apart from that, I certainly had some exciting and truly interesting information to tell!

Finally, our older kids showed up from our surrounding woods, again carrying several fat marmots and other edible critters. Suddenly, I started to feel a little bit nervous. How should I tell Misha I had found many other tasty herbs and spices in our surrounding bushes, next to the yellow 'spice' leaves he always used? Feeling a bit unsure, I decided to wait until Misha again offered me a chunk of his own roasted animal. Would Misha really want to listen to what still was the 'smallest runt' in our camp? Impatiently, I waited...

After Misha had spiced and roasted his own fat marmot, he looked at me, chuckled at seeing my eager face, and again offered me a nice chunk of meat that was flavored with his yellow spice leaves.

Feeling thankful, I started to devour the roasted chunk of marmot. Only, now that I remembered all the other nice tasting 'herb spices', I was now a lot more particular about its bland taste. I was sure that, as a little trapper boy in my past life, our own chunks of roasted meat had tasted MUCH better! How should I tell Misha about my recent discoveries, to make him try out my newly found spicy herbs?

First, I wiped the smear from my face, before I told Misha:

"Misha? Although your roasted marmot tastes good, I am sure it could taste even better. Next time, you might add a little bit of that greenish moss and some tall ferns from near the border of our bushes. You may also add a few tiny blue flowers, but not too many, to enhance its flavor even more. If you wish, I will help you and bring some really tasty spices to you tomorrow..."

Looking very surprised, Misha stared at me while he stammered:

"How the heck do YOU suddenly know about tasty spices? For as far as I know, you've never roasted a marmot or any other small animal yourself. Did our Wise Woman tell you about using that greenish moss and tall ferns and those tiny blue flowers?"

"No, I didn't talk to our Wise Woman about them. But, after yesterday when you told me about those unknown tasty herbs and spices, this morning, I went into our bushes to look for them. Soon, I found LOTS of tasty herbs that can be used to spice both your roasting animals and our daily foods! Shall I bring some tasty herbs to you, tomorrow, so that you can try them out on your next marmot?"

Suddenly looking rather wary, Misha responded:

"WHAT did you say you have done this morning? Don't you know that tasting unknown herbs can be extremely dangerous? Many good looking herbs are deadly poisonous; and, if you don't be very cautious with them, they could make you very ill or even kill you!"

"Yes, I know! Only, I seem to have inherited a very useful 'sixth sense' from my past life that tells me in advance which herb is too dangerous or poisonous. Besides, I have already tasted all my edible herbs and spices; and, as you can see for yourself, I am still alive and kicking! Therefore, I have already proven on my own body that my spicy herbs and tasty plants are absolutely safe!"

"Yeah, well... When my own Dad was still alive, he always told me about remembering his past lives and inheriting his special abilities from them. He even thought I could have inherited those same abilities... Therefore, I am willing to believe you, and, perhaps, I am really going to try out some of your newly found tasty herbs. That is, if I can find them, and our Wise Woman has tested them first and approves of them. But, if the result tastes yucky, you will have to eat the spoiled animal all by yourself!"

"That is okay with me; but only if I can use my own herbs on the spiced animal and roast it all by myself."

"You know that our rules forbid you to do such a thing, unless you have caught your own animal first. Therefore, I am afraid that you still have to be more patient..."

"Then, let me join you tomorrow, to set my own trap and catch my own animal. I already know how to fold a snare from a piece of wire and set a trap, because you've already shown me how to do it."

"To be honest, I would LOVE to let you join us tomorrow; but you KNOW you have to wait until you are dry during the night. And, of course, your parents have to allow you to join us first..."

Because I again started to feel frustrated and angry, I left Misha, stomped towards our green-and-golden Royal caravan, and forcefully kicked it a couple of times while muttering loudly.

Why didn't my tiny body grow up faster so that it finally had its first 'growth spurt'; just like every other 'normal' kid my age had from time to time, at least according to Misha? Why was my tiny 'little runt' body still staying too small and too immature to listen to my full bladder at night? Now, I couldn't even demonstrate my newly found tasty herbs to Misha and to all my other older friends...

My Dad heard my kicking and muttering and showed up in our doorway, to take a look at what I was doing. He saw my angry face, sensed what could have happened, and again told me to be more patient. My time would surely come...

His response made me feel extra furious, so that I sneered:

"Why didn't Mom and you breed me a couple of years earlier? Now, I am still such an impossible little runt! I am finally able to help the older boys by gathering tasty spice plants for them, and I am still not allowed to join them into our surrounding woods, to catch my own animals and try out my newly found spices. I HATE this tiny body that still prevents me from doing really important things..."

My Dad stared at my angry looks and fire-shooting eyes with a frustrated face, slowly shook his head, and went back into our caravan while closing our front door. Was he silently telling me to stay outside until I had calmed down first? Well, that would be understandable as seen from my Dads disappointed point of view...

Fortunately, my fury never lasted long. Soon, I forced myself to calm down, regulated my breath, stepped inside our caravan, and followed my Dad into our living room. There, I climbed onto his lap without saying a word, and enjoyed the happy feeling of his safe arms around my waist. Of course, my lovable Dad couldn't help it!

Soon, both my Dad and I had forgotten my silly frustrations, and we were best friends again. Happily, he joined me in our shower stall, where he washed me while I created enormous clouds of lather that soon covered both my chuckling Dad and me.

My Mom showed up, looked at what we did, and chuckled:

"Janov, I think you've started living through your second youth!"

Still chuckling, both my Dad and I splashed some water towards my suddenly angry looking Mom who quickly retreated into her kitchen. Then, my Dad rinsed me, dried me, put a fresh diaper on me, and put me to bed in my own small sleeping den.

Soon, I was sound asleep, dreaming of finally joining my older friends into our surrounding woods and setting my own traps.

14. From now on, I am our little 'Chief Cook'.

The next morning, our group of older kids queued up and disappeared into our surrounding woods, while I stared at them longingly. However, this morning, I decided to DO something! First, I told my 'diaper friends' to leave me alone again, because I had something more important on my mind. Then, I went into our surrounding bushes, to gather several nicely smelling herbs that 'told' me they would nicely spice Misha's roasted animal and improve its bland taste.

After I was sure that my gathered herbs were absolutely harmless, I first tasted them critically, one by one. Again, the yucky herbs made me feel queasy, while the poisonous ones always radiated fear, sleep, darkness, or danger. Fortunately, this extremely useful 'sixth sense' never betrayed me; even after I grew up and collected unknown herbs from other countries. Soon, I went to our caravan, carrying several nicely smelling herbs, small flowers, and greenish moss.

Unfortunately, my parents weren't home, and I also didn't know in which particular caravan they could be. Therefore, I couldn't ask my Mom to help me chop my tasty herbs into tiny pieces. What should I do now? Well, because I was already very self-supported for an only four-year-old boy, I just put my herbs into our kitchen sink, washed them thoroughly, and dried them using our kitchen towel. Now, I only had to squash my pods and leaves, and slice my herbs into tiny pieces.

Of course, I was sure that my Mom would NEVER allow me to use her sharp kitchen knife; because she always told me I was too young to handle such a dangerous thing on my own. However, this was an emergency! Therefore, I just took my Mom's sharp kitchen knife and her wooden cutting board out of one of the kitchen drawers.

Carefully, I bundled my herbs together and positioned the wobbly string onto my Mom's cutting board. Hesitantly, I took the sharp kitchen knife in one hand; while trying to steer the unwilling herbs bundle with my other hand. Trying not to cut my untrained fingers, I hesitatingly started to slice my bundle of herbs into tiny pieces...

Suddenly, and totally unexpectedly, my untrained hands started to move all on their own; and I was sure I had nothing to do with it!

One hand started to steer my unwilling bundle of herbs, while the other hand adeptly used the sharp kitchen knife to chop my herbs into tiny pieces, at an astonishing speed! After chopping my herbs, my hands just laid the kitchen knife down onto the sink and again started to listen to my will, as if nothing special had happened...

For several seconds, I only gasped from sudden disbelief. What the heck could have happened to my hands? Open-mouthed, I stared at my perfectly chopped herbs, neatly piled up on my Mom's wooden cutting board. Still feeling utterly surprised, I stared down at my still slightly trembling tiny hands. How could my hands suddenly chop my herbs all on their own; without any conscious help from me? I was absolutely sure it hadn't been ME who had chopped my herbs this neatly; because I didn't have any cooking training at all and I had never chopped any unwilling herbs before.

Then, I started to think. Could somebody else have chopped my herbs for me, maybe by pulling my conscious mind into some sort of 'induced trance'? However, I also hadn't felt any outside influence from anybody else around me, except for that my hands suddenly seemed to be taken over by some unknown force that knew exactly how to use a sharp kitchen knife. Of course, this was absolutely IMPOSSIBLE! Yet, the 'absolutely impossible' HAD happened; and somebody else clearly had taken over my untrained hands and adeptly chopped my bundle of tasty herbs for me.

Still feeling utterly surprised, I involuntarily thought of the 'little trapper boy' I had been in my past life. Could my inside have remembered my former cooking skills from my past life; as it also seemed to 'remember' I had once been a powerful Shaman and Cosmic Mage? That would also explain why I suddenly 'remembered' all those unknown herbs I was sure I had never seen before in my present life. Well, IF really my 'little trapper boy' from my past life had 'taken over' my untrained hands, he had been extremely good at handling a wooden cutting board and a sharp kitchen knife!

While my brain started to feel more and more enthusiastic, it also continued to think. What would happen if I asked my 'little trapper boy' to show up again, to help me with the rest of my herbs mixture? Would he again help me by taking over my hands? First, I got a fresh clove of garlic and a small onion from my Mom's stock. Then, I put them onto my Mom's wooden cutting board, took the sharp kitchen knife in my hand, and started to slice the onion into a few parts...

Chapter 14. From now on, I am our little 'Chief Cook'.

Almost immediately, somebody else took over my hands and just started to slice the onion and smash the clove of garlic, again without any intervention from me. Adeptly, my tiny hands mixed everything together on my Mom's cutting board, before they laid the knife down and returned to my own control.

This time, I couldn't deny it any longer. Clearly, my 'little trapper boy' from my past life WAS helping me, by taking over my hands! Wow, this unusual 'help from my past life' could be an extremely useful 'extra ability'! Enthusiastically, I thanked my 'little trapper boy' in my mind; but he didn't respond and just stayed silent.

Now feeling VERY enthusiastic, I scraped my nicely smelling herbs mixture into a cup and mixed it some more. Then, I washed my Mom's wooden cutting board and sharp kitchen knife, dried them, and put them back into our kitchen drawer. After washing my hands and drying them, I trotted outside. Again, I went to my usual bench and sat down, this time taking my nicely smelling herbs mixture with me. Now, I only had to wait until our older kids showed up...

Halfway through the afternoon, our older kids returned into our camp; this time looking even more enthusiastic than usual. Next to carrying their usual marmots and other small critters, they triumphantly carried an enormous porcupine to our campfire!

Immediately, I sat glued to the strange animal and stared in rapt at its razor sharp quills. Clearly, our Mother Nature had provided this particular beast with an extremely efficient defense system; probably to discourage any nasty predator with sharp teeth. Only, its excellent defense had not prevented it from being caught in Misha's snare...

Unexpectedly, my built-in 'little trapper boy' let me sense, without using any audible words, that he wanted to help me again! Therefore, albeit very hesitatingly, I started to help Misha prepare his porcupine. Immediately, my 'little trapper boy' took over completely; and, much to my happiness, he showed me exactly what to do and how to avoid being pricked by those dangerous quills.

At lightning speed, my small hands started to tear quill after quill out of the dead beast and neatly pile them next to each other, as if I already was an experienced trapper and had done this all my life...

Although Misha looked very surprised, he thankfully accepted my unexpected help. Working closely together, we had plucked our porcupine in no time. Now, we carried it to our small butchery next to our parking lot; where I helped Misha clean it out, again helped by my 'little trapper boy' who seemed to know exactly what he had to do.

All the time, Misha looked utterly surprised at my obvious skills, but he still didn't say a word and just let me do. He even let me use his own sharp knife to help him skin the beast. After Misha and I had prepared his fat porcupine, a few older kids helped us put the heavy animal onto a wooden stake, to roast it over our already brightly glowing campfire while turning it around and around.

In the meantime, the other kids had already prepared their smaller animals. They had also gathered many yellow leaves, obviously to 'spice' both Misha's porcupine and their own animal meat. Now, it was MY time, to persuade my older friends to try out my own tasty looking and nicely smelling herbs mixture! First, I took my cup of herbs from my wooden bench, and teasingly held it under Misha's nose. Then, while showing him my best puppy dog eyes, I pleaded:

"Misha? Could you please use MY herbs mixture on your roasting porcupine? You only have to add a little bit of oil to make it sticky; and I am sure your porcupine meat will taste absolutely wonderful."

For a few seconds, Misha still hesitated, looking utterly surprised. Then, he tentatively sniffed my nicely smelling herbs mixture, and sniffed it again while his eyes suddenly grew big! Turning towards the other kids, my older friend exclaimed:

"Please come here and smell THIS wonderful spice mixture! Have you ever scented such exquisite aroma? I think we should use it on our porcupine, and probably on all our other animals as well!"

Immediately, everybody wanted to smell my special herb mixture! One by one, they took my cup, sniffed at it, and nearly all the kids nodded their consent with already watering mouths. However, after a few second of being enchanted, a few kids started to look more warily. With doubtful voices, they told the others:

"Although our little Prince's herbs mixture certainly smells wonderful; how can we be absolutely sure there isn't any poison ivy or deadly pseudo chervil in it? I think we should ask our Wise Woman for her advice first..."

Of course, all the others agreed; looking relieved now that they could be sure my spicy herbs mixture wouldn't unintentionally poison them. In procession, we left our waiting animals and went to our Wise Woman, to ask for her professional advice.

Soon, our Wise Woman showed up from her caravan and asked us what she could do for us. Proudly, Misha explained everything to her. Our little Prince seemed to have sort of a 'sixth sense' that could 'feel' unknown plants and detect any dangerous herbs. Now, they wanted to be absolutely sure that my nicely smelling herbs mixture was harmless, before they used it on their roasting animals. Could our Wise Woman please test the mixture for them, to play it safe?

For several seconds, our Wise Woman only stared at me, until she seemed to feel satisfied and nodded. Now, she took my cup of herbs mixture into both hands, 'sensed' its energy, and sniffed at it. Then, she smeared a little bit of my greenish mixture onto her hand and tasted it. With a broadly smiling face, she finally told us:

"Well, I cannot find any harm in this exquisite tasting mixture, and it certainly smells wonderful! Please, could I have my own slice of roasted porcupine, if there are any leftovers?"

For a second, my friends around me still stayed silent. Then, they started to cheer loudly, while Misha took me onto his shoulders and horsed me back to our campfire. Obviously, my friends were already very eager to taste my nicely smelling herbs on their roasting animals!

Misha offered me their bottle of baking oil; and I put a few drops of oil into my mixture, to make it sticky. Somebody else handed me their brush; and I started to smear our porcupine with the oil and my tasty mixture, while involuntarily trembling with pride. In the meantime, many other kids had started to smear their own roasting animals and small mammals with MY nicely smelling herbs mixture.

From now on, Misha turned his roasting porcupine around and around, while I continued to smear it with even more oil and herbs mixture. Soon, a heavenly aroma started to caress the air, making our mouths water and our hungry stomachs grumble aloud. Even a couple of grownups sniffed the air approvingly and asked to be allowed to taste a small slice of our heavenly scenting porcupine.

Finally, our porcupine was roasted, and Misha divided its meat into several chunks and sliced the chunks into many smaller pieces. Tentatively, everybody took a piece of roasted porcupine and started to nibble on it. Immediately, they looked surprised, took a much bigger nibble, and then a really huge bite. Smiling broadly, they took several more bites, while staring at their little Crown Prince with almost reverence in their proudly beaming eyes!

Much to my delight, our roasted porcupine tasted absolutely exquisite. It certainly tasted much better than any roasted meat had ever tasted before now! Inwardly, I felt relieved, while I savored my own slice of heavenly tasting porcupine. Fortunately, everything had gone extremely well, and I hadn't made any mistakes with my excellent choice of spicy herbs. Silently, I thanked my 'little trapper boy' in my mind; but he didn't answer and only grinned some.

For quite some time, all my friends and a few grownups marveled at the exquisite taste of our roasted porcupine meat, and had second helpings. In silence, they savored their fat slices of spicy meat, with beaming eyes. Finally, they licked their fingers and lips clean, and told me I had done a more than excellent job! At last, we burped loudly, to thank the spirit of our porcupine for offering its tasty meat.

Long after we had devoured our porcupine, everybody remained speechless, still enjoying the nice aftertaste. Now and then, they stared at their slightly blushing little Prince, showing me what looked like lots of awe and reverence in their proudly beaming eyes.

Unexpectedly, a few oldest kids huddled together, obviously whispering about ME! Why did they do that? Could I have done something wrong, and would they now tell me to leave them alone?

After some more whispering, Misha left the group and approached me. Politely, almost reverently, he asked me to stand up because he wanted to lift me onto his shoulders... Very hesitatingly, I obliged. What could Misha be up to? Would I now be kicked out of their older group? Very much to my surprise, Misha started to horse me around our campfire in triumph, while he told me:

"My dear Crown Prince, never did we taste such delicious meat! Thank you very much for what you have done for us; and we want you to be our own little Chief Cook from now on."

This time, my suddenly throbbing heart nearly burst with pride, while my throat choked up so that I could only nod my 'YES'. Wow! Totally unexpectedly, our entire group of 'older kids' wanted to be my friends; and they also wanted ME to be their little 'Chief Cook' and help them spice their roasting animals! This was quite a lot more than I ever could have imagined, even in my wildest dreams! Misha slid me down onto the ground; but my throat still felt too choked up to give my new friends any audible answer. Therefore, I just continued to nod vigorously; until my head nearly fell off and I had to stop nodding before I dislocated my neck...

136 Aad Aandacht is a Dutch psychotherapist who loves writing 'books with a message'

From now on, every afternoon, I first went into our surrounding bushes to gather my spicy herbs, preferably while my Mom was away. Of course, I didn't want to cheat on my Mom, and I still loved her dearly; but I wasn't sure how she would react...

After collecting my herbs, I brought them home and used my Mom's sharp kitchen knife and cutting board to chop and slice them. Only the first few times, my 'little trapper boy' took over completely; until I started to get the hang of it and was able to chop and squash my tasty herbs all by myself. From then on, my 'little trapper helper' took over only when I really needed his help.

Within a few days, I started to experiment by putting several different herbs together, trying to concoct even more refined tastes. I seemed to have a natural feeling for which herbs tasted best and what I could mix together or not. Now and then, my experiments failed, and we had to throw away a yucky tasting animal, but who cares? It was mid-summer, and my older friends always had plenty of animals as a replacement. I learned from every new experience, and my cooking skills vastly improved. And, to be honest, I already loved my self-allotted task as our little 'Chief Cookie' very much!

After a couple of days, my Mom suddenly called me into our kitchen while pointing to her wooden cutting board:

"Harold? What the heck did you do to my cutting board? Since a few days, it starts smelling rather peculiar, and I am sure neither your Dad nor I have anything to do with it..."

"Sorry, Mom, for not cleaning your cutting board well enough; but I needed it to chop my herbs into tiny pieces."

"What are you telling me? You needed it to chop your herbs? Then, you've used my sharp kitchen knife as well? Didn't I tell you how dangerous that knife is? I am sure you are still way too young to handle such a risky thing on your own!"

"But, Mom... Please, don't be angry with me, but I NEEDED your knife and your cutting board! I am our Chief Cook now, and I have to use it every afternoon to chop my gathered herbs. Please..."

"Since when are YOU promoted to be our 'Chief Cook'? And do you really believe that? Please, tell me, for how long have our older kids been making fun of your young age like this?"

"MOHOM... I really AM our Chief Cook; and nobody is making fun of me! For more than two weeks, I have been chopping my herbs and spicing our roasting animals with my tasty mixture..."

"And, you want to use my sharp kitchen knife tomorrow again? Then, let me see your fingers. And your hands and arms..."

Sensing I was winning my plea, I immediately spread my fingers out towards my wary looking Mom; and she looked them over carefully, one by one. Of course, she couldn't find any nasty cut or scratch on my entire body, not even the faintest old scar! Still not looking totally convinced, she hesitatingly asked:

"Could you please show me what you are doing every day? I still think that a four-year-old little boy is way too small to handle such a dangerous knife without any supervision, even if he is 'extremely bright' for his age and promoted to be a 'Chief Cook'..."

Feeling affronted because my Mom called me a 'little boy', I raced towards our surrounding bushes and quickly gathered several nicely smelling herbs. Soon, I raced back to our caravan, washed my herbs in our sink, and dried them. Then, I just took my Mom's cutting board and sharp knife out of the drawer, without asking her first.

After asking my built-in 'little trapper boy' to help me, I started to chop my herbs into tiny pieces at lightning speed, while adeptly steering the unwilling bundle with my small fingers. I had also gathered a few tasty cloves and small pods; and I squashed them expertly by using the side of the knife. Finally, I took an empty cup, and used the huge knife to scrape my herbs mixture into it.

All the time, my Mom stared at my lightning fast ministrations with bulging eyes and baited breath! Obviously, she never thought her little boy could be THAT good at handling a dangerously sharp kitchen knife without injuring himself! Of course, my built-in 'little trapper boy' had showed off awfully; but my Mom didn't need to know that... After regaining her breath, my still gasping Mom first swallowed a couple of times, until she finally uttered:

"My dear Harry, I never knew you could be such a skilled cook! Now, I feel sorry for doubting your unbelievable abilities. Your demonstration absolutely convinced me. From now on, I will trust you with using my sharp kitchen knife and wooden cutting board; but, for heaven's sake, always look out and be very careful not to cut your fingers instead of your herbs..."

Chapter 14. From now on, I am our little 'Chief Cook'.

For several seconds, I stared my Mom down in disdain; because she again questioned my obvious skills as our Chief Cook. At the same time, my inside felt proud that my Mom finally decided to trust her 'little baby boy'. Therefore, I fiercely embraced her and told her I loved her very much. Then, we cuddled for quite some time. At last, for the first time ever, I helped my Mom cook our own 'healthy dinner', of course spiced by my carefully selected tasty herbs!

That evening, my proud looking Dad took me on his lap and held me very close, while he told me:

"You are growing extremely fast, my son! I still vividly remember when your mother told me she was pregnant, and how happy I felt. Now, you are still a young boy and sitting on my lap; but, way too soon, you will leave us, marry a nice girl, and have children of your own. Today, your Mom told me our older kids promoted you to be their Chief Cook, even though you are not allowed to leave our camp. And, tonight, by cooking our exquisitely tasting dinner, you have proven to be an excellent Chef and able to perform real miracles with your tasty herbs! Only, please, always be modest, and never think you are allowed to do more than the other kids just because you are our Crown Prince. They allow you to be their 'Chief Cook' only because you are very good at cooking and you have earned your honorary title. Please, always do everything in a way that allows you to be proud of yourself, and you will be an excellent Gypsy Leader in the future."

Of course, I totally agreed with my wise Dad! From now on, I would always do only those things that would make me feel proud of myself! Feeling both happy and respected, I tried to melt into my Dad's powerful aura, while very much enjoying his tender loving care. Then, I 'octopussed' myself onto his broad chest and marveled in the nice feeling of being cared for and loved by such a wonderful man.

My Dad and I continued to hug and cuddle for the remainder of the evening, until I nearly fell asleep in his arms. At last, my Dad joined me in our small shower stall and washed me from head to toe, while I had lots of fun creating enormous clouds of lather. Finally, my Dad dried me, put a diaper on me, and playfully tickled my belly button; making me squirm and giggle. I always LOVED it when my Dad pampered me and took his time to help me! I still do...

Before I went to bed, I kissed my Mom goodnight and again thanked her for allowing me to use her wooden cutting board and sharp kitchen knife. My Mom smiled at me, kissed me back, and thanked me again for helping her spice our healthy dinner.

Now, my Dad put me to bed in my small den and draped my blankets around my body. Feeling dead tired but still wonderful and totally happy, I closed my eyes and almost immediately fell asleep. Soon, I started to dream of already being a 'Real Big Boy'...

Unexpectedly, my 'little trapper boy' showed up in my dream! He told me he was living in my 'unconscious mind' and always helped me grow up whenever our Beloved Ancestors and Spirit Guides asked him to do so. When I unexpectedly took my Mom's sharp knife and started to chop my tasty herbs, they immediately asked him to take over; because they were afraid I would slice my untrained fingers, and they had promised to protect me always and everywhere.

My 'little trapper boy' from my unconscious mind also promised to help me become 'totally dry', so that I could join my older friends into our surrounding woods and finally catch my own animals!

Feeling elated and totally happy, I stopped dreaming and soon tumbled into a healthy and refreshing sleep.

15. I am dry and allowed to enter our woods.

Early in the morning, I woke up and rubbed the sand out of my eyes, while still remembering my happy dream. Would really my 'built-in little trapper boy' from my unconscious mind help me be 'totally dry', hopefully soon? Of course, everybody knows that dreams are never true... Well, only time would tell.

Then, I thought about my spicy herbs. Today, I would again help my Mom with her cooking, now that she officially allowed me to use her sharp kitchen knife. To please her, I would collect some very rare and extremely special herbs, to spice her healthy food and make it even tastier. After breakfast, I would first go into our surrounding bushes and ask my precious herbs for advice.

Already feeling bright and shining, I first stretched out as far as I could, to loosen my stiffened muscles. Then, I jumped out of bed and went to our small shower stall, to take my usual morning shower. As I had done hundreds of times before, I quickly untied my wet diaper and let it drop to the floor. Now being naked, I turned around to switch on the warm water tap and wash my nightly urine away.

Unexpectedly, something strange started to dawn on my confused mind. Why didn't my naked belly feel chilly from the nightly wetness, as it always did in the morning? I also missed the strong acid smell of nightly urine that always evaporated from my wet diaper. What could have happened to my diaper, or to me?

A split second later, I snatched my diaper from the floor and felt its inside with trembling hands... Then, I started to cheer and dance around from pure happiness! Unlike it had been any other morning, MY DIAPER WAS STILL DRY!

Vaguely, I remembered waking up after I dreamed about my little trapper boy who promised to help me; to take a quick leak. Still feeling sleepy, I had loosened my diaper, emptied my bladder, and again fastened the still dry thing. Yawning from sleepiness, I had crawled back into my bed and fell asleep immediately. Now, my nightly diaper turned out to be totally DRY! Finally, my bladder had warned me in time during the night when I had to visit our toilet.

Finally, I was a 'Real Big Boy' instead of a 'diaper kid', and I could join my older friends into our woods. For the first time, my tiny body didn't betray me any more! Quickly, I stormed to my parents' bedroom, and jumped onto my Dad's stomach with a loud Indian howl:

"DAD; WAKE UP! My diaper is still DRY! Tonight, I suddenly woke up all by myself, to take a real leak! From now on, I don't need to wear a diaper anymore, never again. Finally, I am a Real Big Boy!"

My Dad woke up some and first yawned a few times, while he squinted at me. Then, he started to chuckle at seeing my extremely enthusiastic face. While lazily tickling my dry belly, he mumbled:

"Are you sure you will not wet your bed again tomorrow?"

"Yes, Dad, I am absolutely sure! Tonight, I woke up and had a normal leak. From now on, I will wake up every time I have to pee or poop. Finally, my little body doesn't betray me any more!"

Of course, my enthusiastic baritone voice also woke my sleeping Mom. Slowly, she turned around, yawned, and stared at me with sleep charged eyes. Still feeling very enthusiastic, I told my yawning Mom:

"Mom, from now on, you can throw all my diapers away because I don't need them anymore!"

Smilingly, my Mom put her arms around my still bone-dry little body. First, she pulled me against her breasts and kissed the top of my blond head. Then she assured me:

"From now on, you are my one and only Real Big Boy! Only, you are growing too fast, and I will miss my little baby..."

Although I didn't like my Mom calling me a 'little baby', I still felt extremely happy. Enthusiastically, I started to smother both my Mom and my Dad with kisses, until they both giggled and begged me to stop, or else... Would my Dad now allow me to join my older friends into our woods? Pleadingly, I asked my still giggling Dad:

"Dad, am I now allowed to join my older friends into our woods?"

Again chuckling at seeing my very eager face, my Dad answered:

"Harry, my precious son; finally, you have achieved what you wanted so desperately. Now it is your time to discover some more of our outside world. Tonight, you will sleep without a diaper; and, when your bed is still dry in the morning, your Mom and I will allow you to join our older children into our woods. I can still remember my own first time when I finally could accompany our older kids into our woods, so I know how it feels! Only, please, be very careful while leaving our secluded camp for the first time, and always listen to the older and more experienced children in your group."

"Yes, Dad, I promise I will be very careful; and I will always listen to the older children in our group."

Still feeling extremely happy, I dived in between my parents and closed my eyes. Soon, I fell asleep, and dreamed of accompanying my friends into our woods, setting my own trap, and catching a huge animal in my snare. Everybody cheered and high-fived me, while a few strong boys dragged my caught animal towards our camp...

After I woke up, my Dad and I decided to shower together again. Although we felt a bit cramped in our small shower stall, we washed each other, shampooed each other's hair, almost drowned each other in enormous clouds of lather, and had the fun of our lives. Again, my chuckling Mom teased my Dad about living through his 'second youth', but we couldn't care less and just went on having fun.

At last, my Dad and I dried each other; while I tiptoed to reach his hairy chest and he squatted down to dry my tiny belly and legs. Then, all three of us enjoyed my Mom's healthy breakfast and glasses of milk, of course again spiced with some of my tasty herbs.

Feeling wonderful and absolutely content, I went outside to have my last longing look at our already disappearing group of 'older kids' who soon would be my brand new companions. Today, I was staring at them for the last time! Tomorrow, I would accompany them into our surrounding woods, to set up my own traps and catch my own small animals to spice them and roast them over our campfire!

Although my inside suddenly felt a little bit nervous now that my Big Day approached, I almost couldn't wait to join them. Longingly, I stared along the winding paths that lead through our surrounding bushes into our mysterious woods. Tomorrow, I was finally allowed to enter these mysterious paths and enter our hitherto forbidden woods and dense forests for the very first time!

After the older kids disappeared along the winding paths that led into our mysterious woods, I quickly turned around and gathered our 'diaper kids' around me. First, I climbed onto one of our benches, to be able to oversee them, and also to look a bit taller.

Then, I told my 'diaper friends', with a proud baritone voice:

"Since today, I do not need to wear a diaper anymore because my body now warns me in time, even when I am in a very deep sleep. Therefore, starting tomorrow morning, I will leave you and finally join our group of older kids into our woods!"

Much to my surprise, one of our 'diaper girls' started to cry. Although I knew she was only five years old, I thought she reacted rather 'childish' at hearing my revelation; until I heard her sob:

"Prince Harold, I am sure we will miss you terribly! Who will now teach us how to hide properly? You always were the best hider and seeker in our camp. Could you please stay a little bit longer, to teach us some more, perhaps until you are a bit older and taller?"

To my astonishment, all my 'diaper friends' nodded their agreement; while they assured me they really would miss me! Couldn't I wait for at least a couple more months, before joining our group of older kids into our mysterious woods? What if I got lost, didn't know my way back to our camp, and nobody could find me?

A much taller boy of about six years old stepped towards me and angrily punched my arm, while he grumbled:

"This is not fair! I am a lot older than you are, and I am still wetting my bed at night. Why are you always so early?"

WHAT was this taller boy telling me? For a few seconds, I felt too surprised to know what to answer. Why would this boy think I would be EARLY? Didn't he know I had been waiting for AGES, until I finally would be dry during the night and no longer needed a diaper?

Then, I started to think. Could this six-year-old boy be right, after all? Up to now, I had always assumed I was late in my development, because I was the tiniest kid in our 'diaper group'. However, this boy was already six years old, he was much bigger than I was, and he was still wetting his bed at night. On the other hand, I was only four years and three months old, and I was already completely dry! Could there really be some truth in what this bigger boy told me? Perhaps, he was only jealous of my 'too early' achievement...

Curiously, I looked around at the other 'little diaper kids'; and, for the first time, I estimated how old they were. Suddenly feeling very surprised, I now saw that most of these 'little' kids were a LOT older than I was! This was something important I had never noticed before.

Up to now, I had always thought they were a lot younger, because my too bright brain so easily outdid them. Now, I finally saw that, in reality, I was not only the youngest kid in our 'diaper group', but I was also the fastest developing one! While I gasped for breath, this unexpected revelation almost knocked me down.

For a second, I closed my eyes and put my head in my hands, to digest this new information. Clearly, I was NOT physically retarded; but, on the contrary, I was extremely FAST in my development! My small body should only catch up some in its length; but it was NOT too slow! Feeling strange and nonplussed, I left my diaper friends.

Thinking and pondering, I sauntered into our surrounding bushes and started to gather some fresh herbs in advance. In the meantime, my brain slowly accepted that I could have been wrong all the time, about being too slow in my development. Clearly, I had not been slow at all; but, on the contrary, I really was one of the fastest developing kids in our community! Why had I never realized this before?

After I had gathered several tasty herbs, I went to our caravan, put a few herbs aside for my Mom's dinner, and prepared the remaining herbs to use them on our roasting animals. Then, I stepped outside and trotted towards Michail's caravan, to ask my Big Friend for his advice. Of course, I trusted my own Mom and Dad; but I was a bit afraid they would love me too much to be absolutely honest with me. Besides, didn't every parent always think his own child was the most special creature in the world? I supposed that my parents would be at least a little bit too prejudiced, to tell me the truth and only the truth...

My Big Friend was truly happy to see me; and he immediately pulled me into an enormous bear hug. That felt wonderful! In vain, I tried to put my own small arms around Michail's enormous waist, which made both of us giggle. Obviously, I still would have to grow quite a lot taller, before I would be able to return one of Michail's 'gentle' hugs. Before we talked and I could ask him my questions, Michail wanted to wash his two little sons first. O course, I 'helped' him, by creating lots of lather and smearing both splashing little boys with it, until they nearly disappeared in the thick clouds.

After rinsing both squirming twins, I helped my Big Friend with drying them and powdering their sensitive parts. Then, after a lot of wrestling, I succeeded in putting a clean diaper on a wriggling Michi, while Michail put a clean diaper on a squirming Movi. Finally, we laid them in between their pillows and told them to go to sleep.

Now that Michail's twins were out of the way, we sat down on his leather couch in his living room; and I crawled onto his enormous lap to be comforted and feel a bit safer. Suddenly feeling nervous, I started to ask my Big Friend my most burning question:

"Michail? I want to ask you something important, but it is difficult to find the right words. Am I really developing extremely fast? Up to this morning, I always thought my little body betrayed me, because it still stays too small and too immature. That is, until an angry diaper kid suddenly blamed me for being too EARLY in my development! Of course, he might have been a little bit jealous... but what do YOU think? And, could you please give me a real honest answer, without being gentle or considering my feelings?"

Looking rather surprised, Michail first waited for a few seconds, before he hesitatingly answered:

"Boy, what are you asking me now... A real honest answer? Well, okay, the best thing I can do is give it an honest try! Compared to all the other little kids I have seen in my life, you are the brightest, most special, and fastest developing boy I ever saw. You sat upright extremely early, crawled early, talked almost immediately, and understood every single word we told you from a very young age. Now, you are only four years old and you already stopped wetting your bed. That is very fast too, compared to most other kids in our camp. Plus, we have always been able to talk to you as if you already are a grownup; and, many times, you outdid us with your clever answers and witty remarks! So far, all of your developments have been extremely fast; with maybe one unimportant exception: your body is still a bit too small for your age. Now, please, think for yourself. How many four-year-old kids are able to read the mind of somebody else, or are promoted to be a Chief Cook at such a young age? Therefore, please, forget your silly doubts, and be only PROUD of yourself and of who you are, always and everywhere!"

Oh my... What was my Big Friend telling me now? Before I could give him an answer, I had to think his honest revelations over first, to sort them out in my confused mind. Therefore, I left his cozy lap, slid down onto the floor, and went to his window, to stare at our faintly glowing campfire. Then, I started to think...

Firstly, my Big Friend had confirmed that I really was developing extremely fast; with the 'unimportant' exception that my body still stayed a bit too small for my age. He also confirmed that my body was extremely fast with being dry, compared to most other kids in our camp. Thus, the angry boy in our 'diaper group' was right; although he could have been a bit jealous. Therefore, at least according to Michail, I really was extremely early in my bodily development!

Now that I had accepted Michail's first revelation, I also wanted to think over another important one. Was I really able to 'read the mind of somebody else', as my Big Friend unexpectedly stated? Until now, I never thought about any of my useful 'abilities' or 'sixth senses' as being some sort of 'mind reading'. To me, they just were my 'normal' abilities. However, I remembered how, as a baby, I always knew what other people told me, by feeling the energy of their words. I also sensed the preceding auras of people who planned to pay us a visit; at least ten seconds before they actually reached our caravan. Many times, I knew what my parents or Michail were going to tell me, by 'tuning in' into their minds and listening to their thoughts. While playing hide and seek, I had removed my own picture from the minds of my searching friends, so that they couldn't find me...

Only, up to now, I had never seen any of my Shaman abilities as some form of nosy 'mind reading'. Could I really be such a bad person? Now and then, I had heard our own people snicker about certain gadjo 'clairvoyants' who were cheating on too superstitious people, by reading their minds and telling them exactly the things they already knew but still wanted to hear from a so-called 'medium'...

Besides, private is private, and we Gypsies always estimated our personal privacy VERY highly! Even our Wise Woman always politely asked us first, before she hesitantly entered the depths of our minds to look at our hidden thoughts. Perhaps, I should ask our Wise Woman about my so-called 'mind reading' capacities first, before I again misused any of my 'powerful Shaman abilities'...

Now feeling a lot better, I left the window and again climbed onto Michail's enormous lap, to be held and cuddled. Sitting on a cozy lap always was my most favorite pastime! Immediately, my Big Friend put his strong arms around me and 'gently' crushed my ribs, as usual. That felt wonderful, and I basked in the pleasant feeling of being loved without any restrictions or prejudices. Clearly, Michail didn't care about me being a dangerous 'Shaman' or a nosy 'mind reader'. Fortunately, my Big Friend trusted me enough to know I would never misuse any of my Shaman abilities to satisfy my own curiosity...

At last, our hungry stomachs started to rumble, and both Michail and I started to laugh at the same time. Then, Michail wanted to make a couple of sandwiches. Of course, I immediately offered to help him by spicing his sandwiches with my own special herbs! While my Big Friend boiled some eggs, I raced outside and quickly gathered a couple of tasty herbs. After returning, I chopped them at lightning speed, while Michail looked at my skills with a proud face.

Next, I helped him slice a few tomatoes, prepare some lettuce, and peel the eggs. Soon, our sandwiches were ready; and we took them to the living room to savor them. My Big Friend grabbed one of our sandwiches, sniffed at it, nodded approvingly, and took a huge bite. His surprised face started to beam and he nearly groaned with delight! After devouring a second huge bite, he told me:

"My brilliant Crown Prince, never before did I taste anything this delicious! My young friend, you are an extremely special boy, a real marvel, and today also an absolutely excellent cook!"

Involuntarily, I started to blush, because I didn't expect my Big friend to praise me this much. In the meantime, I devoured my own tasty sandwich. After we finished our sandwiches and drank some healthy juice, Michail's little sons started to wake up from their nap.

Of course, my Big Friend had to tend to his wakening boys, to change their diapers and prepare their baby food. Therefore, I decided to leave him alone. I thanked Michail abundantly for his honesty, and assured him he was the very best Big Friend in the world. I was sure we would always be friends, forever! Then, I went outside, to play for the last time with my 'little diaper friends'.

Surprisingly, now that I no longer felt like the 'tiniest runt' in our diaper group, I suddenly felt much freer and very much enjoyed our 'childish' play! Soon, we were playing our usual games of hide and seek; and, again, the seeker and all the others couldn't find me for quite some time. No, I did NOT cheat on them, absolutely not! I only turned out again to be extremely good at playing our games.

16. Entering our woods for the very first time.

Near the end of the day, I went to my own wooden bench where I always waited for our 'older kids' to show up. Only, today, I also had to tell them some very important news! Tomorrow, their 'little Chief Cookie' would finally join them into our surrounding woods, to set his own traps, and to catch and roast his OWN animals! I almost couldn't wait to see their surprised faces...

Soon, our older kids showed up, again carrying several fat marmots and other edible mammals. Marmots were the most common animals in our woods, and our children always caught plenty of them. Now and then, they caught a bigger animal, like a fat porcupine or a stray hare. On rare occasions, they even caught a small piglet that had enough meat to feed everybody for a few days, next to providing us with its usable tendons and strong leather skin.

Immediately after my friends arrived, they went to our small butchery; to skin and clean out their caught animals. Of course, I accompanied my new friend, Misha, and helped him skin and clean out his fat marmot. Then, I helped him smear its meat with my own nicely smelling herbs mixture. In the meantime, all the other kids had started to smear their own animals with my tasty and again heavenly smelling mixture, while proudly smiling at their 'Chief Cookie'.

When finally all my friends were ready and could listen to me, I climbed onto my wooden bench to look a bit taller. While everybody approached me and looked at me with expectant faces, I told them:

"Please listen carefully to what I have to say! Starting tomorrow, I am going to join you into our surrounding woods, to set my own traps and catch my own marmots or other animals!"

For a second, silence fell over our group, while everybody stared at me with surprised faces. Then, all my new friends crowded around me, ruffled my unruly blond hair, and congratulated me with my important milestone! They told me they were proud of their Chief Cookie who finally would be able to catch his own animals. Although I would be the youngest kid ever who joined them into our woods, they were already sure I would be a valuable part of our group!

Especially Misha seemed to be genuinely happy to have me in their midst; although he also asked me:

"Do your parents really allow you to join us into our woods, as you are only four years old and still a bit too small for your age?"

"Firstly, I am already four years and three months old! And yes; since yesterday, I am completely dry and don't need to wear a diaper any more. Therefore, I am now a Real Big Boy and allowed to join you into our woods; starting tomorrow morning!"

Happily, Misha lifted me onto his shoulders and horsed me around our campfire, while he chuckled:

"Starting tomorrow, our little Prince Cookie is going to join us, to catch and roast his own animals."

Still chuckling, Misha let me slide down onto my own feet. In the meantime, my new friends were already roasting their staked animals, of course again smeared with my nicely smelling herbs mixture. Soon, a delicious aroma started to fill the air, making a few grownups smile at us approvingly. Starting tomorrow, I would prove to my new friends that I could be much more than only a 'little Prince Cookie'! Feeling hungry, I hoped that Misha again would offer me a tasty chunk of his already nicely roasting marmot.

When finally all the animals were roasted, my friends started to divide their meat into many smaller chunks. Unexpectedly, ALL my new friends offered me a fat slice of their roasted animal; so that I could pick my own share! This is what they always did in case one of them hadn't caught an edible animal. Clearly, from now on, I REALLY belonged to our group of older kids!

Almost bursting with pride, I filled my hungry stomach to the brim with their tasty slices of animal meat. Then, my friends and I burped loudly, to thank the animal spirits for offering us their tasty nourishment. Feeling satisfied and wonderful, we went to our own caravans, to wash the smear from our hands and faces, and to join our parents until we became too sleepy and went to bed.

That night, I finally went to bed without wearing any clothes at all, for the first time since I was born as a little baby. Sleeping without wearing my usual diaper, clad only in my 'birthday suit', turned out to be a very nice feeling; as if, somehow, I felt much more alive and more aware of my own body. From now on, I would sleep just like all

Chapter 16. Entering our woods for the very first time.

the others in our Gypsy camp always did, without wearing anything at all. I really belonged to our 'young grownups' now!

The next morning, just before I woke up, I had a beautiful dream that unfortunately turned into a nightmare. In my dream, I was a little 'trapper boy', living in an enormous forest with several steep ravines, dangerous rapids, and swirling water streams. My Mom had died in childbirth; and, from then on, my 'trapper Dad' had raised me all on his own, only now and then helped by our nearest neighbor and best friend who lived in his own log cabin, half a mile away.

From a very young age, I always wanted to help my trapper Dad with everything. Therefore, my Dad soon taught me how to catch wild deer and other strong animals in our cleverly hidden traps. At first, my Dad always tied a long leash around my waist and watched over me; until I became a trained trapper and didn't stumble into hidden ravines or dangerous rapids any more. When I finally could cross the most dangerous water streams all on my own and knew exactly how to rescue myself if I unexpectedly fell into the foaming water, my trapper Dad released me from my leash and told me I could now scour our surrounding forest without any supervision.

From then on, I always helped my Dad skin our caught animals, clean them out, and divide them into chunks, by using my own sharp knife. Then, I helped him roast our chunks of meat, by spicing them with several nicely smelling herbs I had selected from our surrounding forest. I seemed to have a very useful 'sixth sense' that always told me which herb would be poisonous or dangerous; and my 'trapper Dad' soon found out he could trust my strange 'abilities' absolutely.

Suddenly, my dream turned into a nightmare. A hungry grizzly bear showed up and wanted to eat me for a morning snack, while my panicking trapper Dad tried to rescue me with only a small knife in his hand. Unfortunately, my trapper Dad couldn't rescue me; but the bear took revenge by killing him, me, and our closest neighbor and best friend who lived half a mile away...

While my nightmare slowly disappeared, I woke up in shock and at first didn't know where I was. Suddenly, I sat upright in my bed in my own sleeping den, still panting and wheezing and trembling all over. Desperately, I tried tot get rid of my disturbing feelings, because I still smelled the grizzly bear with its stinking breath, while it ripped my small body open with its enormous claws...

Finally, my consciousness started to return into the here and now, while I regulated my breath and forced my body to calm down. Then, I started to think. Had really a hungry grizzly bear killed my Dad, our closest neighbor, and me? Only, who had been our closest neighbor and best friend who lived half a mile away? I was sure that both my trapper Dad and I loved him very much; because he always helped us with everything. Or, had my nightmare put me through another very strange dream? Everybody knows that dreams are never true...

Unexpectedly, a warm and soulful voice in my inside told me:

"My dear young friend; please don't feel shocked, because you only remembered one of your past lives. Soon after the Earth has rounded the Sun two times; you will meet your former neighbor, and you and he will again be best friends. After another two times, you will also meet your former trapper Dad and again be his son."

Immediately, I recognized the warm and soulful voice of our Beloved King of Ancestors who also was my dearest Spirit Friend from our Timeless Eternal Realm! About a year ago, after I said farewell to my beautiful King Admiral butterfly, my dearest Friend had promised to contact me again. I still remembered His soulful voice telling me:

'Within a short time, we will meet again and talk some more. For now, you have to forget everything about me.'

Surprisingly, I HAD forgotten everything about my Beloved King of Ancestors Friend, until now. Would I again have to forget His predicting words? Much to my delight, this time, my strange 'dream' stayed with me. Now and then, its message showed up in my mind, making me think about the earth rounding the sun...

Of course, I already knew that the sun moves around the earth in one day, thus creating day and night. However, I had never heard of the earth rounding the sun! Therefore, I would have to ask my Dad or Michail about this rather strange message. Perhaps, our Wise Woman would be able to explain its hidden meaning to me?

Now that I thought about my dream some more, I found out that my dream also had been a confirmation that I really had been a little trapper boy in one of my past lives, helping my trapper Dad spice our roasting animals with my carefully selected herbs. Plus, I had been very good with using a sharp knife! Now only one important question remained: My Beloved Ancestor Friend had told me that I would meet my former trapper Dad, and that I again would be his son...

Chapter 16. Entering our woods for the very first time.

Only, how in the world could ever my former 'trapper Dad' be my Dad again? That was almost impossible, because I already had my own Dad! I was very fond of my lovable Dad; and I was absolutely sure I could not have two Dads at the same time. Clearly, I had been dreaming only some very strange dream; and everybody knows that dreams are never true. Therefore, I tried to ban it out of my memory, to go on with my life as if nothing special had happened.

Feeling a bit irritated, I shook my head a few times, to get rid of my strange dream. Then, I left my bed and started to think of my pending visit to our surrounding woods for the first time. Immediately, I restarted to feel full of anticipation and energy. Today was my 'Big Day', finally! Today, I would join my older friends for the first time, into the outstretched woods and forests that surrounded our secluded camp. Today, I would finally enter our mysterious woods, set up my own trap, and catch my own first animal!

A few days ago, Misha had already shown me how to fold an effective snare and how to cover my trap with some forest litter, to make it invisible to any wary animals. Now, our woods were waiting! Hurriedly, I left my small sleeping den, went to our living room, and looked outside. Were my older friends already waiting for me?

Alas... Much to my disappointment, nobody was outside, and our camp was still enveloped in darkness. Our wooden benches were still empty, and only our campfire shimmered faintly in the crack of dawn. Where were my older friends, the lazy slackers? Come on, let's go!

Feeling a bit disappointed, I sauntered to my parents' bedroom and crawled in between my snoring Dad and Mom; planning to wait here until the sun showed up and it would be time to go outside and join my friends towards our woods. My Dad woke up, turned around, chuckled when he felt my cold body, and threw his warming arms around me to stop my shivering. That felt safe and cozy; while I tried to let my body melt away into his powerful and lovable aura, as usual. For what felt like only a split second, I closed my eyes...

I woke up at the bright sunlight that peeked through a small gap in our curtains and teasingly tickled my eyes. Quickly, I sat upright, because I felt confused about lying in my parents' bed... Then, reality dawned upon me. WHAT? Had I overslept my first appointment with our waiting group of older kids? Immediately, I was in a tremendous hurry, hastily jumped out of my parents' bed, and raced to our living room, to take another quick look outside.

Feeling shocked, I stared at the already growing group of older kids who were gathering around our campfire; and I was sure they were waiting for ME! Why hadn't my parents woken me up in time, instead of silently leaving their bed to prepare breakfast? Now, I suddenly belonged to those same 'lazy slackers' I always loathed; and this was on my first 'Big Day'...

Angrily, I stormed into our kitchen and whined:

"Mom, please hurry up, because everybody already waits for me!"

My Mom chuckled at seeing my panicking face, while she ruffled my uncombed blond hair and responded:

"Please, calm down! Nobody will leave without you; and you have to wash up and eat your healthy breakfast first."

Because I couldn't stand still for a second, I hopped up and down from frustration while I helped my Mom with preparing breakfast. Then, I raced our plates to our living room and immediately started to wolf my food down, while nervously staring outside. More and more kids were joining our steadily growing group, and they were still waiting for ME! What if my new friends didn't want to wait any longer and decided to disappear into our woods without me?

Hastily, I gulped my milk down; but, now, I had to wait for my much slower parents to finish their own meals... Come on, Mom and Dad, please hurry up, because my friends are waiting for me!

Impatiently, I tried to send my worried thoughts to my Dad:

'Please Dad, hurry up, because I don't want to be a lazy slacker and left behind on my first Big Day!'

My Dad seemed to have picked up at least some of my worried thoughts, because he suddenly chuckled. With an understanding smile, he allowed me to leave our table early. Immediately, I jumped up and raced to our front door; in my sudden hurry forgetting to say goodbye. Quickly, I trotted outside, where I had to stop because I squinted at the bright morning sunlight that suddenly blurred my vision.

A few waiting kids stared at their little Crown Prince who almost broke his neck in his obvious hurry to be in time. Chuckling, they nudged a few others; until nearly everybody started to laugh at seeing my eagerness. Then, a couple of kids started to chant:

"HA-ROLD, HA-ROLD..."

Because I initially felt a little bit ashamed about being tardy, I first slowed down considerably. However, then, my inside started to feel proud to be recognized like this, as if I already was 'one of them'. Clearly, my new friends were chanting my name because they felt happy to have me in their midst! Now, I was even more determined to prove that I could be a valuable part of our older kids group.

When I joined them; several new friends crowded around me and playfully ruffled my unruly blond hair. Again, they told me they felt very happy to have their young Prince in their midst, and they were sure that I soon would be a valuable part of their steadily growing group! Only Misha seemed to look a little bit worried, until he approached me and hesitatingly asked:

"Harold? Of course, now that you are joining us, you don't have to wait any more for a slice of OUR meat, because you will soon catch your own animals and roast them. Only, do you still want to be our Chief Cookie and help us spice our food?"

Chuckling at seeing Misha's worried face, I teased him:

"You really think you could get rid of me this easily? Of course, I will still help you! Now come on, let's GO..."

Looking relieved, Misha ruffled my hair while he responded:

"Not yet! Not everybody is as quick as you are... We first have to wait for three more sleepy kids."

Really? After my new group first had to wait for ME, they still had to wait even longer for three more tardy lazy slackers who didn't show up in time? But, then, I had NOT been the slowest kid in our waiting group, even if I really had been a little bit late. Thus, my friends had not been waiting for ME, as I had assumed in my eagerness to join them. Well, okay... Today, I had to learn that our world didn't always revolve solely around me...

Finally, three yawning sleepyheads showed up from their caravans and trotted towards us. They grinned sheepishly while mumbling they were sorry for oversleeping. Then, they just blended into our waiting group, acting as if this was their normal routine...

Feeling very surprised, I just couldn't understand how those lazy slackers could be so indifferent about being tardy, while our mysterious woods were waiting. However, the other kids didn't seem to mind and just started to walk towards our surrounding bushes.

A few oldest kids disappeared first into one of the narrow winding paths, while beckoning the others to follow them. All the others followed them, frolicking and teasing each other, while on their way creating a long and twisting line. Suddenly feeling a little bit nervous, but also full of anticipation, I too stepped into our moving line, directly behind Misha. Now, we finally entered one of the mysterious paths that were leading towards our unknown woods...

Of course, I had entered our surrounding bushes many times before, while studying Mother Nature and looking for the tastiest herbs. Only, until today, I had never followed those winding paths and always stayed far away from our mysterious woods. While following Misha and the others, I again remembered what my Dad had told me, that first day when I was allowed to play outside all alone...

From a very young age, our parents always told their children to stay far away from our surrounding woods, to avoid any nasty predators or dangerous animals that might attack them. We always had to be very careful; until we were strong enough and knew exactly what we had to do to fend for ourselves.

If we ever happened to meet some dangerous animal, we first had to screech and yell for help as loudly as possible, while grabbing a sturdy branch. Then, we had to push our branch into any open mouth with nasty teeth that showed up, to hurt the attacking animal and hopefully chase it away... Well, I surely hoped I would never meet such a dangerous predator with open mouth and razor sharp teeth.

Today, I found out that our winding path through our surrounding bushes suddenly ended up in an enormous oblong clearing! One by one, all of us entered the huge clearing; where we stopped and waited until all the others were present. Finally, for the first time in my life, I was in the mysterious place where I had longed to be for such a long time, our surrounding woods! I stopped dead in my tracks, looked around in awe, and suddenly felt extremely small and vulnerable.

Around me, many hundreds of enormous forest trees majestically rose high into the sky, having their top branches entwined. Their outspread treetops formed what looked like an enormous cathedral over our heads. The spongy ground and fallen leaves under our feet were dampening all of our usual sounds, thus creating an eerie silence. Beneath my bare feet, the soft and mossy carpet felt like walking on some moving cloud...

Chapter 16. Entering our woods for the very first time.

The unexpected silence felt overwhelming; so that I nearly forgot to breathe from the initial shock. Ultimately, I was only four years and three months old, and the youngest kid in our group...

For quite some time, I felt only tiny and fragile, until the initial shock disappeared and my trembling body forced me to breathe again. For several seconds, I felt a strong urge to cry; while a few tears already welled up in my eyes and dripped onto the mossy ground.

Immediately, I forced myself to be a Real Big Boy and not be some little crybaby! What would my new friends think when they saw their suddenly blubbering little Royal Crown Prince and so appraised Chief Cookie? Quickly, I regulated my breath, repressed my upcoming tears, and furtively looked around at the other kids.

To my utmost surprise, all the others seemed to feel totally at ease in these eerie surroundings. They just acted as if entering this truly impressive cathedral was doing nothing out of the ordinary to them! Had all my new friends already gotten used to this splendid grandeur of our ancient forest? I was sure I would NEVER get used to it and always feel the same overwhelming awe...

Because I was still a small and vulnerable kid, I also missed my Dad, my Mom, or Michail, who always had been near me to help me and comfort me whenever I needed them. For a split second, I thought about turning around and going home, as a little crybaby who became homesick and missed his Mommy. Only, then, I would no longer belong to our 'older kids'; and I would have to play again with our 'toddlers'. Well, that was the very last thing I ever wanted to do!

Hesitatingly, I went to Misha and silently worked my small hand into his much bigger one. Fortunately, Misha didn't think I was a little crybaby that wanted to go home... He only looked at me and smiled, while he squeezed my hand and whispered into my ear:

"The first time in our woods is rather overwhelming, isn't it? Soon, you will get used to all these powerful forest energies, and then they will no longer bother you. Now, let's follow the others into our woods, and find out what we have caught in our traps."

Still feeling small and vulnerable, I nodded my approval, while I regulated my breath and forced my still wet face to produce a feeble smile. Fortunately, Misha didn't tell the others that I was only a little crybaby that needed to be sent home to his Mommy...

Stealthily, I wiped my still dripping tears from my wet face with my free hand, before any other kid could see them. With my other hand safely enveloped in Misha's much bigger one, we started to follow the oldest kids into our mysterious woods...

17. Emptying traps; girls don't have peckers.

Slowly, Misha and I followed our oldest kids across the enormous and impressive 'cathedral clearing', until our group entered another small path. In here, everybody lined up again. One by one, my friends stepped onto a rocky path full of slanting boulders that led along a steep ravine. While forming a long row, everybody started to clamber onto the mossy boulders and follow the dangerous looking path, obviously feeling totally at ease and without any stumbling at all.

Still feeling rather overwhelmed by what I had experienced so far, I left Misha's hand and hesitatingly stepped forward. In absolute awe, I stared at all those overgrown mountain ridges with huge boulders along an outstretched ravine, whose steep borders were nearly hidden behind huge curtains of colored and abundantly flowering vegetation. Seeing this colorful and absolutely splendid sight, I never knew that our Mother Nature could be this beautiful!

One by one, all my older friends moved forward along the ravine; until it was my turn to step onto the first slanting boulder. For a few seconds, I hesitated, while staring into the seemingly bottomless depth of the overgrown ravine next to me. This was the first time I saw such a dangerous creation of Mother Nature, and I felt a little bit shocked. What would happen if I unexpectedly slipped on the mossy surface of such a wobbly boulder and fell down? Wouldn't I tumble into this bottomless deep ravine and probably break all my bones? Stealthily, I peeked around at what the other kids were doing...

Much to my surprise, all the other kids just walked along the rocky path; balancing on the wobbly boulders and jumping across the many dangerous cracks as if they weren't afraid at all. None of them ever slipped on the mossy surfaces or tumbled down into the steep ravine and broke all their bones.

Well; what my older friends could do, I could do too; even while I was the 'tiniest runt' and the youngest kid in our group. I only didn't want to stumble or slip on a too wobbly boulder and disappear into the bottomless depth next to me! Still feeling a little bit hesitant, I approached the first slippery boulder and stepped onto it...

Out of the blue, I suddenly remembered my strange dream, where my 'trapper Dad' and I were living in a dangerous forest. In my dream, as a 'little trapper boy', I had been USED to climbing along steep ravines and jumping across dangerous cracks! Obviously, in my past life, I had been a real mountaineer, climbing all the slippery rocks and jumping across all the dangerous cracks like a 'young gazelle' as my proud looking trapper Dad always called me.

What would happen if I fantasized I was still such a little mountaineer, following my trapper Dad along this not so very dangerous ravine? Would my 'little trapper boy' from my past life help me again; as he had done before when he helped me slice my bundle of herbs into tiny pieces? Silently, I called him in my mind for help...

Still feeling a bit cautious, I decided to trust my built-in little trapper boy. Carefully, I stepped onto the first slanting and dangerously wobbling mossy boulder... Much to my happiness, my untrained legs and feet still seemed to know exactly what they had to do! With only a little bit of help from my 'built-in trapper friend', they just stepped forward and firmly planted themselves onto the rugged boulders with an astonishing confidence. Wow; that felt marvelous!

Enthusiastically, I started to climb even the steepest cliffs and jump across the nastiest cracks, as if this was my daily habit and I had done this all my life. I even didn't need to grab Misha's already outstretched hands, who obviously wanted to help me along this 'too dangerous' rocky path. Clearly, Misha had planned to help me keep my balance on the wobbly boulders and jump across the dangerous hidden cracks, because he had turned around and seemed to be waiting for me with his hands outstretched towards me.

Misha's eyes grew big and he halted his breath, when he saw me climbing even the most slippery slanting boulders and jumping across the nastiest overgrown cracks all on my own, as if I was an already experienced trapper! With bulging eyes, he stared at the unexpected vision of the already happily climbing and jumping 'young gazelle'. Then, Misha got an unreadable expression on his face. He didn't say anything at all, but only stayed close by so that he still would be able to lend me a helping hand IF I needed any.

Although I clearly didn't need Misha's help, I still felt truly happy to have my older friend at my side, and I secretly hoped we would become best friends! I already liked him very much; and, to me, he already felt as a very good friend or perhaps a bigger brother.

Aad Aandacht is a Dutch psychotherapist who loves writing 'books with a message'

Soon, Misha withdrew his outstretched hand, turned around, and just went on climbing, while I followed him at a short distance. Now and then, my older friend stood still, turned around, and smiled at me; and I smiled back at him immediately. Strangely, he still had the same unreadable expression on his face, as if he could be feeling sort of... I wasn't totally sure, but could it be 'respect'?

After we left the steep ravine with its slippery slanting boulders and unexpected hidden cracks that, in hindsight, turned out to be less dangerous than they had seemed before, we started to pave our way through a couple of heavily overgrown bushes with prickly thorns that tried to scratch our unclad arms and legs. Then, we arrived at the bank of another beautiful creation of Mother Nature, a wildly fizzing and foaming water stream! All my friends just started to cross the fast stream full of dangerous rapids, by jumping from slippery boulder to boulder. At its also wet and slippery border, Misha stopped again, turned around, and proffered me a helping hand; although this time looking at me with a questioning face...

Only, my built-in 'little trapper boy' had already told me what I had to do to reach the other side safely, without any help at all. Again, my inside remembered following my trapper Dad everywhere, to help him inspect our traps and set up new ones. For quite some time, he had held me on a long leash, until he was sure I wouldn't drown if I accidentally slipped and tumbled into a too dangerous water rapid.

At last, slipping off a boulder and tumbling into a fast rapid became fun, and I started to be very good at rescuing myself from the foaming water. From then on, my trapper Dad trusted me absolutely, and he allowed me to scour our dangerous forest without any help at all, and all on my own! Now that I had to cross this much easier water stream, I just hopped from boulder to boulder until I reached the other side, without ever stumbling or slipping. This was too simple...

This time, Misha had to follow ME across the many wildly foaming rapids, still with the same unreadable expression on his face; although, clearly, he hadn't expected me to be this good. All the time, he didn't say a word; although he seemed to have a lot of difficulty catching up with my unexpected speed.

Was I really outdoing a fourteen-year-old and very experienced kid who had been scouring our woods and forests all his life? Wow! Then, I really still was sort of a 'young gazelle', as my proud looking former trapper Dad always called me.

After everybody had crossed the fast water stream with its wildly foaming rapids, we started to follow a much easier path along another ravine, until we suddenly entered another huge rectangular clearing. In here, everybody halted again, and waited patiently until all our other friends had shown up and joined us safely and unharmed. When the last kids showed up, the oldest boys counted our heads, obviously to be sure that nobody was lost. This time, we started to pave our path through some dense undergrowth; while avoiding several nasty thorn bushes, rolling boulders, and hidden overgrown potholes.

Suddenly, one of our boys, Joc, disappeared into a thick shrub. A moment later, we heard wrestling and beeping sounds, coming from within the shrub. Then, Joc returned, proudly carrying a fiercely struggling marmot with a glistening snare around its neck! Triumphantly, he showed the fat beast to us; before he adeptly killed it by smashing its ensnared head against a boulder.

For a moment, I felt severely shocked; because I involuntarily pitied the poor animal that couldn't help getting caught in Joc's cleverly hidden snare. Slowly, I got tears in my eyes, while my stomach turned into a knot from frustration. How would I feel, if some huge giant smashed MY head against a boulder, to kill me and eat me?

Then, I started to think it over, until I saw that this marmot hadn't suffered at all, compared to being eaten alive by a hungry predator with dangerous teeth and sharp claws. When I looked at it from this new point of view, Joc's marmot had been very lucky to end its little life like this, fast and painless! After I found this clarifying insight, such a fast and painless death never again bothered me.

In the meantime, Joc had unwrapped his snare from the neck of his marmot. He went to our oldest kids, and put the dead beast into one of the huge string bags they carried. Smiling broadly, he went to another thick shrub, folded the same piece of wire into a new snare, and attached his snare onto a nearby branch next to a faintly visible animal track. Cleverly, he used a little bit of forest litter to cover his trap, before he returned to us and again blended into our group.

All the time, I had watched Joc's ministrations with concentrated interest and scrutinizing eyes. Yes, this was exactly what Misha had taught me to do, when he showed me how to fold a snare from a piece of wire. Only, would this nearby branch be thick enough to withstand a bigger animal, in case it happened to ensnare itself in Joc's trap?

Secretly, I was sure I would have chosen a much sturdier branch, so that my snare would be able to catch bigger animals as well! Again, I remembered being a little trapper boy and setting my own traps to catch wild deer and other really big animals to roast them or preserve their dried meet as stock during our very cold winters. Soon, my remembrances faded away, and I returned to the here and now. None of my friends had made any comments, so I just let it go.

Then, one of our girls, Biny, disappeared into another thick shrub along a faintly visible animal track. Almost immediately, she returned, proudly carrying a fat marmot. She put the already dead beast into a string bag, and adeptly set up a new trap along another animal track. To me, her sturdy and cleverly hidden trap looked much better than Joc's trap had been! Only, how did I suddenly know this, while I had never set up a trap in my present life? This was strange...

Now, a much younger boy, Jonno, disappeared behind one of the surrounding thorn bushes. Soon, he returned with a disappointed face, shaking his head because his snare was empty. He took the same snare and clumsily set up another trap at the back of the same bush. Involuntarily, I shook my head, because my bright brain thought that Jonno would never be a good trapper. He was too clumsy; and his still clearly visible trap would warn any alert animal from miles away!

Again feeling surprised, I shook my head to get rid of my strange thoughts. How the heck did I know how a good trap should be, while I had never set up a trap in my present incarnation? This was becoming eerie... unless my 'little trapper boy' could have a hand in it. For a moment, I thought I sensed him in my inside, softly grinning...

For quite some time, we went on and on; on our way also looking for any edible nuts, fresh footprints, or interesting animal tracks. One by one, our kids disappeared into a shrub to look after their snare, collect the next animal, and set up a new trap. Only now and then, a trap turned out to be empty; but the kid just shrugged it off and set up a new trap along another animal track. Mostly, the snare had done its work, and another beast was added to our slowly filling string bags.

One time, everybody started to laugh and point at the next boy:

"Look, Jaspi caught a rat! Jaspi is a ratter, Jaspi is a ratter..."

Jaspi glared at his teasing friends with a sour face while he threw the dead rat far away into the bushes. Of course, everybody in our Gypsy community knew that rats could infect us with nasty diseases.

Therefore, we never ate any roasted rats, not even if we were out of food and nearly starving to death! Still looking sour, Jaspi set up his new trap along another animal track. Then, we went on; looking after our traps, collecting our caught animals, and setting our new traps, mostly along other fresh animal tracks.

All the time, I continued to observe how my experienced friends folded their snares, attached them to nearby branches, and covered them with some forest litter. Every time, I tried to understand what exactly my friends were doing, and why they were doing it like this. Now and then, I thought they were making slight mistakes, and I was sure I could have done better.

Only, all the time, I also wondered how I already knew how to set a trap and make it invisible to the wary animal, without ever having done it myself. This was very strange... unless I really had been a 'little trapper boy' in my past life and still remembered my own trapper skills from my past incarnation...

After some time, my friends and I started to feel a bit thirsty from all our climbing, paving through the thick undergrowth, collecting our caught animals, and setting our new traps. Therefore, we stopped for a moment and went to one of the many water streams, to drink its cool and refreshing mountain water. My thirsty friends just squatted down next to the stream and scooped some water into their mouths, using their folded hands as a provisional cup.

Of course, I tried to copy them; but I did it a bit awkward and spilled most of the water before it reached my mouth. Secretly, I wished I had brought a real cup... Fortunately, after some more trying, I got the hang of it and succeeded in drinking enough water before it again seeped through my fingers. At last, I could drink just like the others were doing; folding my hands as a cup, splashing some water at my friends, and having lots of fun. Still chuckling, we went on and wandered towards the next trap.

Now and then, one of our boys had to 'take a leak', probably to get rid of the excessive water. Then, he always went to a tree, pointed upwards, and tried to squirt as high as he could. When a couple other boys saw their friend, they immediately accompanied him, having lots of fun trying to cross their streams and outdoing each other dislodging bugs from the leaves. Sometimes, I joined them in their splashing contests and tried to equal them; but my small body and little pecker didn't let me squirt that high.

Aad Aandacht is a Dutch psychotherapist who loves writing 'books with a message'

Chapter 17. Emptying traps; girls don't have peckers.

Misha tried to tease me about my lack of success, by telling me I had to grow some hairs first... Yeah, well; in our group, only a few older boys had already grown some tiny hairs, down there and under their armpits. When a growing boy got more hairs, he always left our older kids group, neatly dressed up, and then started to chase after an attractive girl to try to court her and perhaps even marry her.

Chuckling, I turned around, scowled at my teasing friend, forcefully punched his arm, and rebuked:

"Just look at yourself, with your tiny wisp of fuzz! And just wait until I have had my first growth spurt..."

However, Misha only laughed at seeing my indignant face. Teasingly, he tried to catch me; but I quickly ducked away and ran off, to escape his wrath. Soon, a couple other friends started to help me, by laughing at my teasing older friend and admonishing him not to pick only on the tiniest kid.

Of course, we were only teasing each other; and it was lots of FUN to have Misha as my older friend. Besides, Misha had been right. I really had to wait for at least a couple of years, before I would be able to outdo the others in their peeing contests.

After some time, I started to wonder why our girls never accompanied us boys in our funny peeing contests. I supposed they too had to pee from time to time, because they always drunk about the same amount of water. However, for as far as I had seen, they only laughed at our bragging efforts and commented on our splashing successes; but they never joined us to a tree to try to outdo us.

Why didn't our girls accompany us to partake in our peeing contests and perhaps prove they could do better? Could they be ill, or were their bladders not strong enough to squirt high and cross our streams? Could this be the reason why they were called 'girls' and we were called 'boys'? What else could be the difference?

Secretly, because I didn't want to be obvious about not knowing the difference between boys and girls, I started to observe our girls, until I unexpectedly detected something very strange I had never seen before. When a girl had to take a leak, she never went to a tree but always squatted down over a hole in the ground and let her pee flow freely! Why did she do that? Why didn't she join us to a tree and squirt high? Dislodging bugs from the leaves was much more fun!

Feeling more and more curious, I waited until one of our girls had to pee and squatted down over a hole in the ground. This time, I went to her and tried to take a good look at what she was doing...

Suddenly, I felt shocked into my deepest core, because I nearly couldn't believe my own eyes! This particular girl didn't seem to have any visible pecker, as we boys so proudly used to aim our pee through! She only had sort of a small cleft between her legs, from where her pee splashed down into a hole in the ground.

Why the heck was that poor girl 'handicapped' like this? Did she involuntarily lose her pecker one day, perhaps because she had some nasty accident; or could she have undergone some nasty 'surgery' in a far-away 'gadjo' hospital that I once heard about?

Fortunately, the girl didn't seem to mind my curiosity. She only smiled at seeing my bewildered face, winked at me, and just went on peeing. Still feeling severely shocked, I left the peeing girl, returned to our group, and stealthily looked around at our other girls...

Immediately, I felt even more shocked! To my astonishment, I found out that NONE of our girls had peckers. They all had the same small cleft between their legs, and none of them seemed to have anything usable to pee through. A few older girls were developing tiny breasts, and one of them had a faint trace of dark hair down there. But, none of them seemed to have any visible pee-thing on the outside! Could THAT be the difference between 'girls' and 'boys'?

Still feeling dumbfounded, I suddenly couldn't understand why I had never seen such a clear and obvious difference between boys and girls before. Did I really think I could be a 'clever brainiac' that was extremely 'early' in his mental development? Yet, I was sure I had never seen any differences between boys and girls, although I instinctively seemed to know which of my friends were girls or boys.

Could I have seen their bodily differences only unconsciously; while my conscious mind never paid any attention to their bodily differentiations, perhaps with the exception that most girls had slightly longer hair on their heads? Secretly, I wondered why, for goodness sake, our Supreme Being had created such an enormous difference between boys and girls. Or, did our girls lose their peckers one day, because they had broken it off accidentally? Involuntarily, my hand went to my own little pecker, as if to protect it from being broken off. My Dad always called it my 'pee-nis'...

Chapter 17. Emptying traps; girls don't have peckers.

Although I desperately tried to understand why all our boys were having a 'pee-nis' and our girls obviously didn't have anything at all; I just couldn't come up with a reasonable explanation. Clearly, I had to ask my Dad or my Mom about it, or perhaps my Big Friend, Michail. Or, would my new friend, Misha, be able to explain to me why girls didn't have peckers? Quickly, I made a mental note, to ask my older friend about it, first thing when we could have a private talk.

Now, an even more urgent question came to mind that involuntarily made me shudder with the unwelcome idea. Would I too be at risk to lose my own pecker and thus turn into a girl? I absolutely didn't want to lose my own little pee-nis, because I was already way too used to it! Although I had only a tiny one, I hoped it would soon start to grow and finally become at least as big as Misha's.

For quite some time, I went on thinking and pondering. Should I pity our poor girls who clearly had to live without any pee-things to pee through, probably for the remainder of their lives? Or, could it be 'normal' for our Gypsy girls to be 'handicapped' like this? Was this how every Gypsy girl was born, without anything usable to pee through other than only a small cleft between her legs? Why had I never seen this obvious difference between boys and girls before?

Feeling more and more frustrated, I sat down on a mossy boulder, with my head in my hands. Silently, I tried to remember how my Mom's naked body looked, the last time I saw her in our shower stall... Of course, I had seen my Mom's naked body several hundreds of times. However, so far, I had never really looked at how she was built. Now, I decided to have a very close look at her, as soon as I would return home and she would wash me in our shower stall.

Apart from that, my inside was already sure my Mom too wouldn't have a visible pee-nis on her outside. Therefore, as soon as I got home, I could better ask my Dad my burning question about my own bodily risk of turning into a girl! In the meantime, I would be very careful with my own little pecker, because I absolutely didn't want to lose it.

Still feeling strangely nonplussed, I trotted back to Misha and my other friends; now and then still folding my hands around my own little pecker, as if trying to protect it from falling off accidentally. Fortunately, nobody seemed to have missed me; because all my older friends just walked on towards their next traps, to empty them and set up their new ones along other animal tracks.

Around noon, we finally had emptied all our traps; and all my friends had set up their new ones. Our now rather heavy string bags were full of caught animals; and a couple of strong boys carried them on their shoulders, now and then switching turns.

Clearly, we were ready for today; and I thought we would go home now, to roast our caught animals over our campfire. As our Chief Cook, I would first go into our surrounding bushes and gather several nicely tasting herbs, to spice the roasting meat. Then, all my new friends would again offer me fat a chunk of their own roasted animals, so that I too could fill my hungry stomach to the brim.

Okay, let's turn around and go home...

18. Setting up my own trap; and showering.

Much to my surprise, nobody turned around to go home. Clearly, all my friends were still waiting for something to happen, while they were staring at ME... Why were they looking at me so funny? What were they still waiting for? Or, what could they be expecting from me? Had I done something wrong, maybe unknowingly, and would they now tell me I was still too young and therefore had to leave our older group? But, I didn't WANT to leave our group of older kids who had become my new friends! What should I do now?

Suddenly, Misha stepped towards me, put a hand on my shoulder, and pointed to a small hill while he asked me:

"Harold? Do you want to set up your own trap now, perhaps on that small hill over there?"

Immediately feeling unburdened, I heaved a deep sigh of relief. So, that was what everybody around me had been waiting for... Of course, I was more than ready to set up my first trap, anywhere Misha wanted it! Broadly smiling at my older friend, I vigorously nodded my head while feeling both very relieved and totally happy again.

Why the heck was I always afraid that other people wouldn't accept me, or tell me they didn't want me to be around them any more? Was that because, in spite of being such a clever little 'brainiac', I still was the 'tiniest runt' in our camp and a tad too small for my age?

Now that my big moment approached, I started to feel nervous. Was I really ready to set up my first trap? What if made a stupid mistake; and my new friends would be disappointed in their too clumsy little Crown Prince? Suppose I forgot how to fold an effective snare, and Misha had to correct me; or, even worse, he had to do it for me? What if no marmot or other animal would be interested in my first trap; and, tomorrow, my snare turned out to be empty? Or, even worse, what if I caught a RAT in my first snare? I didn't want to be laughed at, the first time I set up my own trap...

Fortunately, Misha seemed to understand what I felt; because he smiled reassuringly while he took a new and glistening piece of wire.

With slow movements, he showed me again how to fold an effective snare and attach it to a nearby branch, so that it would strangle the caught animal. With another reassuring smile, he offered the glistening piece of wire to me...

Hesitatingly, I took the glistening piece of wire in both slightly trembling hands and stared at it. Now, I had to prove that I really was a valuable part of our group of 'older kids'; although I was our tiniest member. Would I, with my trembling hands, really be able to fold an effective snare? Suddenly, I took a deep breath and forcefully willed my unwanted emotions down, so that I would be calm and concentrated. My Dad once told me to be ALWAYS proud of myself, and I would do just that! Therefore, after I had calmed down, I just started to fold my first snare, trying to copy Misha's example.

At that same moment, without any warning, my built-in 'little trapper boy' took over and quickly folded a totally different snare for me! Again, my untrained hands started to move all on their own, as if they already knew how to fold a much more effective snare. Again, faint memories showed up in my mind, of me helping my trapper Dad set up our rigid traps, to catch wild deer and other strong animals.

Within a few seconds, my hands had folded a strangely formed snare that didn't look at all like the much simpler snare that Misha had folded before. Yet, my inside was sure this snare would do its work much more effectively, by catching and strangling even the strongest animals very effectively and without any problems!

All the time, Misha had looked at me with an unreadable face, but he didn't say a word and only nodded at me to go on. Still sensing my 'little trapper boy' in my inside, I went to the small hill and looked for an animal track. Soon, I found a fresh one, obviously from some huge animal, leading into a dark tunnel across a thick bush. First, I looked at the animal's footprints, to see where it had left its wariness and sped up to reach its safe place. There was the point where I wanted to set up my snare, so that the animal wouldn't see it in its hurry to get home. Hesitantly, I started to lay out my strangely formed snare in front of the dark tunnel, hoping I was still doing everything right...

Again, my 'little trapper boy' took over! At lightning speed, my hands started to form a strange looking knot around a sturdy branch that surely was strong enough to hold at least a struggling wild deer. My hands also bent a couple of twigs towards my trap, so that the twigs would force the animal to put its head straight into my snare.

Chapter 18. Setting up my own trap; and showering.

At last, my hands covered my trap with some forest litter, to make it invisible to even the most wary animal. Imagining I was such an animal myself, I wasn't able to see my own cleverly hidden trap! While I crawled backwards, my 'little trapper boy' wiped out my own trail, so that any approaching animal wouldn't get alarmed. Then, he released my hands and just retreated into my inside.

Still feeling very strange, I needed a few seconds to recover. Then, suddenly feeling very PROUD of setting my first trap, I returned to our patiently waiting group. Would we now go home to prepare and roast our caught animals? Come on, let's go!

After a moment of waiting, I hesitantly looked up at my silent friends, because nobody said anything. Much to my surprise, all my friends still stared at me, this time as if they couldn't believe their own eyes... What were my friends waiting for? Why did nobody tell me anything? Had I unwittingly done something extremely stupid, and would they now send me home?

Slowly, I started to feel more and more nervous, while staring at my own wriggling feet. Would the older kids now send me away, and tell me to wait until I became older and wiser and had grown up some more? Ultimately, I was only four years and three months old, and I still was the tiniest 'runt' in our group of older kids...

Unexpectedly, Misha threw his strong arms around my faintly trembling little body, while he exclaimed:

"Wow, little man, I cannot believe my own eyes! All the time, you did everything like an experienced trapper! First, you climbed all the wobbly boulders and jumped all the hidden cracks as if you have been scouring our mountains all your life. Then, you crossed our dangerous water stream at lightning speed, without ever stumbling or slipping and without any help. Now, you suddenly folded a strange looking snare, using some special knot I have never seen before but I am sure it will be a lot more effective than our own knots are. Plus, you are the only kid in our experienced group who thought about wiping his own trail, so as not to alarm any approaching animal. As you have been doing all these clever things for the first time, I am sure you are a 'natural trapper', probably from a past life; and I am really proud to be your older friend and guide!"

At hearing Misha's praising words, I felt VERY surprised! Still a bit hesitantly, I looked up at my older friend, now feeling all warm and mushy inside. Misha had said I had done everything like an 'experienced trapper'. Now, THAT was a compliment!

While all my new friends around me started to cheer and ruffle my hair, I almost started to cry from sheer happiness; but immediately repressed my tears and forcefully regulated my breath. From now on, I should always behave as a proud Gypsy Prince, for crying out loud, and NOT as a little crybaby that wanted to go to his Mommy!

After their cheering around me finally calmed down, all my new friends wanted to compliment and high-five me, telling me they were very happy to have me in their midst! They also hoped I would soon catch my first marmot or other tasty mammal in my special snare with its extremely rigid knot, so that I finally could roast my own animal over our campfire, of course spiced with my own tasty herbs from our surrounding bushes. Would I still be willing to provide their caught animals with my spicy herbs as well?

Of course, I would still spice their caught animals, as I was their 'little Chief Cookie' and very proud of my honestly earned title!

Then, we decided to go on. Today, we had gathered enough edible animals to fill our hungry stomachs. Our strongest boys took the filled string bags, and we followed them through the dense undergrowth towards what I thought would be home. Frolicking and chasing after each other, we returned to the wildly foaming stream full of dangerous rapids. Again, we crossed the stream without any accidents.

Following the oldest boys, our group sauntered back to the first steep ravine. Again, we climbed all the slanting boulders and jumped across the nasty cracks without any accidents. Now, we reached our huge 'cathedral' clearing from where we had started our journey. Here, the oldest boys counted our heads again; to be absolutely sure that everybody was present and nobody was left behind or got lost.

Of course, I thought we would go home now, to roast our caught animals and eat them. However, much to my surprise, our group clearly decided to take another route. Instead of walking home along our winding paths, we suddenly turned to the right and entered another winding path that brought us back into our woods!

Feeling very surprised, I asked my older friend:

"Misha? Why are we going back into our woods? Don't we go home now, to roast our caught animals over our campfire?"

Smiling at seeing my surprised face, Misha responded:

172 Aad Aandacht is a Dutch psychotherapist who loves writing 'books with a message'

"Well, as the sun is still high in the sky, we're having time enough to take a shower and perhaps a swim."

Feeling extremely surprised, I looked up at Misha. What did my older friend tell me now? Had I heard this correct? Were we really going to take a SHOWER, here, in our woods? For several seconds, I didn't know what to think of it. Had really somebody built an enormous shower stall, somewhere around here, that would be big enough for all of us? Feeling speechless, I didn't dare ask any more questions but just continued to follow my friends along the winding path.

Within a minute, we arrived at the mossy banks of a small but amazingly nice looking ravine. Again feeling totally in awe, I stared with bulging eyes and open-mouthed at the most magnificent thing that our Mother Nature had ever created! Across the ravine, I saw an absolutely beautiful waterfall that continually displayed a splendid rainbow full of wonderful colors in the bright sunlight. Feeling almost shocked, I stopped dead in my tracks and nearly gasped from my sudden and very powerful emotions.

A huge colorful curtain of swirling water streamed down from the rocky borders across the ravine and splashed into the wildly foaming river below. Never before had I seen anything this marvelous, and its sheer beauty totally overwhelmed me! This superb play of light and colors, sparkling in the bright sunlight, was the most beautiful grandeur I had ever seen! There was our enormous 'shower stall', obviously created by our Mother Nature itself...

Because I unintentionally got a few tears in my eyes from my too overwhelming emotions, I hastily wiped them away. Silently, I went to Misha and again worked my small hand into his bigger one. Again, my older friend didn't say a word, but he just stepped nearer and softly squeezed my trembling hand, as if wanting to tell me he understood... I looked up at Misha, and saw that he too had tears in his deep brown eyes. Fortunately, I was not the only crybaby here that became emotional from feeling too overwhelmed!

After a couple seconds of feeling sentimental, Misha and I walked towards the mossy banks. Several kids were already climbing down into the ravine; and we just followed them downwards. Again, my untrained legs seemed to know exactly how to jump from ridge to ridge without ever stumbling, as a real 'young gazelle'.

Seemingly effortlessly, I hopped down until I reached the bottom of the ravine, with only now and then a little bit of help from my built-in 'little trapper boy'. Obviously, I WAS a 'natural trapper'!

When we reached the bottom of the ravine, we first waited until all the others had joined us safely. Then, cheering enthusiastically, everybody tumbled over each other to reach the swirling curtains of foaming water. Immediately when my friends reached the waterfall, they dived under the inviting looking water spray, threw their bodies under the splashing shower, and started to jump up and down.

Enthusiastically, I followed my friends towards the huge waterfall. Carelessly, I stepped under one of its forceful water streams that turned out to be icy cold. Then, within a second, I thought I was going to die! Almost immediately, my chest started to heave and feel upset, my throat choked up, and I suddenly couldn't breathe any more. My body started to cramp and shiver in the cold water, and I was sure this had to be the miserable end of little Crown Prince Harold and his way too short life. What the heck could be happening to me?

Still unable to breathe and feeling desperate, I tried to yell to the other kids for help, but my blocked throat refused to produce any audible sounds. Therefore, as quickly as I could, I turned around and fled from the dangerous waterfall, as fast as my small legs could carry me. This alluringly beautiful waterfall turned out to be a real death trap; because it almost KILLED me, for crying out loud! Fortunately, I could escape from it just in time...

At a safe distance from the deathly waterfall, I stopped running, turned around, and glared at it. Fortunately, my cramps and shivers were already diminishing, while my throat slowly opened up until my lungs were able to breathe again. Only, although I was still alive and kicking, I didn't trust that beautifully foaming waterfall anymore. What could have happened to my suddenly choking lungs? What strange phenomenon had tried to kill me, by taking my breath away?

From my safe distance, I glared at my former 'friends' who now turned out to be my eternal foes. Why hadn't they warned me to be careful, or told me in advance what I could expect from this waterfall shower? Why had my former 'friends' tried to KILL me, by letting me step under such an extremely dangerous quirk of Mother Nature, without any warning? Or, didn't my former 'friends' know that this too beautiful creation of Mother Nature was a treacherous murderer? Would they now undergo the same fate of choking up?

Chapter 18. Setting up my own trap; and showering.

Much to my surprise, all my 'former friends' seemed to have the fun of their lives under the murderous water shower! All the time, they cheered loudly and playfully splashed even more water at each other. Now and then, one of the kids left the swirling stream; only to return and quickly dive under it again. Why didn't the cold water choke them and kill them, as it had tried to do me?

This strange phenomenon was extremely eerie! Could my tiny lungs be too small to be able to survive such an unexpected danger? Or, could I be the only kid in our Gypsy community who turned out to be 'allergic' to such a splashing colored waterfall?

After a few seconds, Misha saw me, still glaring at the murderous waterfall from some distance while looking scared. Enthusiastically, he waved at me and beckoned me to come over and join him.

Only, I plainly refused to come over, because I didn't want to undergo such a murderous attempt for a second time!

Then, one of our older girls, Biny, saw me too; and, together, they walked towards me. When they reached me, Misha looked at my still frightened face and asked, with sudden concern in his voice:

"What is your problem, little man? Why don't you join us any more under our waterfall?"

Nearly crying at hearing such a concerned voice, I stuttered:

"I... I couldn't breathe any more bec... because that waterfall cho... choked me up and tried to KILL me!"

Much to my surprise, both Misha and Biny first looked at each other, and then they started to bellow with laughter! Why were my 'former friends' laughing at me; while I could have been DEAD, for crying out loud? Or, had I unwittingly done something stupid, obviously without knowing what I was doing? Again, I nearly started to cry from my welling emotions and sudden embarrassment...

This time, Biny put her arms around me while she explained:

"Please, little Prince, don't cry any more and dry your tears! You only forgot to jump up and down under the cold water stream until your body gets used to the sudden cold and your breath returns. Now, come on, dry your tears, and let's go back to our waterfall. Then, you only have to jump up and down for a few seconds."

Although still a bit hesitatingly; I decided to trust my friends and accept their invitingly outstretching hands. Ultimately, our waterfall hadn't killed anybody else, so why should it kill me? Besides, all the other kids HAD been jumping up and down, immediately after they entered the cold water stream. Therefore, Biny could be right!

Walking hand in hand, we went back to the 'dangerous' waterfall. Still guided and reassured by both Misha and Biny, I stepped under the forceful cold-water stream. This time, I started to jump up and down immediately; and my friends turned out to be absolutely right. Within a few seconds, my skin started to tingle, my body stopped shivering and cramping, and I could breathe again!

Misha smiled at seeing my relieved face, while Biny told me:

"See? Just jump up and down until your breath returns."

Now that I could breathe again, the splashing of the initially cold water stream on my naked body felt really nice! Soon, I joined my frolicking friends and started to cheer and dance with them under the foaming water curtain. They playfully splashed some more water at their happy looking little Prince, and I splashed them back in return. Immediately, we were in a ferocious water fight, trying to drown each other in even more huge splashes of water! Fortunately, nobody else had seen me panic or flee away from the cold waterfall.

Today, I found out that I still had to learn quite a lot more before I could be a REAL trapper! Obviously, just being a 'natural trapper' was not enough, in spite of also having sort of a built-in 'little trapper boy' that sometimes helped me.

For quite some time, my friends and I continued to play under our waterfall, having lots of fun. Then, the oldest kids gathered us around them and told us we had still enough time left to go swimming!

Obediently, everybody started to follow the oldest kids along the whirling water stream that soon turned into a slowly broadening river. Where were we going now? Within five minutes, I found out that the broadening river ended into a beautiful lake that was surrounded by several steep ridges and abundantly flowering bushes.

All my friends started to cheer loudly, while they stormed towards the lake and happily 'cannonballed' their bodies into the inviting water. Immediately, they started to swim around and playfully chase after each other while trying to dunk each other under the water surface.

Chapter 18. Setting up my own trap; and showering.

That is... everybody else started to swim around in the huge lake, except for me! Warily, I went to the edge of the water and stared into its dark and bottomless depth in severe doubt. Nobody had ever taught me how to swim. Therefore, would it be safe for me to plunge into this enormous bathtub without knowing what to do and how to do it? What would happen if I sank down towards the bottom of this way too deep water basin and couldn't return to the surface?

Ultimately, I was only a 'tiny runt' and still the smallest kid in our older group. Would any of my older friends be able to rescue me in time, before I sank deeply under the water surface and drowned? Besides, how would anybody around me ever know I was drowning when they couldn't see me anymore?

Tentatively, I sat down on some mossy bank, put my feet into the crystal clear water, and splashed a bit. In the meantime, I started to think. Would my built-in 'little trapper boy' know how to swim; and would he be willing to teach me? Or, would he be able to help me in time IF I took the chance and just plunged into the uninvitingly deep water below my feet? However, what terrible things could happen to me if my built-in little trapper helper did NOT know how to swim or how to rescue me? Would drowning be painful?

Suddenly, I saw a small ridge under my feet, seemingly just below the water surface! Feeling curious, I tried to estimate how deep down it would be. Could that small ridge be able to rescue me, in case I dived into the water and my 'little trapper boy' couldn't help me? Well, there was only one way to find it out!

Curiously, I slid down from the mossy bank and probed around with my feet, until they felt the small ridge that turned out to be not too deep down. Feeling like a little adventurer, I stepped onto the small underwater ridge and probed around a little bit further, to see how far it stretched out into the lake. 'Safety first', as all our grownups always told their kids! Fortunately, the underwater ridge turned out to be safe enough to step onto it without any immediate danger.

Standing upright on my ridge, the water came up to only my waist. Now, I had to decide what I wanted to learn first... Therefore, I looked around at what the other kids were doing. Most kids were swimming around, chasing after each other, or diving under the water surface and resurfacing again. A few kids just floated around, moving lazily or lying still and looking at the clouds over our heads.

Yes! Floating around was the first thing I wanted to learn, because it seemed to be easy enough to do. Thus, I took a very deep breath, closed my mouth, and slowly went down on all fours.

After my face disappeared into the water, I first waited until my ears were used to the sudden silence. Then, I had to come up to breathe again. Well, so far, being in the water seemed to be easy enough! After taking another deep breath, I went down on all fours again. Then, I slowly turned around until I was on my back.

Much to my delight, my body automatically started to float, just below the water surface. My face stayed out of the water so that I could breathe; while my body sank down when I breathed out, but it floated up again when I breathed in. Therefore, I had to breathe in every time before I sank too deep and my face dived under the surface.

So far, floating around turned out to be really easy!

19. Drowning; and us boys differ from girls.

For quite some time, I went on drifting on the water surface, while lazily staring at the moving clouds over my head. Then, I started to feel a bit bored and therefore decided to go towards the next stage. Now that floating had turned out to be really easy, I supposed that swimming would be easy too. Instead of only floating around, I also wanted to join my frolicking friends and partake in their splashing water games! However, before I tried to swim, I first wanted to look at the others, to find out what they were doing to propel forward. Very slowly, while trying to keep my face above the water surface, I stretched my legs downwards and started to feel around for my ridge, to stand upright and look at what the others were doing...

Suddenly, without any warning, I PANICKED, so that I involuntarily swallowed a gulp of water and started to cough! Where could my safe ridge be that I was sure had been just below my probing feet? WHERE WAS THAT RIDGE? I needed it to stand on it, because I almost couldn't breathe any more and my body already started to sink down into the bottomless depth! Slowly, my head disappeared under the water surface, so that I really couldn't breathe any more. Clearly, I had drifted off too far into the huge lake; and now I was unable to find any solid ground under my feet.

Because I couldn't refill my lungs with air, my body slowly sank down into the bottomless depth beneath my desperately searching feet. Feeling more and more hopeless, I started to kick around and splash with my arms; thereby involuntarily swallowing even more water, as nobody ever taught me what I had to do to resurface. A nasty pressure started to build up in my ringing ears, while my poor heart started hammering in my chest like crazy.

Obviously and very clearly, I was DROWNING, because I didn't know how to surface and breathe again! This time, even my built-in 'little trapper boy' couldn't help me any more, because my desperate panicking prevented him from showing up and taking over. Today, I had lived through my last adventure on earth, towards the sorrowful end of little Crown Prince Harold Janovski Romani...

Would my parents be very sad after my friends found my dead body, probably near the end of the day? Would now everybody have to move away from our camp; or was I dying far enough away to let my people stay in our secluded place? Our Gypsy belief forbade us to stay in the same place where one of us had died; but I absolutely didn't want to be such a nuisance to them...

Unexpectedly, a hazy figure showed up next to me in the water; and two strong hands gripped my arms and quickly pulled me back to the surface! Immediately after my head resurfaced and I could breathe again; I coughed out a lot of inhaled water, refilled my longs with fresh air, and started to cry my heart out. This drowning adventure had been the most humiliating experience that I had ever lived through in my whole life! Still feeling desperate, I blindly wrestled around until I could clamp myself onto my unknown savior.

Then, I saw that I was clamping onto my older friend, Misha. Clearly, today, Misha had been my earthly guardian angel, because he had rescued me from drowning! Looking at my panicking eyes and still very upset face, Misha chuckled:

"Please loosen your death grip on me, so that I can dive under you. Now trust me, let yourself float for a second, and then climb onto my back; so that I can swim us to the banks and you can recover."

Patiently, Misha helped me loosen my death grip on him, so that I could float again. Then, he dived under me, helped me climb onto his back, and swam us to my small underwater ridge. He sat down on the ridge, pulled me onto his lap, and then firmly pressed his fists against my upset stomach. Patiently, he waited, until I had coughed all the swallowed water out of my lungs and my stomach.

Fortunately, now that I was able to breathe again, my panic quickly subsided. Within a few minutes, I stopped crying, regulated my breath, and immediately started to feel curious again. What could have gone wrong so that my head went under the water surface; and why had I not been able to resurface, as Misha and all the others seemed to do so easily? And, why hadn't my built-in 'little trapper boy' helped me, instead of letting me drown?

Misha looked very relieved when at least some life returned into my eyes; but he also apologized:

"Sorry, little man, for being too late! All the time while you floated around, I've kept a very close eye on you. Until, suddenly, I didn't see you any more because you disappeared under the water surface. Immediately, I dived down and pulled you upwards, so that you could breathe again. Now, I want to teach you how you can surface all on your own, without any help from me. Please, sit down on this ridge, and look at what my legs are doing..."

First, Misha helped me sit down on my underwater ridge, with my head just above the water surface. From here, I could look down at what Misha was doing while he swam in front of me. Fortunately, the water was crystal clear, so that I was able to see all his movements.

Misha put his arms high into the air and slowly sunk into the bottomless depth, until he was deep under the surface. While I watched intently, he started to open and close his legs while forcefully kicking at the surrounding water with his feet. Soon, his smiling head popped up again; and he spit out some water while he grinned:

"Now, trust me and let yourself glide into the water next to me. I will hold your hands."

Two minutes later, I left Misha's guiding hands and dived under the water surface. When I had dived deep enough, and the by now well-known pressure started to build op in my ears, I forcefully kicked at the surrounding water and resurfaced all on my own!

Up to now, I never knew that diving under water and swimming up again would be this easy and could be so much fun. Thanks to my older friend and rescuer, Misha, I now knew exactly what I had to do to resurface and keep myself from panicking. Fortunately, all my fears about drowning were gone, and I already started to enjoy my older friend's swimming lessons very much!

Now that I didn't panic any more and was able to rescue myself; Misha showed me how I had to move both my arms and my legs at the same time, to propel myself forward. Soon, he and I were swimming next to each other; while I tried to keep up with him.

Unfortunately, my rather erratic movements were still way too uncoordinated; and I also still didn't feel my built-in 'little trapper boy' helping me. Maybe, he really couldn't swim; although, now and then, I thought I sensed him in my inside, chuckling at my idle tries...

Well, even without his help, I just went on trying to swim faster and faster. Teasingly, I dived under Misha, swam as fast as I could, and then popped up at his other side and spit some water at him!

Misha only chuckled at my playful antics, until he suddenly turned around and forcefully DUNKED me, by pushing my head under the water surface! For a moment, I lost my orientation and panicked while I sank deeper and deeper. Then, I remembered what Misha had taught me about using my legs to resurface. Soon, I showed up again, spluttering and coughing, and also feeling ready to murder my former 'friend' and now 'eternal foe'! How did Misha DARE do this to me, after I nearly drowned and still couldn't swim properly...

Again, Misha chuckled at seeing my sudden fury. Teasingly, he stuck out his tongue, and then he dunked me again!

This time, I was mad as hell at Misha, and felt ready to chase my 'former friend' to hell and back, to get even with him. Still splashing erratically, I swam towards my former 'friend' and now eternal foe, and tried to push his head under the water.

Of course, my thoroughly trained 'former friend' was way too fast for me and escaped easily, still laughing at me and sticking out his tongue. Immediately, I launched myself at him again, while trying to swim less erratically. How could I ever catch up with my eternal foe, to teach him a lesson he would never forget?

For quite some time, I went on chasing my 'former friend' across the lake; still feeling angry and trying to get even with him. At the same time, unnoticed, I started to swim better and better. Gradually, I found out how I could use my arms and legs more rhythmically, so that my little body was gliding even faster through the water. All on my own, by using my anger as a powerful driving force, I was teaching myself how to swim fast and properly!

Now, I also sensed that my built-in 'little trapper boy' could swim as a water rat and maybe even better; but he had wanted me to learn swimming all by myself! Therefore, this wise boy in my inside really was my built-in best friend; and, from now on, he would always help me and teach me everything that he knew...

At last, I could swim almost as fast as Misha. Quickly, I pulled up next to my 'eternal foe', who suddenly seemed to be tired and went slower and slower. Or, was he doing this on purpose, perhaps to tease me even more? Still feeling angry, I dived under Misha, popped up at his other side, and mercilessly DUNKED him; by forcefully pushing his head under the water and sitting on it. Hopefully, that should teach my eternal foe a lesson he would never forget!

Chapter 19. Drowning; and us boys differ from girls.

Of course, Misha just dived a little bit deeper and easily swam from under my sitting body. Immediately, he popped up next to me and smiled broadly at seeing my still very angry face. Much to my surprise, he also complimented me:

"My dear friend, this is exactly what I wanted you to do! I hoped you would be mad at me, so that you could use your anger to teach yourself how to swim faster and more rhythmically. Now that you discovered all by yourself how to swim properly, you are a real 'water rat'. Come on, let's join the others and take part in their fun."

Feeling ashamed, I now understood that Misha had dunked me and made me angry on purpose, because he wanted me to discover all by myself how to swim properly. But, then, Misha still was my best friend and rescuer; and he had only teased me to HELP me! Feeling happy again, I smiled broadly at my ex-foe and now re-found older friend. Next, I followed him towards the other kids, to join them and partake in their fun. All the kids accepted me immediately; and we had lots of fun dunking each other and being dunked in return.

Today, I discovered that dunking and being dunked was a funny water game; and I started to like it very much! From now on, I was a real 'water rat'; and I always wanted to go for a swim whenever I had a chance to go to our beautiful waterfall and follow its broadening river towards our bottomless mountain lake.

Near the end of the day, the sun sank too low and the mountain air became too chilly, so that everybody wanted to go home. All of us felt dead tired; and, being soaking wet and shivering from the afternoon cold, we hoped that our grownups had put some more logs onto our campfire. Immediately after we returned into our 'cathedral' clearing and the oldest boys had counted our heads, we raced along the winding paths towards our camp!

Feeling thankful, we gathered around our already brightly glowing campfire and started to warm and dry our now almost uncontrollably shivering bodies.

Soon after my shivering body had warmed up, I first went into our surrounding bushes, to perform my self-allotted task as our little Chief Cookie. In the meantime, everybody else had started to prepare their caught animals. Again, all my friends smeared their roasting animal meat with my nicely smelling herbs mixture, of course painstakingly controlled by me.

A very nice aroma started to fill the air, making several grownups sniff approvingly while winking at their so clever little Chief Cookie. Would they again ask us for a chunk of our nicely roasted animals, as they had done before?

When our animals were roasted, all my friends sliced them into several parts and again offered me, and a few unlucky others, a fat slice, so that everybody had more than enough food to fill our hungry stomachs. Again, the spiced animal meat tasted delicious; and we burped loudly to thank their spirits for their healthy sustenance.

Happily, I mused that, starting tomorrow, I wouldn't need my friends' fat slices any more, because I would be roasting my OWN caught animal! That is, if really an animal decided to follow the faint track and ensnared itself in my cleverly hidden trap with its special knot... At last, being dead tired but feeling wonderful, we went to our caravans, to greet our parents and wash the smear off our faces.

Immediately when I stepped inside our caravan, my Mom took me into our kitchen and started to clean my dirty face and hands with lots of soap. However, this time, I just let her do as she liked, without making much of a fuss as I normally always did. Today, I had another, and certainly more important, thing on my mind!

After my Mom was ready, she teasingly kissed my wrinkling nose; and I kissed her back twice before going to our living room. In there, I crawled onto my Dad's safe lap, kissed his prickly cheek, and tried to melt into his enveloping arms and powerful aura. For a few seconds, I sat still and enjoyed our close togetherness very much. Then, I decided to ask him my burning question:

"Dad? Today, I suddenly found out that our girls don't have any usable peckers to pee through. They only have sort of a cleft between their legs, from where they let their pee stream freely into a hole in the ground. Why are our girls this different from us boys? Did they lose their peckers one day, or did they undergo some kind of surgery to remove them? And, should I be careful with my own pecker before I too turn into a girl? How can I protect it, because I'm way too used to mine and certainly don't want to lose it?"

Involuntarily, my hands went to my own little pecker and covered it, as if trying to protect it from falling off; while my Dad stared at me with a surprised face. Suddenly, he started to bellow with laughter, in the process nearly squashing me in his strong arms. He tried to say something, but had to hiccup and immediately started to laugh again.

Chapter 19. Drowning; and us boys differ from girls.

My Mom left her kitchen and entered our living room; probably because she had heard my unexpected question and wanted to partake in our conversation. She too started to laugh, although she also stared at me with what I thought could be a lot more respect in her eyes...

Fortunately, no grownups in our Gypsy community ever taught us kids to feel 'ashamed' of any parts of our human bodies, or of any of our natural bodily functions. In our own Gypsy language, we didn't even have any proper words for 'being naked' or 'indecent', because nobody in our camp ever needed to use those silly 'gadjo' words.

During the entire summer, all our children always ran around completely naked and absolutely free; except for our little 'toddlers' who had to wear diapers until they became 'dry' during the day. In our secluded Gypsy camp, wearing clothes was only perfunctory or functional, for example because the outside air felt too chilly or we had to visit a gadjo town; and dressing never was a 'must'!

My Dad had already told me that the 'gadjo' world outside our camp had very strange beliefs concerning their unclothed bodies. Those strange gadjo's had created their own so-called 'nudity laws' that FORCED everybody in their gadjo towns to hide certain parts of their bodies from everybody else. Otherwise, the 'sinners' could be punished severely, for walking around 'indecent'! Although I tried to understand those strange gadjo's, I never found out why even their smallest kids were forced to feel ashamed of certain normal parts of their natural bodies that they called 'private parts'. They had to be extremely strange people, those so-called gadjo's!

Therefore, I was absolutely sure I hadn't asked my parents a too impossible question. Patiently, I waited until they stopped laughing, calmed down, and were able to answer me; because I HAD to know the truth about boys and girls, before I did something stupid and involuntarily turned into a girl. What if I lost my own pecker while I could have rescued it, by knowing what I had to do?

After my parents stopped laughing, my Dad responded:

"My so extremely quickly maturing son, you certainly are a clever one as well! Didn't you take a closer look at one of our girls, while she sat down to let her pee stream into a hole in the ground?"

"Of course I did! This morning, I took a close look at Biny while she squatted down to pee into a hole in the ground. Then, I saw that her pecker is totally gone! It only left sort of a pink cleft behind, with small crumpled lips around it. Therefore, I certainly don't want to look like her! I just want to stay a boy and become a real man, and finally grow a huge penis like yours or Misha's."

Again, my parents started to laugh, making me feel even more confused. Had I really asked them such a funny question? How could my concern about losing my masculinity be this hilarious? When would they finally stop laughing and answer my important question about the risk of losing my own little 'pee-nis'?

Finally, my Dad ruffled my unruly blond hair while he told me:

"Okay, my way too early maturing little brainiac. I once promised I would talk to you as if you already are a grownup; and I will do it now as well. Although you might be a tad too young to understand everything about our sexual organs, I will try to clarify some bodily differences between boys and girls. Basically; boys and girls have the same sexual organs. Only, where boys have them on the outside, girls carry them inside their bodies. Try to imagine a girl's pecker is inside her belly; but its skin is folded inside out, thus creating a pee hole between her legs. Does this explanation make any sense to you?"

Of course, I had to think this unexpected information over first. Therefore, I slid off my Dad's lap, went to our windows, and stared outside. In the dusk, a man was raking our faintly glowing campfire; while another man discarded its burnt ashes and charred cinders. My Big Friend, Michail, was talking to my Grandma while carrying his squirming twins in his safe arms. A few people sat together on our benches; having some small talk and laughing while keeping their voices down. Everything in our secluded Gypsy camp felt quiet and peaceful, as it always did around this time of the day. This was my safe and lovable home, and I felt blessed to be living here, in my own Gypsy community in our own green-and-golden Royal caravan.

Now, let's get back to what my Dad told me; about a girl having the same organs but they are inside her body. In my mind, I imagined folding my own little pecker inside out, by pushing it into my belly. That way, I really could create sort of an inward hole! Therefore, my Dad's explanation did make sense. And, when I folded my crumpled little sack together; it really looked like two 'crumpled lips' as I had seen on Biny and on a few other young girls when they had to pee.

But, what about my two tiny 'beans' in my outside sack that would once grow into the much bigger 'balls' that all our grownup men hung in between their legs? Would a girl have the same two balls, but were they growing inside her belly, instead of on the outside? Curiously, I returned to my Dad to ask him my next question...

For quite some time, my parents patiently answered my questions. They explained how our sexual organs are basically the same, but the man's outside 'penis' replaces the woman's inside 'vagina'. The man's outside 'balls' are the woman's inside 'ovaries', creating little eggs every month, to make new babies if she becomes pregnant. Only, the man's inside 'prostate' is the woman's inside 'womb'; where a little 'fetus' grows for nine months, until it leaves the woman's stretching vagina and becomes a new human baby.

Immediately, I had ready another question for my Dad:

"Dad, what is a 'prostate'? That is what Jonno's father complained about when he suddenly couldn't pee any more."

My Dad explained that a prostate is sort of an inside container that temporarily holds the man's 'sperms' that originate from his outside balls; until he 'ejaculates' his sperms into the woman's womb, where they try to find a ripen egg. If they find a ripen egg, they try to kiss it so that it can become a new baby that grows up in the woman's womb until it is big enough to be born. Sometimes, two little sperms are kissing two eggs, so that the woman gets twins. That is what had happened to Felicia, Michail's deceased spouse...

Immediately, I had my next burning question ready, about how such a 'sperm' could find a ripen egg to make it 'pregnant'...

After thinking over my question, my Dad explained that Mother Nature had thought out a wonderful way of making babies. To be able to do this, once a month, a woman created a few eggs in her ovaries that descended into her womb. At the same time, a man had created millions of 'sperms' in his outside balls that stayed in his inside prostate until they left through his penis and tried to find an egg.

Therefore, to make new babies, a man had to put his penis into a woman's vagina, to send his sperms towards her womb. Only once in a few years' time, one of the man's many sperms could find a ripen egg in a woman's womb and make it 'pregnant'. Then, a tiny fetus started to grow in the woman's womb until it was big enough to show up as a brand new baby, mostly around nine months after the woman got pregnant. This is how every man and woman on our planet earth is born, as a brand new little baby...

Finally, I felt satisfied and decided I had heard more than enough explanations for today. I started to yawn, hopped off my Dad's lap, and let my Mom wash me and put me to bed. Of course, I again slept without a diaper, feeling much happier and freer in my 'birthday suit'.

Now that I didn't need a diaper any more, I finally belonged to our 'older kids' group, and I would sleep just like all the others in our Gypsy camp always did, clad in only our 'birthday suits'.

Feeling dead tired from strolling around in our woods and swimming in our lake, I closed my eyes and fell asleep almost immediately. Soon, I started to dream, about millions of tiny sperms that tried to find a little egg to kiss it and make it pregnant in my Mom's womb. If they succeeded and the little egg became a growing fetus, I would finally get a little brother or sister...

20. As stiff as a dead tree; I catch a real pig.

The next morning, I woke up full of anticipation and immediately wanted to jump out of bed. Only, much to my dismay, my strained muscles had become stiff and painful during the night, making me grunt from the unexpected aching. Clearly, my tiny body wasn't used yet to paving through our dense woods, climbing along steep ravines, and learning how to swim and dive in our mountain lake. Therefore, I now nearly couldn't move my arms and legs!

Gritting my teeth, I slid out of my bed, hobbled to my parents' bedroom, and crawled onto my Dad's broad stomach to be held and comforted. From there, I complained:

"Dad? This morning, my arms and legs are aching terribly, and my body feels as stiff as a dead tree..."

My Dad woke up, and first squinted at seeing the already very bright sunlight. Then, he looked at me and started to laugh at seeing my sour face and hearing my grunted complaints. Teasingly, he tickled my also painful belly, while he chuckled:

"Well, I think that, after scouring our woods and playing in our mountain lake for the first time, you've caught 'baby stiffness'."

Of course, I became angry with my teasing Dad for calling me a 'baby'. Couldn't he show some more respect to my painful misery? Angrily, I sat upright and punched his stomach. Ultimately, I was no longer a 'baby' but already a Real Big Boy; and I had already folded my first snare and set up my first trap...

Suddenly, I was in a tremendous hurry, wrestled free from my Dad's enveloping arms, and raced towards our kitchen; because I couldn't wait to enter our woods and take a look at my trap! What if I had NOT caught my first animal, and my snare was still empty? Or, what if I had caught a rat, and all my friends laughed at my misfortune and called me a 'ratter'? Oh no... Please, let it be a small marmot, or maybe nothing, but NOT a rat...

My Mom was already busy in our kitchen; so that I started to help her prepare her so-called 'healthy breakfast', of course spiced with my tasty herbs. Now that I was moving along, my initial 'baby stiffness' magically went away, and my body felt again enthusiastic and full of energy. I wolfed my healthy breakfast down in a tremendous hurry, and then almost choked while gulping down my glass of milk. Again, my understanding parents allowed me to leave our table immediately, telling me to go join my friends and have lots of fun.

Happily, I bolted outside, in my tremendous hurry again forgetting to say goodbye. Come on, lazy slackers; where are you? Let's GO!

Teasingly slowly, our still yawning group gathered around our campfire, until even our laziest slackers were present. Again, the oldest boys disappeared into the winding path first; and all of us followed them, again forming a long and twisting line.

For the second time, I entered our huge 'cathedral clearing' with its majestic trees and all those entwined branches over our heads. Much to my surprise, this time, I didn't feel any more like the smallest and most vulnerable 'tiny runt'. This time, the soft moss under my feet felt really nice; and it was as if the huge cathedral already welcomed me! Had I really matured this much, in only one day?

My older friend, Misha, tried to take my hand; but, this time, I refused politely. Perhaps, I needed his help if we crossed an extremely steep ravine full of nasty cracks, but not now. Misha looked a little bit dejected, and I could feel him pout; but I just turned around. None of the other kids needed a reassuring hand, so why should I?

Feeling full of enthusiasm, I just started to lead the way, while beckoning the others to follow me! Obediently, my friends started to follow their over-enthusiastic little 'leader' towards our first ravine, nudging each other while chuckling at seeing my obvious eagerness.

Again, we clambered along our steep ravine with its wobbly boulders, and crossed our dangerous stream full of foaming rapids. This time, my built-in 'little trapper friend' helped me only now and then, probably because I was already learning to perform most 'trapper abilities' all by myself! Silently, I thanked my built-in friend for his lessons and much appreciated help. Although I didn't hear his answer but only sensed some faint chuckling, being thankful felt great.

Soon, we reached our rectangular clearing; where we waited until everybody else had joined us safely and unharmed. After the oldest kids had counted our heads, we again started to pave our path through the undergrowth, towards our snares and hopefully caught animals.

Chapter 20. As stiff as a dead tree; I catch a real pig.

Again, Joc went into the same shrub from yesterday, where he had set up his new trap along another faint animal track. This time, his snare was empty; but he just shrugged it off and set up another trap along a different animal track. Next time, he would have more luck. After we walked a bit further, Biny went to her trap and returned, triumphantly carrying another fat marmot. She put it into a string bag, set up a new trap along another fresh animal track, and we went on.

One by one, all my friends looked after their snares, gathered their caught animals, and set up their new traps along faint animal tracks. Nearly everybody had caught at least some small critter; and the few kids who hadn't caught anything, just shrugged it off and set up another trap. Of course, their luckier friends would provide them with fat slices of their own roasted animals; so that, again, nobody would be left hungry. Besides, in our Gypsy camp, our most heard device was 'live and let live'! Nobody in our camp ever cared about 'owning' any 'possessions' or 'personal belongings'.

From their first days as newborn babies, all our Gypsy kids immediately got used to sharing everything among everybody. Therefore, nobody in our camp ever accused any others or was in a fight about 'stealing' or 'taking away' things. Nothing on earth could ever be 'owned' by you, simply because you couldn't take it with you towards your next incarnation! You were allowed to use things temporarily; until you passed away and had to leave your 'possessions' to others.

We proud Gypsies never really understood how those gadjo's, the 'others' that were living outside our camps, ever could be living the way they were doing: stealing from each other, fighting, accusing, and denouncing each other, and still feeling happy about it...

Just like yesterday, more and more marmots and other small animals joined the steadily growing piles in our string bags. Again, we had gathered more than enough mammals to feed everybody in our group. Six-year-old Jonno had caught a big frog that jumped up and down in its snare and caused lots of laughter. Looking disappointed, Jonno let the frog escape into the bushes and clumsily set up another trap along the same already disappearing trail.

Again, I was sure I would have done Jonno's job quite a lot better; but I wisely kept my mouth shut. Who knows what we would find in MY trap! Would my first trap still be empty, because no animal had put its head into my special snare? Where were those rats...

Finally, all my friends had emptied their snares, put their caught animals into one of our steadily filling string bags, and set up their new traps along faint animal trails. Now, we were on our way to the last trap that was set up on a small hill, being MY trap...

Involuntarily, I started to feel a bit nervous, while I hesitatingly followed the other kids from a small distance. What kind of animal would be in my snare? Or, would my first trap be empty?

Suddenly, a loud screeching sound caught our surprised ears, still reverberating across the forest trees! Immediately, my friends halted and looked at each other in sudden shock, while they perked their ears up to listen even better. What the heck could be happening? I was sure I had never heard such an eerie sound before...

For a few seconds, everybody remained silent, obviously waiting until the animal repeated its screech and they could determine what animal it was and where its unexpected sound came from. Then, all my friends stormed towards MY hill, now cheering loudly:

"It's a PIG! We've caught a pig! We've caught a real pig!"

Racing towards my hill, trying to be there first, my happy looking friends quickly gathered around MY trap. In obvious awe, they stared at the again loudly screeching animal that desperately tried to get away from all those unexpected onlookers.

Hesitatingly, I followed my over-enthusiastic friends at a much slower pace, still not comprehending what could be happening. Why was everybody so extremely enthusiastic, all of a sudden? And, what was that loudly screeching sound that I faintly recognized from a 'past life' but couldn't identify, because I was sure I had never heard it before in my present life? Could this really be a small piglet?

When I reached my trap and wrestled through the already forming circle of enthusiastic onlookers, my mouth almost fell open from sudden surprise! For a few seconds, I even rubbed my eyes because I couldn't believe them. Clearly, my snare was holding an enormous, fat, ugly, again screeching, and still desperately wrestling PIG!

The huge beast stared at us with watery eyes, while in vain trying to free itself from my rigid snare with its special knot. Again, it pulled at the strangling snare, jumped up and down, and even tried to bite the strangling thing, but it couldn't free itself. After some time, the pig gave up struggling, stopped screeching, and just glared back at us...

Chapter 20. As stiff as a dead tree; I catch a real pig.

Now, I was very happy to have such a clever built-in 'little trapper friend'! Thanks to him, I had attached my strangely formed snare to an extremely sturdy branch, while using his special knot! Now that I saw this enormous pig, I was absolutely sure that most other knots couldn't withstand the way too strong muscles of this huge beast. Fortunately, for me and for our group, the fat animal had chosen MY special snare with its rigid knot to put its fat neck into it. Only, what should I do now, with such an enormous beast?

In the meantime, my surrounding friends had fallen silent. They were still speechless, while staring open-mouthed at my enormous pig. Obviously, none of them had ever thought that their 'littlest runt' could catch such a valuable animal in his first trap ever!

Suddenly, I was in severe doubt. How would I ever be able to smash the enormous head of this fat beast against a boulder, to kill it? That was what my friends always did when they caught an animal that was still alive. Because this pig was caught in MY snare, it was MY responsibility to kill it and put it in our string bag! Would I be able to take some huge boulder and forcefully smash it against the thick skull of my fat pig, to kill it? Besides, wouldn't our string bags be way too small for such an enormous beast?

Before I could decide, Misha threw his arms around my waist, nearly breaking my ribs in his over-enthusiasm. First, he lifted me high into the air and started to dance around my pig like crazy, while my pig tried to turn around to follow us with its wary looking eyes. Then, Misha put me back onto my feet while he told me:

"Little man, you really DID it! The first time you set up your own trap, you immediately caught an enormous PIG in your snare! You really are an extremely special kid! This is almost unbelievable..."

Misha took a sturdy branch with a thick end from the ground; and handed it to me while he explained:

"Please, Harold, take this branch and try to hit your pig directly behind its ears with the thick end; but swing your branch with all the force that you can bring forth, because this is an extremely strong animal with a very thick neck and an almost unbreakable skull!"

Still very hesitatingly, I took Misha's heavy branch into both trembling hands. Only, what should I do now? I had never killed a pig before; and I didn't want to cause the animal any unnecessary pain.

Perhaps, I should practice some first, before I tried to hit the again squirming beast directly behind its ears...

Stealthily, I looked around for a usable thing to practice on, until I saw an old and rotten stump. Yes, this stump might be a good dummy, being soft and having the correct height! Enthusiastically, I started to hit the stump with my branch, while trying to aim its thick end directly behind a darker spot that represented the pig's ears.

All my surrounding friend looked at my ministrations curiously, now and then stepping out of the way to avoid being hit by my swinging branch. My enormous pig still wriggled around, while staring at us with suspicion. Within a minute, my untrained arms started to tremble from swinging my heavy branch that still swayed too much from left to right. Desperately, I went on and on, trying to steer it correctly; until, after several more tries, I finally was able to hit the dark spot with enough force and reasonably accurately.

Now, I thought I would be ready to hit the enormous beast exactly where I wanted, hopefully with enough force to kill it in one blow. Therefore, I went back to my wriggling pig; and looked at the spot directly behind its ears where I hoped to break its fat neck, while my friends still kept a safe distance from my swinging branch.

First, I waited until the wriggling beast had turned itself into the right position and stood still. Now, I took a very deep breath, strained my muscles, and swung my branch towards the neck of my pig with as much force as I could bring forth. My branch swished through the air, while I deliberately steered all of my force into its thick end. Much to my delight, the thick end of my heavy branch hit the pig exactly where I intended, directly behind its ears! Unfortunately, my sturdy branch also broke into two halves from the impact, with a loud cracking sound. Feeling shocked, I stared at the broken pieces...

A second later, I heard my enormous pig fall down with a dull bang that made the mossy ground tremble under my feet. Its huge body shuddered, heaved a deep last sigh, and laid perfectly still!

Misha poked my silent pig with his finger; but it was already DEAD. Obviously, my swinging branch had broken its fat neck! Now, I felt very happy to have such strong muscles for an only-four-year-old 'little man'. Oops, sorry, of course, I was already four years and three months old, and I would be four years and four months old within two weeks from now.

For several seconds, my friends only stared at my dead pig and at me, still open-mouthed and with surprised faces. Clearly, none of them had expected their 'littlest runt' to kill such an enormous animal this effectively... Then, a real pandemonium of cheering voices broke loose. Everybody started to dance around my pig and me, high-fived me, ruffled my unruly blond hair, or slapped my shoulders!

To their utmost surprise, their tiniest 'older boy' ever had killed an enormous pig using only ONE blow, thus doing it like an experienced trapper! They never thought that such a tiny imp would ever be able to perform such a grown-up accomplishment this easily... Their happy congratulations and well-meant compliments made me blush over and again; while I felt absolutely and totally PROUD of myself!

After quite some time of cheering and dancing around my dead pig and me; my over-enthusiastic friends finally calmed down. Then, we decided to carry our enormous beast home. The oldest boys fabricated sort of a transporter from a couple of sturdy branches and long twines. They dragged my heavy pig onto it, tied it up, and attached a couple of pulling ropes. In triumph, everybody started to drag our makeshift carrier, with my pig on it, towards our camp.

Of course, because this was MY pig, I had to lead the way, proudly pulling the longest rope and still feeling on cloud nine. All the time, I felt extremely proud of myself and of my unexpected accomplishment. My powerful feelings of pride nearly suffocated me; and I had to force myself not to cry from sheer happiness. Today, I had PROVEN to be a valuable part of our older kids group! Ultimately, I had caught a real PIG in my first snare, being our 'smallest runt' and only four years old. Oops, sorry... Of course, I was already four years and three months old, and soon even four months...

After dragging, pulling, and hauling our heavy pig across all the nasty cracks and slippery boulders, we finally reached our camp. Feeling dead tired but also very happy, we towed our transporter towards our campfire in triumph. Then, we slumped down on our benches, to catch our breaths and take some much-needed rest.

My Big Friend, Michail, was the first grownup who saw our pig, and he immediately warned the others:

"Look at what our older kids are bringing home today! This time, they have caught an enormous PIG in their snares! Wow, and it is an exceptionally FAT one too. Who caught it?"

"Prince Harold caught it in his first snare; and he killed it by using only ONE blow behind its ears, as an experienced trapper!"

"Really? That is almost unbelievable! Our littlest imp, killing such an enormous pig using only one blow? Wow..."

Happily, Michail scooped me off my bench and nearly squashed my tiny ribs against his enormous chest, while he exclaimed:

"I KNEW you would be something truly special! I just knew it... Accept my honest congratulations, Crown Prince Harold, for catching such a valuable animal in your first snare."

Many more grownups showed up; and, working together, they helped Michail carry my enormous pig towards our butchery that was next to our parking lot. Together, they lifted our carrier upright, so that Michail would be able to open the heavy beast and clean it out.

In the meantime, even more people showed up and stared at my enormous pig in obvious awe. Everybody slapped my shoulders or ruffled my unruly hair, and congratulated me with such a fat catch! Then, they started to praise my superb trapper skills, over and over, making me blush fiercely. Had I really done such an extremely special achievement? I, who still was our 'littlest runt'? Wow...

Now that my pig stood upright, Michail took a sharp knife and first showed me how to skin and prepare my huge pig without making too much of a mess. Then, he offered me another sharp knife and asked me to help him. Feeling even more proud, I helped my Big Friend opening my animal, tapping its blood, removing its organs, and cleaning out its heavy carcass. In the meantime, Michail explained exactly what we did and why we did it.

Much to my surprise, we could use almost everything of my valuable pig! Its leather skin, its edible organs, its tendons, its blood, and even its enormous length of intestines to make smoked sausages... I never knew that a pig could be such a usable animal!

Jaspi turned out to know quite a lot about anatomy, from an old learning book his Dad once bought him as a birthday present. From him, we learned many interesting things about how the body of a pig functions and what all those organs are called. Jaspi also told us that the insides of our OWN bodies are looking nearly the same... All that blood, and all those strange looking organs and enormous lengths of intestines, were in MY body too? Yuck!

Chapter 20. As stiff as a dead tree; I catch a real pig.

After Michail and I had cleaned my pig out, and my Big Friend had saved its useful leather skin and many edible organs; I first went into our surrounding bushes to collect several carefully selected and nicely smelling herbs. Now, a couple of strong men attached my pig's heavy carcass to a sturdy pole and hung it over our campfire. While they started to turn my pig around, I smeared its roasting meat with its own lard and with my heavenly smelling fresh herbs mixture.

Now that we had to wait until my pig would be ready, everybody who had helped us went inside their caravans, to wash all the blood and smear from their bodies. Quickly, I followed them and went to my own caravan; to take a shower, wash up, and feel clean again. Of course, both my Mom and my Dad were very curious to hear about how I had caught such an enormous pig in my first snare...

Vividly, I told them how I folded and attached my special snare onto a sturdy branch, using an effective knot nobody else had ever shown me before. I also told them about my strange 'memories' of having been a 'little trapper boy' in my past life, always helping my 'trapper Dad' setting traps and roasting our caught animals, using my own sharp knife. Finally, I told them how my tasty herbs and other edible plants always 'talked' to me in my inside, to let me know how they tasted and on which food they could be used best.

After I had told my parents everything that I knew, my broadly smiling Dad lifted me onto his lap. With a proud voice, he told me:

"Harry, my dear son, you surely know how to make a good first impression! I am also sure that you will soon have quite a lot more surprises in store for your friends and for us. Only, please, never think you can be something special because of only having some good luck. Please, never brag about your early achievements; and be grateful that this particular pig has chosen YOU for offering itself to your snare. You should thank your pig's spirit in your mind..."

Huh? I should THANK my pig's spirit for offering itself to me? Really? Could my wise Dad be right? Should I be grateful that my pig had chosen ME to offer itself to, and not one of the other kids? Had my pig really offered itself to me, or to our Gypsy community, by choosing my rigid trap with its special knot to ensnare itself?

Because I wanted to be absolutely honest, I decided to think my Dad's words over first; and therefore retreated towards our windows and stared at our brightly glowing campfire with MY roasting pig...

After some heave thinking, I saw that my wise Dad really could be right! Out of all our snares, my pig had chosen exactly MY snare to put its fat neck into; because mine was the only rigid one with a special knot that would withstand its powerful wrestling. Therefore, I just closed my eyes and thanked the pig in my mind; by telling it we were very grateful for its meat, skin, and many other useful parts such as its lard and tendons. Much to my surprise, I suddenly thought I heard the faint voice of my pig's happy sounding spirit in my inside! With a slightly oinking voice, its animal spirit told me:

'You are welcome, my human friend! Thank you for practicing first, so that you could kill me instantly without causing me any pain at all. You are a good and respectful human being!'

For a few seconds, my brain still doubted. Could I have made up this faint oinking answer in my inside; perhaps because I hoped to get an audible response from my pig's spirit? I wasn't absolutely sure; but being thankful certainly felt GREAT!

After I thanked my smiling Dad for his wise advice, I went back to our campfire, to take over and look after MY roasting pig.

One of our men still turned its pole around and around, while another man brushed even more lard and tasty herbs onto my huge animal. My older friends were still roasting their own caught animals on smaller stakes, also smearing them with my spicy herbs, this time also using a little bit of lard from MY roasting pig.

Happily, I went to the brushing man, thanked him for his help, and took over. From now on, I wanted to smear and brush my own pig, to let it brown nicely until its meat was ready and could be eaten.

21. Washing and our ancient bonding ritual.

After roasting their own animals; the older kids sliced them into a few chunks, divided the chunks into fat slices, and offered everybody a nicely smelling slice of roasted meat. This time, several hungry looking grownups joined us around our campfire and gratefully helped us with eating. Much to my surprise, everybody still talked with very much affection and respect about their 'little imp', killing an enormous pig using only one blow! Again, their praising words made me blush, over and again...

When my pig was ready to serve a feast meal, Michail and a few others divided its roasted meat into huge chunks, and divided a few chunks into fat slices. Everybody got a slice of my roasted pig; and we started to devour it with a mouth-watering frenzy, while nearly swallowing our own fingers because of its heavenly taste. My roasted pig tasted absolutely delicious; so that all our people took second helpings and again complimented me with its absolutely exquisite taste. Again, their praising words made me blush fiercely...

In the meantime, Michail took a piece of my roasted pig, sliced it into tiny parts, and let his little sons chew on their own slices. Happily, Michi and Movi started to munch on them, with beaming eyes and tiny streams of fat dribbling from their chins. They almost grunted with the delight while devouring their slices; until their parts of pig were entirely gone. Finally, Michail cleaned their dirty faces with a few tufts of fresh grass and brought them back to his caravan.

Soon, everybody else in our camp was stuffed to the brim and burped loudly, to thank my pig's spirit for offering us its tasty meat. Then, for quite some time, our grownups continued to talk to each other about catching huge pigs and killing them using only one blow. Again, they made me blush fiercely, over and again. At last, I secretly thought they could be doing it on purpose...

Near the end of the day, Michail started to gather all the remaining chunks of roasted pig, to smoke them and preserve the many hams as a welcome reserve during our upcoming cold winter. He also gathered all its usable things like its organs, intestines, tendons, and blood.

Then, he started to smoke all the edible things, to bring them to our hidden caves along our special cooling ravine. With a very proud face, my Big Friend complimented me again. He also explained:

"Thanks to you, my beloved Crown Prince and young Friend, we now have more than enough meat and other useful things to survive most of our upcoming cold and snowy winter!"

Again, I blushed fiercely; while, at the same time, I felt PROUD. From now on, I really was a valuable part of our Gypsy community!

Several mothers had started to take their 'diaper kids' home, to wash them and put them to bed. Much to my delight, his time, my Mom did NOT take me to our caravan, as she used to do until now. Because I now was a Real Big Boy and didn't need to wear a diaper any more, I really belonged to our young grownups! Therefore, from now on, I could join my older friends around our campfire until I started to feel too sleepy and decided to go to bed all by myself.

Happily, I looked around at my older friends, while all the little 'diaper kids' were tucked in. Now, I REALLY was a Real Big Boy, although I was not even four-and-a-half years old and still a bit too small for my age. Of course, I felt dead-tired from my adventures in our woods; but I just didn't want to leave our group until sleep forced me. I BELONGED to them now; and, from now on, nobody around our campfire could get rid of me until I had decided for myself!

After tucking their diaper kids in, the mothers returned to our campfire and again joined us on our wooden benches. Again, a few grownups started to talk about the nice aftertaste of my roasted pig, about those heavenly tasting herbs they never knew existed until their little Crown Prince found them and started to use them, and about such a little imp killing such an enormous animal using only one blow. That is, until my Dad rose from our Royal bench and suggested:

"I think we should go now, before the sun disappears and the mountain air becomes too chilly."

Immediately, everybody nodded their consent and stood up. After a short deliberation, Biny's parents and two older women decided to stay in our camp, to look after our already sleeping kids. Now, all our grownups with clothes on hastily disappeared inside their caravans, including my own parents! What were they doing in their caravans? I thought my Dad had suggested we were going to leave our camp before the sun disappeared and the air became too chilly?

Soon, our grownups returned to our campfire, this time clad only in their 'birthday suits', just like all our older kids were. A few women were carrying small baskets filled with what looked like yellow lumps. Where could we be going, at this time of the day? And, why had everybody shucked all their clothes; and what could these baskets with yellow lumps be for?

Hopefully, I would find out soon, because my Dad already took the lead and beckoned everybody else before he disappeared into our surrounding bushes.

Quickly, I stepped into the forming line that followed my already disappearing Dad, until I saw that we were entering the winding paths towards our surrounding woods, followed suit by everybody else. Now, I started to feel extremely curious! What were we going to do in our surrounding woods, at this time of the day?

Because I didn't have the faintest idea, I was very eager to find it out; plus I was sure the already setting sun would soon go down completely, and then our woods would be too dark to see anything at all. Therefore, I stopped and waited until Misha showed up in our winding path, walked next to him, and whispered:

"Misha? What are we going to do in our woods, and what are these baskets with yellow lumps for?"

Misha started to chuckle at seeing my questioning face; but then he decided to tease me by telling me:

"Don't worry too much and just walk on. You are now 'one of us', as you will see soon enough."

Yeah, well... thank you very much, my friend, for your valuable 'help'. Thanks to you, I still don't know anything at all. Again, I had to be patient, although 'patience' had never been my strongest quality...

Soon, we entered our 'cathedral clearing', where we waited until everybody else had arrived; just like our group of older kids always did before we counted their heads. What were we doing here? Now that the shadows were stretching out further, our already darkening clearing suddenly looked rather spooky! Feeling even more curious, I looked around for my Dad, to take his hand and feel a bit safer.

However, before I could find my Dad among all our grownups and older children, we were again on our way. Much to my surprise, we now started to follow the winding path that led towards our waterfall!

Were we going to play under our waterfall or swim in our mountain lake, accompanied by our grownups? That could be a lot of fun!

Within a minute, we reached our waterfall ravine; and, again, I stared in awe at its splashing and foaming water curtain. Now that dusk approached, its environment looked different; with much longer shadows and an almost unearthly atmosphere. For a few seconds, I enjoyed its beautiful vista that I saw only for the second time. Then, everybody started to clamber down into the ravine; while a couple of grownups helped their kids along the many descending ridged.

Of course, I just hopped down from ridge to ridge, without any help from anybody, until I reached the bottom of the ravine all by myself. Because I had my 'built-in little trapper friend' to help me if needed, I didn't need any assistance with such an easy descent.

A couple of grownups looked surprised at seeing their so skillfully climbing 'young gazelle'; but they didn't comment and just went on. Chuckling inwardly, I again remembered my past life as a little trapper boy, where my trapper Dad had held me onto a long leash around my waist while teaching me how to climb safely, until he was absolutely sure I wouldn't slip and drown in some wildly foaming stream, and he started to trust my 'young trapper' abilities.

Soon, we gathered at the bottom of our waterfall ravine, unharmed, and waited for the last slackers to join us. Now, all our kids broke free and raced to our splashing waterfall; where we threw ourselves under the cold water stream and jumped up and down until our bodies were used to the cold and we were able to breathe again. Then, we started to frolic, yell, tease, and splash even more water at each other.

After a couple minutes of splashing and having fun, my Dad left the waterfall, called us, and beckoned us over. Now, I finally saw why our women were carrying those small baskets of yellow lumps. This evening, we were going to wash and scrub each other under our natural shower! Wow! This was a brilliant idea; and it certainly was a lot better than showering in our own small caravan stalls.

Happily, we kids left our waterfall and raced towards our already gathering grownups; where we leaned into a nice man or woman. Of course, I stormed towards my own Dad and enthusiastically leaned into his broad stomach. From the corners of my eyes, I saw that Biny went to my Mom, because her parents were guarding our sleeping children during our absence. Misha went to Michail, who threw his arms around my older friend and 'gently' crushed his ribs.

Chapter 21. Washing and our ancient bonding ritual.

Suddenly, I felt happy for Misha; and I hoped that Michail and he would become good friends! I knew that Misha had lost his own Dad, a few years ago, due to a nasty caravan accident. Therefore, I thought it would be good for Misha to get some tender loving care from my Big Friend with his enormous heart full of love and compassion!

Now, all our grownups took some yellow soap and started to lather their kids up and wash them. My own Dad started to wash me from head to toe; still looking very proud at his young 'trapper son' who had caught an enormous pig and killed it using only one blow.

My Mom washed a happily smiling Biny who seemed to like being washed very much. Misha had lots of fun teasing Michail by mock squirming around like a naughty little kid. That is, until Michail swatted his naked bottom, making Misha squeal in mock anger. A second later, they were laughing and teasing each other again.

Now that all our kids were looking like soapy clouds of lather, we left our grownups and quickly raced back to our waterfall. First, we helped each other rinse all the soap out of each other's hair, and then we painstakingly checked every nook and cranny of each other's bodies for any remains of yellow soap.

Finally, we started a vigorous play-fight of splashing each other with even more water, until we were absolutely sure that all our kids were spotlessly clean. After everybody was ready and absolutely satisfied, we left our waterfall shower and returned to our still patiently waiting grownups.

This time, all our grownups sat down onto one of the many flat rocks and mossy boulders along the water stream, clearly wanting to be washed by us in return! Several kids took a yellow lump of soap and started to lather up one of our waiting grownups. Taking turns, all our kids waited until they got a yellow lump of soap, and then went from grownup to grownup, to lather them up everywhere while washing their naked bodies thoroughly.

One by one, our older kids washed and scrubbed our grownups from head to toe, especially in their 'dirty' and 'private' places. Of course, those 'dirty' places had to be scrubbed the most thoroughly; to remove any left behind traces of poop or pee, exactly as our grownups always did to us when we were still little. Fortunately, none of our happily scrubbing kids had any idea what any so-called 'dirty places' or 'private parts' could be.

To read all our famous 'Gypsy Series' books, please visit www.gypsyseries.com

Nobody in our Gypsy camp had ever taught our children to feel ashamed of any 'secret' or indecent' places on or in our unclad bodies. To us kids, all these places were just normal parts of our human bodies that needed to be cleaned. As a direct result, no young child or grownup in our community ever had any 'bodily shame' or felt 'embarrassed' by touching or washing each other, anywhere on or in our unclad bodies. In our secluded Gypsy camp, both our children and our grownups always felt totally free and unrestricted.

Later on in my life, when I resided in a foreign 'gadjo' country and thought back about my own youth, my inside was absolutely sure that our ancient 'bonding ritual' of our grownups and our children washing each other thoroughly, without any restrictions, had been a truly sacred experience! I was sure that, in our secluded Gypsy camp, our mutual washing ritual had brought our already very close people even closer to each other, by bonding our grownups and our children together even more effectively. This way, none of us kids ever had any 'dirty secrets' or 'danger stranger' restrictions; and we always were totally at ease with our naked bodies and all of its bodily functions. To be honest, we didn't even have any proper words for such things!

Many years later, when I resided in another country in the so extremely frustrated 'gadjo' world outside our Gypsy communities, I really pitied their poor mislead children! In their gadjo world, both the grownups and their children were FORCED to feel ashamed of certain parts of their own bodies, by their so-called 'leaders' imposing their strange 'nudity laws' on them. Therefore, their gadjo children were never allowed to feel unrestricted, not even for a few hours. Otherwise, their 'sinful' parents could be at risk to be arrested for displaying 'indecent behavior', and put in jail or lose their children!

Because all those gadjo children were forced to cover their 'private parts' all day long, they soon started to feel ashamed and inhibited even when nobody else was around to look at them. Therefore, I always felt very happy that my own Gypsy people had raised me as a totally and absolutely FREE child! What the heck were those totally confined gadjo people doing to their poor mislead children...

Now that our grownups were spotlessly clean, they too raced to our waterfall, this time also frolicking and teasing each other as little children. Under our foaming natural shower, all our kids helped our grownups rinse the lather away, until all the nooks and crannies of their bodies were absolutely clean and free from soap.

Of course, we splashed our grownups with as much extra water as we could gather; until a few people started to chase after us. Immediately, we had lots of fun making them stumble or slip on the many wet boulders. Fortunately, all our grownups loved us children very much; and nobody ever got irritated or angry with us for being teased or challenged. They just started to laugh and teased us back.

In unison, we decided to go for a quick swim in our lake, before darkness set in and the mountain air became too chilly. Immediately, all our cheering kids raced downstream along the widening river; bumping into each other on purpose while trying to be there first. Soon, they plunged into the inviting water; followed by our grownups at a slower pace. I followed my friends as fast as I could, although my small legs prevented me from winning our race.

When I arrived at our lake, I ran towards it at full speed and happily 'cannonballed' my tiny body into the water. Then, I swam back to the surface, turned around, and looked for my Dad to tease him. When I saw my Dad, I splashed a couple handfuls of water at him. Chuckling at seeing his surprised face, I shouted:

"Come on, lazy King! I want to dunk you too before we go home. Or, are you afraid of your own son?"

My Dad seemed to feel surprised when he found out that I was already able to swim, because he stammered:

"Who taught you to swim? I had planned to teach you myself; but I see you are already a real water rat..."

"Misha taught me yesterday. Look, I can already dive under the water surface and hold my breath for a very long time!"

Still looking truly surprised, my Dad told my older friend:

"Wow, Misha, you have done an excellent job! Thank you very much, for looking after my son and teaching him how to swim and dive. Thanks to you, he is now our youngest water rat ever..."

Misha started to blush fiercely at hearing my Dad's well-meant compliment, while he teasingly cannonballed himself next to me. When he showed up again, he suddenly tried to dunk me...

This time, a 'little trapper devil' in my inside whispered this could be an excellent opportunity to tease my older friend back for what he had done to me earlier!

After thanking my little trapper friend for such an excellent idea, I dived under water, swam towards Misha, took hold of one of his legs, and forcefully pulled him under the water surface!

For a few seconds, Misha didn't understand what was happening when he suddenly disappeared under the water surface. Then, he looked down and saw me clinging onto his leg! Immediately, my older friend started to kick around with his free leg, as if desperately trying to get rid of his little limpet. Only, I just continued to hold on to his leg with all of my might! In the meantime, I only hoped I would be able to hold my breath for long enough...

When Misha saw that he couldn't get rid of his little 'limpet devil' this easily, he suddenly breathed out and slowly sank down towards the bottom of the lake. Patiently, he waited until I had to resurface. The cheater! Of course, my tiny lungs were a lot smaller than his were; so that, way too soon, I had to come up for fresh air. Soon, I left Misha's leg and popped up next to his side, panting and wheezing while inhaling lots of fresh air into my lungs.

Misha didn't say a word but only chuckled, while he tried to catch me to teach me a lesson. Fortunately, I could escape from his wrath by diving under the surface again. This time, I swam under him and popped up at his other side, teasingly splashing handfuls of water at him. Then, I stuck out my tongue towards my mock-angry looking friend, before I tried to escape across the lake.

In the meantime, my Dad had already entered the water. Now working closely together, both my Dad and Misha swam after me and threatened to punish me for my audacity! Of course, working together, they caught me in no time, and got hold of my arms before I could disappear under the surface again. Suddenly, my chuckling Dad lifted me out of the water and threw my shocked little body across the water surface, as far into the mountain lake as he could!

For a moment, I felt too disorientated to react. I only flailed my arms and legs around while yelping from the unexpected sensation. I hit the water surface, went under, and involuntarily started to panic; until I remembered what Misha had taught me about resurfacing. Immediately, I did what Misha had taught me and kicked at the surrounding water until I popped up. Then, I started to look around for my attackers. When I saw them, I quickly swam back to my Dad and enthusiastically asked him to throw my little body across the lake again! Of course, my chuckling Dad happily obliged.

Aad Aandacht is a Dutch psychotherapist who loves writing 'books with a message'

Chapter 21. Washing and our ancient bonding ritual.

From this day on, I absolutely LOVED our ageless water games of dunking each other and being thrown far away. I just couldn't get enough of our splashing games; which also vastly perfected my own swimming and diving skills. Even after many years of absence without swimming, I still was an excellent swimmer and diver!

After throwing me across our lake some more, my 'old' Dad felt too tired and therefore told us he wanted to take some much-needed rest. Of course, Misha and I started to tease him about 'being too old'; but then we left him alone and swam to the other kids to partake in our own water games. Looking thankful, my Dad swam to the surrounding banks and slumped down on some soft moss.

While I teased and challenged my bigger friends, I unexpectedly found out something that was very important! Surprisingly, being our 'littlest runt' was not always a disadvantage, as I had thought before. Now and then, thanks to being so small, I was able to wriggle myself through almost impossible escape routes, by diving under the surface or in between my friends, who suddenly didn't see me any more! Many times, although I still was the smallest kid in our group, I also was the fastest escaper, and I could outdo my much bigger friends with ease. Now that I knew how to do this, I had even MORE fun!

At last, our shivering grownups called us towards the surrounding banks and told us we had to go home, because the mountain air was becoming too chilly. Reluctantly, we left our lake and trotted back to our waterfall. With a little help from our grownups, we climbed up the ridges. From there, we raced back to our huge clearing, crossed our surrounding bushes, and gathered around our brightly glowing campfire, to warm our now fiercely shivering wet bodies.

Fortunately, our helpful grownups had guarded our camp and their sleeping kids very well during our absence. They had already raked the brightly glowing fire and even put more logs onto it, so that we could warm our shivering bodies in its nicely radiating glow.

When we had dried and warmed up sufficiently, we first went to our own caravans, to put on some warm plaid or another cozy garment. I followed my Mom and Dad inside and grabbed a nicely colored plaid from our couch, while they quickly donned their own warm evening clothes. Together, we returned to our still brightly glowing campfire, while I draped my warm plaid around my naked body, to protect it against the icy cold mountain wind.

When everybody had returned and sat down on the many wooden benches around our campfire, all our children climbed onto a warm and cozy lap to sit on, be cuddled, and feel safe and loved. Of course, I crawled onto my own Dad's lap, next to my Mom; feeling very tired and a little bit sleepy but also wonderful.

This time, Misha sat opposite us on Michail's lap, from where he waved at me with a proudly beaming face. My gut feeling told me that Misha still missed his own Dad terribly, who had died in a nasty caravan accident. Therefore, I felt very happy to see that Michail and Misha were becoming such good friends. My Big Friend with his enormous heart full of Real Love would certainly be a wonderful 'replacement Dad' to my fourteen-year-old buddy!

Again, I felt absolutely wonderful and extremely happy to be living here, in our own secluded site in the Rumanian mountains with their snow-clad tops that always glowed in the bright sunlight; while we were surrounded by our outstretched woods and vast forests that were full of brand new discoveries and exciting adventures.

Only two burning questions remained...

My first burning question was: when would I finally have my first 'growth spurt', as Misha once told me every healthy kid in our Gypsy community should have from time to time. Up to now, I was still the tiniest four-and-a-half year old 'little runt' in our community.

My second burning question was: my Beloved King of Ancestors once told me that I would meet my former 'trapper Dad' soon after our earth had rounded our sun two times. My former trapper Dad also was my Eternal Soul Mate, and he had been our 'Beloved Gypsy Monarch Harold the Great' while I was our Vice Leader and his best friend.

During my present life, I would meet him again; and he would be my new Dad and help me grow up, until I would be our next Gypsy Leader and raise my own little Gypsy Prince. Only, when the heck would our earth have rounded our sun two times? Would my wise Dad, or perhaps Michail, know the answer?

Or, would I again have to be more patient...

# # #

99. You've reached the end of my first book.

Although you've reached the end of my FIRST book about me, it is NOT the end of my adventures as our little Crown Prince! In the SECOND book of my 'Gypsy Series', which is called 'a Boy loves a Man -2- a little upcoming Shaman', I am growing up healthy and prosperously, while again living through several happy, sad, funny, and sometimes dangerous adventures; until I am five years old. I am also a more and more valuable part of our secluded Gypsy community, helped by my devoted friends, parents, Spirit Guides, and sometimes our Beloved Ancestors from our timeless Eternal Realm.

#

In the meantime, my new Dad has started writing his OWN ongoing 'Gypsy Series' of several books about a retired psychotherapist who meets a badly burnt little Gypsy boy and takes him into his house. Soon, the boy turns out to be a powerful Shaman, the vanished Gypsy Heir to the Throne, and his Eternal Soul Mate. This heartwarming emotional rollercoaster full of Love and Happiness also hints at many 'alternative' things as there are 'Past Lives', 'Spirit Helpers', 'Karma', 'Magic', 'Power of Love'; and it contains many practical psychological concepts and useful daily-life hints...

#

Please visit our own Internet site; www.gypsyseries.com ; to stay informed about our newest 'Gypsy Series' books; and please send us a stimulating email... May our Supreme Being always be with you, bless you, and send you lots of Real Love and Happiness in your life!

#

Aad Aandacht is a retired Dutch psychotherapist, living in a small country called The Netherlands. Just like in all his beautiful Gypsy stories, he has been married but divorced, and he has two lovable grown-up daughters but no grandchildren to spoil.

After writing many books in his own language, Dutch; he decided to write his next series of books in a to him foreign language, hoping that writing them in the International Language would spread their important messages all over the world more easily...

Aad still loves writing 'emotional roller coasters' and 'books with a message'; and he plans to go on writing them for a very long time! Next to being a psychotherapist, he studied several 'alternative' and 'paranormal' treatments and remedies; for example 'aura reading and healing', 'contacts with Spirit Guides and Helpers', 'past lives' or 'reincarnations', and the 'Laws of Karma'. He always interweaves his lifetime of vast knowledge and experiences into his stories, so that his readers can pick up his important lessons easily.

Although Aad retired in 2004, he is still very active; helping many so-called 'sensitive children', 'new-age children', 'indigo children', 'crystal children', or 'Aquarius children' get a better life; with more understanding from their parents and surrounding grown-ups.

Enjoy Aad's powerful books, and please send him an email:

www.gypsyseries.com

gypsy@gypsyseries.com

# # #